"Do you think  always win

Frustration, longing, th... ...to hold Gwyn in his arms ... ...anger. The sheriff's convinced I killed Frannie and buried her on property I knew would one day be mine. When your archaeologist friend asked to dig there, I refused her so adamantly she had to get a court order forcing me to allow it. How do you think that looks?"

"It's circumstantial evidence. It doesn't prove a thing," she insisted.

"And how do we know there won't be other circumstantial evidence that's even more damning?"

There are secrets at Beaumarais, she recalled Jed saying.

"If you're trying to scare me, you're not doing a very good job. You didn't kill your foster mother. There is no proof to the contrary."

"That we know of. In any case, we have to be practical and realistic. Until this murder is cleared up and I'm free of suspicion, I can't let you get involved with me—"

She squeezed herself tightly to him. "Just love me, Jed," she whispered against his chest. "That's all I ask of you. Just love me."

Dear Reader,

I suppose all of us have our own mental images of Texas. The open prairie and semidesert ranges of the south and west. The gently rolling pastures of the central Hill Country. The flat plains of north Texas. They're all accurate, of course. After all, Texas is big.

But when Roz Denny Fox, Eve Gaddy and I were asked to set a trilogy in Texas, we wanted people to see a different aspect of the Lone Star state. That's why we went to east Texas, to the narrow strip of land along the Louisiana border. It has tall trees, dense pine and deciduous forests, as well as honest-to-goodness swamps—goodness being a relative term, of course. Not everyone uses that word to describe alligators and water moccasins!

In doing our research, we happened upon a wonderful place on Caddo Lake called Uncertain. The name alone attracted us, but so did the land and the people—and the tales of intrigue they had to spin.

I must tell you right now, though, that while the setting is real, none of the characters are. They're not based on actual people, living or dead. We made them all up. None of the events, as far as we know, bear any resemblance to things that might have happened there, either. In short, we let our imaginations run wild.

I hope you enjoy this RETURN TO EAST TEXAS trilogy. We "certainly" enjoyed writing it.

K.N. *Casper*

P.S. I love to hear from readers. You can write to me at P.O. Box 4062, San Angelo, TX 76902, or find me on www.superauthors.com.

The Millionaire Horseman
K.N. Casper

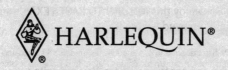

HARLEQUIN®

TORONTO • NEW YORK • LONDON
AMSTERDAM • PARIS • SYDNEY • HAMBURG
STOCKHOLM • ATHENS • TOKYO • MILAN • MADRID
PRAGUE • WARSAW • BUDAPEST • AUCKLAND

ISBN 0-373-70978-1

THE MILLIONAIRE HORSEMAN

Visit us at www.eHarlequin.com

Printed in U.S.A.

Our special thanks to Jim McMillen and
Lexie Palmore, riverboat pilots, who gave us a tour of Caddo
Lake on the *Graceful Ghost*, an authentic wood-burning, steam-
powered paddle wheeler,
and who generously filled us in on so much of the fascinating
lore and legend of Uncertain, Texas.

PROLOGUE

Uncertain, Texas
Tuesday, May 4, 1982

"WHERE'S THE admission request?" Jed asked as he bolted through the kitchen door from his bedroom. He rifled among the bills and other papers Frannie kept in a square, shallow basket on the end of the counter, pulled out the form and scowled.

"I didn't sign it," Frannie told him over her shoulder as she scooped up the cornflakes Emmy or Will had carelessly spilled on the counter. Probably Will. The sixteen-year-old was still having a hard time learning to clean up after himself. She should make him take care of it, but everyone seemed to be running behind this morning, and Frannie had more important things on her mind than worrying about a few spilled crumbs. She wasn't looking forward to the confrontation she knew she was in for.

"Sign it now," Jed demanded. "I have to turn it in this morning."

"I'm not going to sign it," she responded in as calm a voice as she could muster. "I told you that last night."

"Damn it, you promised to help me." His deep

voice was raised enough that Emmy and Will, busy gulping cold cereal at the kitchen table, stopped their chewing and gaped at him. Frannie adjusted the waistband of her loose-fitting work jeans and moved to the sink.

"Watch your language, young man," she warned. "This isn't a locker room." She glared at him, her anxiety starting to rise. "I agreed only to think about it, and I did. But I haven't changed my mind, Jed." To the others she said, "Hurry or you'll be late."

She could feel the angry tension pulsing in the towering teenager. *Where did he ever get his incredible size?* Frannie wondered for the umpteenth time. His mother had been a pale wisp of a thing, and his father...well, maybe that was where the dark hair and lanky frame had come from.

"You can't do this to me," he shouted at her, his blue eyes blazing. "You can't screw me like this."

"Jed Louis," Emmy yelled in her high-pitched voice from the table, "don't you dare talk to my Mom Fran like that."

"Keep out of this, Emmy-M," he said offhandedly to the thirteen-year-old while he continued to glower at Frannie as she wrung out a dishrag at the sink. "This is my big opportunity," he pleaded.

"Jed, you're a good fiddle player. I don't deny it. You're very talented, and I'm proud of you. But you're not concert quality—"

"Maybe not yet," he admitted reluctantly, frustration ringing in his voice. "That's why you've got to sign that paper. So I can go to Juilliard."

"Jed—" Frannie's voice went soft with sympathy "—if I believed you were another Isaac Stern or Itzak Perlmann, I'd sign that piece of paper without a second thought. But all the Juilliards in the world aren't going to put you on the stage in Carnegie Hall. Go to college, son. You're good in science, and you've been offered a basketball scholarship—"

"I want to play the violin," he insisted.

Frannie shook her head. "Do you have any idea how hard it is to make a decent living as a professional musician, especially playing classical violin?"

"I don't have to make a living," he reminded her. "In three years and two months, when I turn twenty-one, I inherit Beaumarais. I'll have all the money I need."

Frannie leaned against the counter and crossed her arms. "Is that what you want to do with your life, Jed—live off your uncle's money? You have an obligation to yourself to earn your own living, to be self-supporting—"

"Oh, I get it," he scoffed. "Other people can inherit wealth, but not me. I'm nothing but a bastard. Bastards don't deserve anything."

Appalled at his bitterness, Frannie replied kindly, "Jed, I never said that."

"The hell you didn't."

Will got up from the table and carried his empty bowl to the sink. As he passed by his foster brother he muttered, "Hey, Jed, cool it, man."

"Mind your own damn business," Jed snapped at him.

Emmy shot Jed a withering glance, then bolted from the table. "We're going to be late for school." She dashed into her room and retrieved her books.

Jed held the form out, stiff-armed, to Frannie. "It has to be turned in today."

"I'm sorry, Jed—" she shook her head in heartfelt commiseration "—I won't sign it. It's not right for you."

Jed slammed the paper down on the table. "Damn it. Every time I want to do something, you tell me it's not right for me. I can't even take Amanda Jennings on a date without you saying she's no good—"

"Amanda, huh!" Emmy sneered. "That stuck-up snob. Just because she's got big boobs—"

"Emerald Monday, you watch your mouth, too," Frannie warned. "I don't ever want to hear you talking like that again. Do you understand me?"

"Yes, ma'am," Emmy said contritely. "But you ought to see the way she keeps coming on to Jed and Will, rubbing up against them and practically sticking her tongue in their ears," she added belligerently.

"That's enough, young lady." To the boys, Frannie said, "I want both of you to stay away from Amanda—"

"Why?" Jed challenged. "Isn't she good enough for me, or am I not good enough for her? After all, her daddy owns the only bank in town, and I'm nothing but a bastard."

Frannie took a deep, fortifying breath. "Jed, stop it. I don't approve of Amanda Jennings because she's a troublemaker. As for Ray Jennings—" she paused, choosing her words carefully "—he owns the bank only because he married into it."

"Oh, so now he's not good enough in your estimation, either." Jed snorted contemptuously. "Does anybody live up to your high standards? Well, look around. You have to close in the porch so Will and I can have our own rooms. This isn't exactly a mansion we're living in.''

Frannie's lips quivered and her eyes grew suddenly moist. She swallowed hard before answering. ''No, it's not, Jed,'' she said softly. ''But it's the best I can do. I want you to do your best, too. It's the only way you'll ever find peace of mind.''

''Peace of mind. Yeah, right. You're ruining my life!'' he shouted. ''I'll show you.'' He grabbed the piece of paper and strode to the back door. ''You'll be sorry you didn't help me.''

CHAPTER ONE

Uncertain, Texas
Tuesday, April 3, 2001

GWYNETH MILLER liked small towns, which was
why she'd chosen Uncertain, Texas. She'd asked
several residents how it came by its curious name
and had received a slightly different version of its
history every time.

One was that back in the 1880s when the location
was little more than a campground and fishing site,
it was "uncertain" if a horse-drawn wagon could get
through on the muddy roads after a heavy rain. Another was that when the town was established and
the residents wanted it be recognized, a county clerk
erroneously recorded the preliminary request on
which the name of the place was still "uncertain,"
instead of the final version.

Not that it mattered. The place had appeal. It was
quiet, clean, unhurried and friendly. Gwyn wasn't
fond of big cities or even living in their shadows.
This little town on the Texas-Louisiana border was
well beyond the pale.

Its location wasn't exactly convenient for her business as an animal manager, which involved making

animals available on a short-term basis for private and commercial projects. Texas roads were so good, however, that being off the beaten track wasn't a serious problem.

Having finished feeding all her animals, Gwyn headed toward a family restaurant in town for a second cup of coffee. She'd stopped at the Caddo Kitchen on her first visit to the area. It was every bit as shabby as it was cozy. The walls were covered with fishing nets, poles, reels and mounted trophies above pea-green vinyl-upholstered booths that were faded and cracking. When she'd remarked to the waitress that she was looking for a house to rent and some pasture to graze horses, the four men drinking coffee around the one occupied table had unanimously recommended she check with Jed Louis. He apparently owned a considerable number of lease properties in the area, as well as farm and ranch land. They knew his telephone number by heart.

This morning, middle-aged men wearing baseball caps with farm equipment logos on them were finishing up platters of sausage patties and eggs or biscuits and gravy at most of the tables. Gwyn found an open stool at the counter and slipped onto it.

"What can I get you, hon?" a gum-chewing woman, who probably wasn't much older than Gwyn, asked from behind the counter.

"Just coffee, thanks."

"Coming up." The woman snagged a heavy china mug from a stack behind her, plopped it down in front of Gwyn and filled it in one quick confident motion without spilling a drop. "You're the gal who was asking about land for horses."

Gwyn smiled. "You have a good memory." It had been almost two months since she'd been in the place and then just the one time.

The woman proudly patted the exaggerated-red curls on her head. "Always was pretty good with faces. I don't imagine any of the guys around here forgot yours, either."

The compliment was so unexpected Gwyn felt a rush of heat to her cheeks.

"Cassie, you planning on serving number six or jawing all day?" a sweaty-looking, overweight man in soiled cook's whites called out from the window behind her.

"Hold your grits, Jake. I'm coming. Men," Cassie huffed. "Always want it hot and quick."

Gwyn snickered and sipped the steaming brew. Her instant coffee back at the house tasted better.

"Somebody told me your horses are those little ones," Cassie commented over her shoulder a minute later while she loaded a couple of slices of white bread into an old-fashioned rotary toaster. "Bet they're cute. My daddy bought me a horse once. A Shetland. Pretty as a new button and mean as the dickens. Never cared much for the critters after that. But those little ones now...I just might change my mind. Do they bite?"

Gwyn chuckled. "Mine don't, if you treat them right."

"I heard you can potty-train them. Is that true?"

Gwyn laughed. "I wish."

"That's what I figured. Like trying to housebreak a man. Not in this world." There was more affection in her voice than complaint. "Maybe I'll drop by sometime and you can let me pet them."

Gwyn just smiled. She would gladly show Cassie the horses if she visited, but Gwyn didn't want to encourage everyone in town to do the same. She was grateful that the grazing field Jed Louis had leased her was well off the road, beyond the piney woods, and safely out of sight. The miniature palominos were natural attractions, which made them extremely marketable, but they needed careful guarding, too. If they were too close to a road, there was a distinct danger of their being lifted over a fence and stolen.

"Heard you're renting Frannie's old place," Cassie prattled on as she tore open a foil bag of ground coffee, dumped it into a paper filter and set a glass pot under the drip spout of the coffeemaker. "Reckon you're going to be in for a few official visitors."

Gwyn's ears perked up. "Official visitors? What are you talking about?"

Cassie reached around and grabbed the abandoned newspaper a couple of places down the line. "I guess you haven't seen this."

Gwyn stared at the headlines, then slowly read the article. She seemed to have opened Pandora's box. She finished her coffee and pulled a couple of dollars from her jeans pocket. Throwing them on the counter, she went out to her Rover. Maybe it was time to mend some fences.

SIPPING DARK, rich Cajun-style coffee, Jed Louis sat at the massive polished walnut desk in the library at Beaumarais, reviewing his calendar for the coming day. He had a meeting with a racehorse owner from New Orleans to discuss breeding one of his Percheron mares to the man's Thoroughbred stallion. "Thercherons," as the combination was known, made excellent show horses. This afternoon he'd scheduled negotiations for the selective cutting of timber from a section of land he owned south of town.

Jed rested back in his chair. On the business front, things were going well. If this new equine venture worked out as he hoped, he'd not only make a nice profit on the crossbreed foal, but he would be expanding the reputation and market for the high-quality stock of Beaumarais Stables. About his private life he was less sure.

Two months had passed since Gwyneth Miller had knocked on his door. He wasn't one to gape at strange women, but he had gaped at her. Something about the soft curve of her mouth had instantly intrigued him. Or maybe it was the spark of interest he'd seen in her pale-blue eyes as she looked at him. Whatever it was, he'd noted she wasn't wearing a ring on the third finger of her left hand when she explained she was an animal manager and she was looking for a house to rent and pasture to lease for a dozen harness horses she owned. He hadn't thought twice about renting her Frannie's house next door and granting her use of the field abutting it on his side of the fence.

She'd moved in before he discovered her horses didn't even stand three feet tall. She could have told him her animals were miniatures, but she'd chosen not to. Knowing she wasn't completely honest and open didn't sit well with him.

Then, two weeks ago, Tessa Lang, an archaeologist working on her doctorate, had turned up in Uncertain. She'd come to Jed and requested access to his ancestral estate, so she could dig for Indian artifacts. He'd refused. That should have been the end of it, and it would have been if that damn Yankee woman, Gwyneth Miller, hadn't suggested to Lang that she obtain a court order overriding his decision. As soon as Jed found out, he marched to his rental house and confronted Miller about her gall in advocating this legal violation of his private property. She'd listened to his harangue, then quietly closed the door in his face. He'd simmered down some since, but it still rankled.

Last Wednesday, Tessa Lang reported finding a skeleton at what she claimed was a Caddo Indian burial site. Well, what was so startling about that? Dig in a cemetery and you're bound to find bodies.

Jed slipped the *Uncertain Times* out of the plastic sleeve in which it arrived every morning. He flattened it out and glanced at the headline: Mystery Bones Near East Texas Lake Identified.

Old news, he thought and took another sip of cooling coffee. Then a name in the text below jumped out at him: Frannie Granger. The cup clattered as he placed it on its saucer. With hands suddenly shaking, he picked up the paper and read the article:

The mystery of Frannie Granger's disappearance may finally be solved. The forty-seven-year-old Harrison County woman vanished nineteen years ago this spring. Her remains were recently found close to an Indian burial ground near Caddo Lake. She is believed to have been murdered.

Jed closed his eyes, which only intensified the sick feeling in the pit of his stomach. Nervous sweat broke out on the back of his neck. Inhaling deeply, he opened his eyes and read on:

On March 28th of this year, upon the discovery of human remains obviously not those of a Caddo Indian of the early-nineteenth century, archaeologist Theresa Lang turned the skeleton over to the authorities for identification. This week, comparison with local dental records proved the bones to be those of Frannie Granger, a widow who was housekeeper for various local residents and who provided foster care for unadoptable children in her own home in Uncertain. Granger was well-liked in the community, and her sudden disappearance caused quite a stir. Sheriff Logan Fielder could not be reached for comment. The question remains, who murdered Frannie Granger, and why?

Jed sagged against the chair, his mind slipping back to a time when hope had been dashed, when a part of his life that had always been tenuous at best, was shattered.

Frannie.

He had been one of those unadoptable children.

Who else would take in a bastard child? His uncle definitely hadn't. When Jed's mother died unexpectedly of an aneurysm, Uncle Walter couldn't wait to turn his six-year-old nephew over to Frannie Granger, like old clothes tossed to the Salvation Army. She had been Jed's salvation, too. The close to twelve years he'd lived with her had been good—until the end.

Their last meeting and the violence of his emotions that day would always haunt his fond memories of the petite woman who'd showered him with affection and occasional tough love. He could still see the pain and sadness on her face when he shouted at her that last morning about what he blindly saw as her betrayal.

The crunch of gravel and the sputtering of a sick engine in the driveway outside his window interrupted Jed's reverie. He looked up and recognized the vehicle instantly. Pushing back his chair, he rose, wended his way around a large globe, past the leather couch and chairs and walked out into the wide central hallway. Morning sunlight beamed through the glass side panels of the broad front door. He turned the polished brass door handle and stepped out onto the wide, stone porch.

Silently Jed watched Gwyneth Miller alight from her faded-green Land Rover. If the buxom woman in trim khaki pants and yellow blouse was inclined to heat his blood, the car that pulled up immediately behind hers turned it cold. The sedan was newer, shinier and definitely more eye-catching with the red-white-and-blue light bar clamped over the roof. Only one word was stenciled on the door: Sheriff. Involuntarily, Jed's stomach muscles tightened.

Logan Fielder climbed out of the patrol car, slammed the door harder than was necessary and sauntered around the hood of his vehicle. The lawman had been lean and mean when Jed first encountered him twenty years ago. He hadn't changed much, nor had his hostility toward Jed.

"Louis," he said, leaving off the "good morning" part. He tipped his Stetson politely to Gwyn. "Ma'am."

She gave him a silent, quizzical nod.

"What brings you out here, Sheriff?" Jed asked without warmth.

"I think you know." He leaned casually against the right fender of the tan-and-white county vehicle. "I see you got the *Times*."

Jed glanced down at the newspaper clutched in his hand. He hadn't realized he'd carried it outside. Forcing a lazy grin, he asked, "Checking up on the newsboy's delivery record?"

"I'm officially informing you, Louis," he said without humor, "that I've declared the site where that archaeologist woman is digging to be a crime scene. That means it's off-limits to you, your people and your animals."

"I can't say I'm surprised," Jed acknowledged. He slouched casually on one hip. "When can I collect Frannie's remains? I want to arrange for a proper burial."

"Not till the D.A. says you can," Fielder replied forcefully. "They're evidence in a murder investigation. I remind you there's no statute of limitations on murder.''

Unwilling to be intimidated by the belligerent tone or the subtle threat it seemed to harbor, Jed commented, ''I suppose investigating will be a bit easier now than it was nineteen years ago. At least someone's found a body for you.''

For a split second, Fielder's lips pursed, and Jed had the feeling his eyes narrowed behind the mirror-lensed sunglasses.

''I heard you're planning to retire in a couple of years,'' Jed continued conversationally. ''Think that'll give you enough time? Or do you plan on running again for reelection?'' He smiled ironically. ''I wonder if the slogan I Got Unfinished Business To Tend To will garner many votes.''

Fielder's ruddy face darkened even further, but he ignored the jab. ''I'll be questioning everyone who gave statements at the time of Granger's disappearance,'' he announced. ''That includes you, Louis, so don't leave town.''

Without bidding farewell to Jed or his visitor, Fielder turned around and climbed back into his patrol car. Again he used undue force to shut the door. Kicking up gravel, he steered around the Land Rover and scrambled down the long driveway to the main road.

Jed emitted a rough, mirthless chuckle.

Gwyn shifted her attention from the departing lawman to the wealthy landowner standing a few feet away. Plainly, there was a history between the two men, and just as plainly, they weren't friends. She might have mixed feelings about Jed Louis, but she'd taken an instant aversion to the sheriff.

"I have the impression you and Sheriff Fielder don't like each other," she commented.

Cocking his head, he narrowed his eyes in an attitude of bemusement. "We've never been real close," he replied in obvious understatement. "I don't imagine he's very happy about having to reopen a two-decades-old case. People might think he botched it the first time."

"Did he?"

All humor drained from his face. "Frannie's dead."

Gwyn's eyes widened. The statement was blunt but not cold. Who was this woman he referred to by her first name? A relative? A friend? Could she have been his mother? The blank expression on his face didn't tell her much.

"Fielder never even figured that out," Jed added.

According to the press account, the woman disappeared without a trace. Even if the authorities had concluded she was dead, there probably wasn't much they could do without a corpse.

"He apparently doesn't have a very high regard for you, either," she muttered.

Jed chuckled, but it seemed more a release of tension than enjoyment of something funny. "Why are you here?" he asked, ending that line of discussion. "Has a commode backed up, or did the roof leak last night?"

She took a deep breath. He was still angry with her for what he perceived as her siding with Tessa Lang. In fact, the suggestion to seek a court order had been a passing comment, one of many offered in commiserating with the doctoral candidate over a missed opportunity. Now that the archaeologist had found a murder victim on his property, he had one more reason to be resentful. Gwyn had to admit she'd handled both incidents poorly, but she wasn't about to apologize. As far as she was concerned, she hadn't done anything illegal, immoral or fattening.

"I wondered if you'd seen the story in the paper."

He flashed the folded *Times*. "Obviously, I have."

She gazed at him for a second, at the square jaw and cleft chin, the black hair and icy blue eyes. Too bad she couldn't take a step back to their first meeting. Maybe if she'd been more forthcoming then, he wouldn't be so hostile now. She sighed. What was done was done.

"I told you no good would come of your interference," he continued. "Thanks to you and Ms. Lang, I've not only lost the use of valuable pastureland, but I'll have strangers traipsing all over the place, upsetting my animals—and yours. The next thing I can probably expect is for the representative from some high-and-mighty-sounding federal agency I've never heard of to tell me they're confiscating my land under some arcane national regulation I haven't heard of, either."

Not a word of sympathy for the dead woman, she noted. "Mr. Louis, I think you're exaggerating."

"Am I?" He slipped his fingers into the slash pockets of his western-cut tan trousers. "I've seen how bureaucracies work, Ms. Miller. They're devoted to rules, not the people the rules were designed to help or protect." He took a deep breath. When he spoke this time, his voice was very low and infinitely sad. "Thanks to you, I'll also have to relive a tragedy I thought I'd put behind me."

She stared at him, stunned. Surely he wasn't telling her he knew Frannie Granger was buried there.

"I had no idea Tessa Lang's excavation would be so disruptive," Gwyn said to justify herself. "She certainly didn't expect to find the remains of a murder victim. I just hope justice can be done for the poor woman."

"So do I," he snapped. "Frannie Granger was a good woman who deserved to live a long happy life."

The force of his statement surprised her. She wanted to know more, but first she had to mend some fences.

After folding her lips between her teeth and taking a deep breath, she said, "Mr. Louis, I owe you an apology. I should have told you my harness horses were miniatures." The admission drew no immediate reaction, forcing her to go on. "It was clear you thought they were normal size."

He locked eyes with her. "Why didn't you?"

"I guess I was afraid you'd refuse to lease me the grazing land I needed." It distressed her to realize she'd acted like a typical Miller, manipulating him into giving her what she wanted.

He drew in a deep breath, then let it out again. "Ms. Miller, I don't see much point in miniature horses or miniature anything, for that matter, but I had pastureland to lease. Unless your animals threatened it or my other livestock, I had no reason to turn down a paying customer."

"I am sorry," Gwyn assured him. "I should have realized that. Do you think we might be able to get back on a first-name basis? Being addressed all the time as Ms. Miller makes me feel like a Boston matriarch."

He raised an eyebrow. Her accent certainly betrayed her Yankee origin, but matriarch? Hardly. Matriarchs had silver-blue hair and cobwebs of wrinkles, not shimmering auburn tresses and flawlessly smooth skin.

"Okay, Gwyn." His chuckle this time was one of genuine humor. "I'm about to have my second cup of coffee. If you have time, perhaps you'd care to join me. Since my most convenient field is about to be tracked all over, we better decide how we're going to deal with this new situation."

With a welcoming gesture, he swept his arm, then followed her through the wide front door.

Gwyn had admired the classic antebellum plantation house the first time she'd seen it from the road. Two and a half stories high, with six massive Ionic columns across its front and a red tile roof with several small dormers, Beaumarais sat on a hill overlooking Caddo Lake. On her one and only visit inside, she hadn't gone beyond the small room off to the left of the central breezeway—a room that, in her estimation, hadn't suited its owner at all. It was fussy and feminine with its antique Victorian settees and fiddleback chairs. This time he led her down the white wainscoted hallway past an elegant staircase to another door on the left.

"This is the morning room," he announced as he allowed her to precede him inside.

The walls were painted forest green, but the room was far from dark. The finely milled woodwork was glossy white and one entire wall was composed of floor-to-ceiling French windows that filled the interior space with bright morning sunlight.

Beyond them, spring growth had the oak and elm trees blooming in soft-green pastels. Past a stand of darker pines, along the irregular shore of Caddo Lake, ubiquitous azaleas, both wild and cultivated, were glorious in their various shades of white, pink, coral, magenta and every tint in between. Their brilliant colors contrasted sharply with the smoky-gray Spanish moss that draped the cone-based cypress trees like dull tinsel. Through the screens of the open windows, Gwyn caught the delicate scent of wild rose and the heady sweetness of hyacinth.

"Jed, this view is breathtaking." Gwyn gazed out, her heart pitter-patting at the beauty of the world before her. "It's like…like…I don't know how to explain it."

"Like the beginning of time," he suggested.

She spun around, surprised by his observation, but it was exactly right. "You like this room, don't you?"

"It's one of my favorites," he admitted.

"And the others?"

"There's only one other. The library. I'll show it to you later."

Two rooms, she thought. One filled with nature, the other with books. She liked what that said about the man.

A tall, fine-featured black woman in a simple gray-and-white uniform came through a side door.

"June, this is Ms. Miller."

She nodded a greeting, which Gwyn returned.

"Will you bring us coffee, please."

"Yes, Mr. Jed. Right away." The woman turned and left the room.

He held a cushioned, white wicker chair for her at a matching glass-topped table.

"Jed, I know none of this is any of my business, but can you tell me what's going on? Who was Frannie Granger? Why was she killed? And why is the sheriff so hostile?"

Jed was torn. He liked to think he saw sincerity in her alluring blue eyes, genuine concern on her part that he might be in serious trouble. After all these years, he was surprised to realize he actually wanted to talk about what happened so long ago.

If he was in the mood for reminiscing, he should probably call Riley Gray, his lawyer. He and Riley had grown up and gone to school together. They'd stayed good friends over the years. But Riley wasn't here now. This woman was. He knew he shouldn't confide in her. After all, a man could lose himself in those beautiful blue eyes of hers.

"It's a long story," he said.

CHAPTER TWO

JUNE RETURNED carrying a tray. She set it down on a side table and presented Gwyn and Jed with large cups and saucers, bread plates, a dish of butter curls, another of preserves and a white linen napkin-lined basket of still-warm croissants. After pouring their coffee and being thanked by Jed, she quietly left the room.

"This looks and smells wonderful," Gwyn said, suddenly uncomfortable, not with the elegance, but with the man sitting across from her. She studied his hands. For all their size and strength, there was tension in them. Their calmness seemed a facade.

He smiled wanly but made no comment. Stealing a surreptitious glance at him as she broke open one of the crispy pastries, she found only thoughtful introspection.

"Frannie Granger was my foster mother," he said at last.

"Foster mother?" Not adoptive mother or stepmother. It didn't seem to fit. Wealthy, socially prestigious families might have nannies and tutors to bring up their children, but they didn't give them to foster parents. Unless she'd been misinformed about his inheriting Beaumarais. Perhaps he'd purchased it.

"My own mother died when I was six—"

"I'm sorry. And your father?"

"He was killed a couple of years earlier. In a car accident," Jed added. "My nearest relative was my Uncle Walter, this was his place. Beaumarais has been in the Louis family for 150 years. Unfortunately he was middle-aged, a confirmed bachelor and not at all suited to bringing up a young boy."

Gwyn sipped her coffee. "Not suited?" she asked over the cup's rim. "In what way?"

Jed chuckled. "Aside from the fact that he had no interest in doing so, he was lazy and tightfisted. He sold off most of the antiques in this house, as well as several unattached pieces of land, rather than work for a living. He piously attended church every Sunday, made a big deal about giving small contributions to charity and the rest of the time forgot the greatest commandment of all."

Gwyn raised an eyebrow, her butter knife poised over the end of a flaky croissant. "Love thy neighbor as thyself?"

"Or thy family." The mild humor of a minute earlier had receded.

"So he was a hypocrite," she concluded. It wasn't exactly a rare breed.

"He and my mother didn't get along. He disapproved of her lifestyle and didn't hesitate to ostracize her for it."

Gwyn might have told him every family had its black sheep, nonconformists who didn't toe the mark, were disappointments or refused to fit the mold. In a sense, she matched all those descriptions.

"So he hired this Frannie Granger to look after you."

"More like shoved me off on her," Jed corrected her. "Still, I can't complain. Everything I've achieved I owe to her."

More than thirty years had passed since he'd been abandoned, but Gwyn sensed a smoldering hurt still lingered behind his words. She'd been told by one of the locals that Jed was thirty-seven and unmarried. Gossip didn't suggest, however, that he was anything like his uncle. There had apparently been a few women in his life, but he'd handled the affairs discreetly.

"So you didn't grow up in this house?"

He shook his head and sipped coffee. Not the chicory blend he'd brewed for himself before June arrived that morning but a rich Colombian roast.

Gwyneth Miller suited this room, he decided. She was beautiful, but she was also at ease in its quiet elegance. Not everyone was. As she helped herself to the cream June had put out, he was struck by the natural, inbred grace of her movements—grace that was mesmerizing and uncomfortably erotic.

"Actually, I grew up in the house you're living in," he informed her. "It was Frannie's place."

"Was she married? Did she have any kids of her own?"

He shook his head. "Her husband died several years before I got to know her. Apparently Frannie wasn't able to have children, but her mothering instinct was very strong," he added. "A friend of hers convinced her to become a foster mom."

Gwyn balanced a dollop of blackberry preserves on the end of her flaky bread. "So it was just the two of you?"

He laughed and buttered the last piece of his own roll. "Just the *four* of us."

"Four? In that small house? Who were the others?"

For a fleeting moment, his eyes seemed to fade, a man recollecting. Not with displeasure, but nostalgically and maybe with a bit of regret.

"A year before Uncle Walter sent me to Frannie, she'd taken in a foundling girl. Her name was Emerald Monday. Everybody called her Emmy. She and I grew up together, doing all the things siblings do." He chuckled fondly. "She was my kid sister, and I was her big brother, a very heady experience."

"Where is she now?"

Jed inhaled deeply, his body sagging. "I don't know."

The desolation in his words was unmistakable, and for a moment Gwyn hesitated to ask the next, logical question. "How come? I mean if you were so close…"

"I'll get to that," he said almost sharply, "in a minute."

Gwyn nodded quietly, aware she'd inadvertently touched a raw nerve. She didn't get a chance to dwell on it, however, before he continued.

"For eight years it was just Frannie, Emmy and me. Then Frannie took in another kid, a boy a year and a half younger than me, a troublemaker by the name of Will McClain. My world was disrupted when my mother died. His life had been just plain rotten from the beginning. His mother was a junkie. The various men he was told to call daddy or uncle were mostly alcoholics and drug addicts. All of them were abusive. At thirteen, Will was headed down the same dead-end road when Frannie agreed to foster him. She was Will's last chance before the authorities sent him to reform school.''

"Sounds like Frannie was taking quite a big chance bringing him into her home.''

"Everyone said she was crazy to do it, that he'd corrupt me and maybe hurt Emmy. They hadn't figured on the force of Frannie's personality or her brand of tough love. She never failed to praise good, but she was like the wrath of God if you messed up. Will messed up a lot those first few months, and she let him know it, but she also gave him something he'd never had before—genuine affection. She talked to him the way no responsible adult ever had. It took him a while, but eventually he came around.''

June entered the room and asked if they needed anything. Jed requested more hot coffee.

After she left he continued, "With time, Will and I got to be pretty good friends.'' He chuckled. "Sharing a bedroom we didn't have much choice. It was either get along or kill each other and I guarantee Frannie wouldn't have let the survivor live.'' The humorous words were out before he seemed to realize what he'd said. When he did, he rushed on as if to cover the blunder. "And Will was absolutely fierce in protecting Emmy-M.''

"Emmy-M?''

Jed cocked an eye and grinned. "That was my pet name for Emmy."

Gwyn didn't miss the genuine affection in his reply. But he hadn't kept in touch with her. A cold shudder crept down Gwyn's spine. Frannie was dead. Was Emmy, as well?

"You not only had a little sister," she commented, trying to sound conversational, "but a younger brother, too. Did you keep in touch with Will?"

Jed shook his head. Gwyn waited, eager to learn what happened to these people who had apparently played such a significant role in his growing-up.

"Everything changed one day." Jed leaned back in his chair and stared out the windows. He spoke softly and slowly, like a man remembering, reliving a distant past and recounting it as much to himself as to her.

"I was almost eighteen," he said, "a senior in high school, about to graduate, and..." He didn't complete the sentence. "Will was sixteen and a junior. He was doing well in school by then, passing all his courses, and was a running receiver on the football team. Emmy had just turned thirteen, still in junior high and starting that mysterious transition from bratty girl to aggravating young woman."

Jed's face was a mask, as if the man inside were somewhere else, but Gwyn could feel the emotion emanating from him. Still staring out the window at the swampy lake in the distance, he shook his head.

"Frannie received government support for Emmy and Will and my uncle's trust paid for me, but teenagers eat more than average and go through a lot of shoes. She cleaned houses for various people in town during the day, but she didn't go to work until after we left for school, and she was usually home by the time we returned. Until one day.''

Gwyn shivered. ''What happened?''

Jed filled his chest full of air and let it out slowly, as if gathering strength to go on. ''On May 4, 1982— it was a Tuesday—we came home in the afternoon, but Frannie wasn't there. On the rare occasions when she had a late cleaning appointment, she'd leave a note telling us where she was and when we could expect her back. We looked for a note that day but didn't find one.''

Gwyn could almost see his mind working, sorting through memories, selecting the details he wanted to reveal.

''She didn't come home that night, either,'' he said. ''We never saw or heard from her again.''

Gwyn discovered she was trembling. ''Just like that?''

''Just like that. Without a trace. All her clothes were still in the house. Her car was in the driveway, but there was no sign of her.''

''That's unbelievable, Jed. People don't just disappear without a trace.''

He smiled. ''You'd be surprised how many do. In the years that followed, I read up on cases of missing persons. It's amazing how many fathers go out for a pack of cigarettes and are never heard from again.''

''How does someone live? You can't get a job without identification, a Social Security number, a checking account. You can't even buy an airline ticket without showing a driver's license.''

"It was easier twenty years ago, but even now, with a little planning it can be done.''

"But why, Jed? You said—at least you implied—you were a happy family.''

"We had the usual problems of teenagers growing up, things of little or no real consequence but that seemed to take on monumental proportions at the time. Were we happy? In the great scheme of things, I guess we were. Of course,'' Jed continued, ''we know now Frannie didn't disappear of her own accord. She was murdered.''

"Murdered.'' Gwyn said the word with a sort of vague wonder. Characters were killed in books and movies. Like most people, she'd never come face-to-face with premeditated, violent death.

June returned with a fresh pot of coffee, poured and left as quietly as she'd entered. Gwyn admired the woman's discreet professionalism. Servants were great sources of gossip and inside information, but Gwyn had the feeling if she tried to pump June about her employer or his background, she'd hit a stone wall.

"It was quite a shock when I read the paper this morning,'' she commented as she sugared and creamed her second cup.

He sipped his own black. "I knew all along she was dead.''

Gwyn clutched her cup with both hands and hoped he didn't notice how badly her fingers were suddenly shaking. Was he telling her he knew because he'd killed her? He implied there were strains in their relationship, though Gwyn couldn't tell if he was referring to a specific issue or, as he'd said, the usual melodramatic crises that were part of being a teenager. "You knew? How?"

He brushed crumbs back from the edge of the table. "Frannie wouldn't have gone away voluntarily without telling us. There was no reason for her to leave. We were her life. She worked hard at cleaning other people's houses, but she also took very seriously her role as mother, moral guide and protector. Even if she'd had enough of Will's capers and was tired of my wanting to have my own way all the time, she would never have abandoned Emmy. She'd brought Emmy up from infancy. They were as close as any mother and daughter could be."

Jed looked over to the side and gazed out the window to the forest and the lake. "There was only one reason Frannie didn't come home that night. She was dead."

Gwyn felt a shiver tumble down her spine. She closed her eyes for a moment, then opened them and asked, "What happened after that?"

He pursed his lips pensively. "I told you the other day that I know about bureaucracies." The rancor from his earlier words when he'd discussed her advising Tessa Lang to get a court order so she could complete her research was missing now. Gwyn didn't think he'd fully forgiven her for her interference, but it seemed the heat of his anger was largely spent.

"Frannie had a set housecleaning routine, so I phoned her Tuesday clients. She hadn't shown up at their houses. I called some of her friends, but none of them had seen her or knew where she was.''

"You must have been frantic," Gwyn observed soberly.

"*Scared* is a better word. We knew something was terribly wrong. Frannie was as dependable as the sunrise.''

"Did you notify the sheriff?"

Jed snorted derisively. "I thought about it, but I didn't want to deal with the law. We'd had a few run-ins over Will, and I'd seen the way Fielder and his men treated Frannie, the snide comments and insults like she was some bag lady collecting welfare. They'd knocked Will around a couple of times, too, and Frannie made it pretty clear she wasn't going to tolerate their harassment. So, no, I didn't call the sheriff.''

Gwyn saw now why Jed had been so disdainful of Logan Fielder. Under the circumstances, she couldn't blame him.

"If Frannie had been in an accident," Jed continued, "I figured they'd contact us. Being the oldest, I took charge that night, told the others to do their homework and fixed us something to eat. The next morning I made sure we all got off to school on time.''

Gwyn wondered how his foster siblings had reacted to his playing man of the house. They could have been grateful for his taking charge, or they might have resented his bullying. Jed had said something about always wanting his own way. Gwyn had certainly had a taste of his lordly manner.

Jed fingered his china cup. "Social Services got wind that Frannie was missing, I guess from one of the people I called looking for her. That Wednesday, after Frannie disappeared, two women from Social Services showed up at Emmy's school, pulled her out of class, escorted her home, packed some of her things and took her away. Will and I came home and found the note they'd left for Frannie, telling her they'd relocated Emmy."

Gwyn drew back. "Just like that? Surely they—"

"I told you," he interrupted sharply. "Bureaucrats are interested in rules, not people. Frannie hadn't been home the night before. No one knew where she was. As far as they were concerned, she'd violated their rules about being a trustworthy foster parent."

"Well, I guess they had a point."

The anger in his eyes turned to ice. "Gwyn, they took Emmy away from the only home she'd ever known," he said with ire that had his neck muscles tightening and his deep tan darkening. "They did it without telling anyone, without letting her even say goodbye to us, her family, the people she loved. When I tried to find out where she was, they refused to tell me. A friend of ours, Riley Gray, went down to their office and demanded to know what they'd done with her and where they'd taken her. The reward for his concern was that they called the cops and had him arrested for disturbing the peace."

Gwyn shook her head. "I can't believe they were so heartless."

"Believe it," Jed said tightly. "They only thing

public servants care about are their pensions and their petty power trips.''

She could see the vein in the side of his neck throbbing. He hadn't raised his voice, but he was bitter and still very angry.

"What about Will?" she asked. "What happened to him? And what about you?"

Jed shrugged stiffly. "Since I hadn't been placed with Frannie through Social Services, I wasn't their immediate concern. Eventually, they might have tried to get involved, but in a couple of months I would turn eighteen, and they'd have had to turn me loose, anyway.''

He twisted his cup thoughtfully. "Will was another matter. He'd been in the system long enough to know it was only a matter of time before they came for him. As soon as he read the note they'd left, he grabbed a few extra clothes and hightailed it out of there." Jed paused. "I haven't seen him since." Another longer pause. "I looked for both of them for a couple of years," he finally added, "and then gave up. I figured if they wanted to get in touch, they knew where to find me. They'd disappeared without a trace—just like Frannie.''

"Jed, you don't think they're…" She couldn't finish the sentence. They couldn't be dead, too. Not like Frannie. After all, Jed knew *why* they'd disappeared.

He didn't answer.

"Excuse me, Mr. Jed.'' June had came into the room so quietly Gwyn hadn't even heard her, or maybe Gwyn's mind was so distracted by the man telling his story she'd blocked out the other sounds around her. "Mr. Sedgwick is here. He says he has an appointment with you for ten o'clock."

Jed raised his left hand and checked his watch. "I completely lost track of time." He rose from his chair. "Where is he now?"

"In the sitting room," the housekeeper replied.

"I'll take him to the library. Tell him I'll be with him in a minute."

"Yes, sir." June left.

As Gwyn started to get up, Jed moved behind her chair. "We still haven't decided what we're going to do about moving your horses."

"I think they're safe enough for the time being. After all, they were there while Tessa...Ms. Lang was digging."

"She and her people were at least civilized. While I disagree with what they were doing, I have to admit they showed respect for the land and the animals. Chances are the sheriff will have an army tramping through bushes, cutting fences and poking around. I'll check out a couple of other fields I have available and get back to you later today or early tomorrow."

Gwyn could feel the heat radiating from him as he escorted her down the hallway to the front door. She caught a glimpse of a corpulent man in tweeds in the fussy front room as they passed by. Jed walked her to her Rover and held the door for her.

"Thank you for the coffee," she said as she turned the key in the ignition. The aging car coughed once and started.

He rested his hand on the door frame. "I enjoyed having someone to share it with."

She looked in the rearview mirror as she putted down the driveway. He stood at the base of the steps to his mansion and watched her for a moment before going back inside. She shouldn't be impressed by her landlord, she told herself. After all, she'd met beautiful people before. When you're one of ''The Millers'' of the fabled Miller Millions, you meet them all: movie stars, athletes, business tycoons, the idle rich, diplomats and presidents. She'd learned a long time ago to discount good looks and practiced charm. Beneath their veneers of sophistication, the rich and famous were phonies and connivers, selfish, manipulative creatures out only for their own interests and pleasures.

For that reason, jaded as she was, she couldn't understand why Jed Louis threw her so completely off balance.

She turned right on the paved road and drove the couple hundred yards to the house that had once belonged to the dead woman who'd been found less than a quarter of a mile behind it.

The grave would have been fresh nineteen years ago. It seemed strange that Logan Fielder hadn't found it at the time. Obviously, the man had been incompetent as an investigator then. That didn't explain, though, why he was so antagonistic toward Jed now. Clearly, there was more behind his hostility than an ancient record of teenage pranks and mischief.

Jed's was a heartbreaking story. Four people living ordinary, peaceful lives one day, their security totally shattered the next. Yet Gwyn didn't doubt he was telling the truth…or at least that everything he'd told her was the truth. She was convinced he hadn't told her everything. There was something very disturbing about the way he recounted the events of nineteen years earlier.

When Jed had ranted at her and accused her of lying about her horses, which was at least partially true, and then complained about her supporting Tessa Lang over the archaeological dig, he'd looked her straight in the eye. Defiantly. He hadn't backed off, because he knew he was in the right. She understood and respected that, even though it put her at a disadvantage.

His eye contact had been unsure when he talked about Frannie Granger, as if he were trying to gauge the reaction of his listener. He'd stared out the window, at his plate, sipped cold coffee and nibbled on his crumbly roll, but he'd determinedly avoided looking at her straight on.

Were his the actions of someone not at peace with what he was saying, the behavior of a liar, of someone with a guilty conscience?

CHAPTER THREE

JED BATTED his hand across his face at the incessant bee buzzing around his head. He opened his eyes. Not a bee, a chain saw, he thought. He'd arranged yesterday for some trees to be thinned out on the property south of town. Then logic kicked in. He wouldn't be able to hear the cutting from here.

Engines. Motorcycles. Someone was on the grounds of Beaumarais. Jed sat bolt upright.

Fully awake now, he streaked naked from his bed and went to the window. He couldn't see anything, but there was no mistaking the keening whine. The sheriff's department? He didn't suppose the forensics guys would be here for another hour or two. Besides, this wasn't the sound of people seriously, conscientiously, doing a job. This was the racket of thrill seekers.

His bedside clock said seven. June wouldn't arrive for another hour. After throwing on a pair of worn jeans and a knit pullover, Jed bounded down the stairs two at a time. He stopped in the library, opened the gun case, removed a twelve-gauge, loaded it with birdshot, put a handful of extra cartridges in his pocket and stomped out the back door.

A sprint along the edge of the pines on the north

border of the back lawn brought him to the site the sheriff had cordoned off. The screech and roar of hard-charging engines grew in volume as he approached the barn where Gwyn kept her horses.

Three men old enough to know better were gouging deep tracks in the soft turf with their dirt bikes on the outside of the yellow tape Fielder's people had stretched around the excavation. Nearby, Gwyn's silly little horses were prancing, rearing and neighing in panic at the noise and disruption around them.

As Jed paused to catch his breath, one guy parked his bike, climbed over the wooden fence into the corral and tried to corner one of the miniature palominos. Had he not been so consumed with his own nefarious entertainment, he would have seen someone running toward him, but he was too self-absorbed to even notice Jed's bright-red shirt.

Pointing the shotgun into the air and taking heed that the pellets would land harmlessly, Jed pulled the trigger. The blast cut through the shrieking of the engines and reduced them to a rattling purr. The man on foot froze in his crouched position.

"Turn off your engines," Jed called out to the guys straddling their cycles. "You," he shouted to the leather-clad man in the corral, "get out of there. Now!"

"What the—" one of the bikers snarled.

Before he could finish the sentence, Jed aimed his shotgun at him, the muzzle trained low. The guy flinched when he realized where the damage would likely occur. Both hands went straight up, palms out.

"Okay, man, okay."

The other two fun seekers shut off their engines. Jed motioned them to get off the bikes. Leather-man climbed self-consciously over the whitewashed fence, his eyes never leaving the weapon leveled at him.

The sudden twitching of an eyebrow and leering smirk on the face of one of the others made Jed instantly aware of someone behind him. A fourth cohort? Where had he been?

"What's going on here?" a female voice demanded.

Jed marginally relaxed. He knew that clipped northern twang. Resisting the impulse to turn and face her, he said, "We have some visitors who seem to think tearing up other people's land and terrifying little horses is great sport."

"Well, I don't. I'll go phone the sheriff."

"No, don't," the guy in leather, apparently the leader of the pack, implored. "Look, we didn't mean any real harm. Just having some fun."

"Fun?" she repeated in alarm. "You call this fun?"

"Okay, so we got a little carried away."

"Well, as far as I'm concerned, mister, the sheriff can carry you the rest of the way. To jail." More calmly, she said to Jed, "I'll go ring him."

"Wait," the leader practically begged. "We'll pay for whatever damage we've done."

Jed laughed without humor. "Are we supposed to take that as an offer of generosity?" He narrowed his eyes. "You trespass on private property, tear up the ground, endanger harmless domesticated animals, then think you can write a check and walk away? This isn't an amusement park.''

He finally allowed himself to look over his shoulder at Gwyn. Definitely a mistake. Her hair was pulled back in its usual braid, but the woven coil was untidy this morning. Obviously, she'd just woken up. It took determined concentration not to think about her head on a pillow with that frazzled rope of auburn hair snaked over her shoulder. She wasn't wearing lipstick, either, and the natural softness of her lips in this early-morning light was an intoxicating invitation to taste.

He was suddenly uncomfortably aware he had nothing on under his threadbare jeans. To keep from embarrassing himself further, he concentrated on the men.

''How'd you get on my property, anyway?''

''The gate on the lake road was wide-open, man,'' the leader said.

Jed emitted a soft curse. ''Call the sheriff's office while I watch our visitors,'' he told Gwyn.

Half an hour later, after she verified none of her horses was injured, the good-time boys were hauled away and Logan Fielder stood, legs set apart, thumbs hooked in his wide belt, scowling ferociously at Jed.

''Who the hell do you think you are, Louis, pulling a shotgun on people?''

''A man defending his property,'' Jed replied caustically to the belligerent tone. ''I wouldn't have had to if your people had done their jobs. They left a gate open last night.''

"That's your problem. You should have checked it," Fielder snapped back.

Jed had, but either he hadn't examined it closely enough or the detectives had come back again afterward.

"I promise you, Sheriff, I'll make sure no one gets on my place again."

"And I warn you, Louis, don't try to restrict access to a crime scene or I'll charge you with obstructing justice."

Threats might have worked twenty years ago. They didn't now. "Fail to take the proper safeguards, Sheriff," Jed countered just as strongly, "and I'll bring charges against you for neglecting your duty to protect the public and willfully allowing the destruction of private property."

"It'd never stand up in court."

"Maybe not," Jed conceded with a lazy smile. "Then again, maybe it would. It's a matter of proving intent."

"Gentlemen, please," Gwyn interceded. "This isn't getting us anywhere."

"She's right," Jed agreed, satisfied he had the lawman on the defensive. "I'll make a deal with you, Sheriff. You take due care and so will I." Without waiting for a reply, he extended an arm in invitation to Gwyn and turned back toward the mansion.

Half expecting a shouted command from behind to halt, Gwyn tagged along but found herself having to nearly run to keep up with Jed's long stride. "Am I a villain in this piece, too?" she asked.

He stopped and gazed at her. "What?"

"I understand you're angry, Jed. So am I. Believe me, I don't like to have my horses upset, but do you think you could slow down enough for me to keep up with you without breaking into a full gallop?"

An embarrassed smile crept across his face. "Sorry. I don't know which gets me more ticked, those lamebrains on motorcycles or that lamebrain wearing the star."

"Geniuses are all unique," Gwyn offered. "Lamebrains are all alike."

Jed laughed. Impulsively he put his arm around her waist and pulled her up against his side. "Not only beautiful, but wise."

An amused grin came readily to her lips, but the sensation of his hard warm body touching hers was suddenly very disconcerting. She glanced up at him. The friendly smile she met in his twinkling eyes could easily have been the prelude to a kiss. The harsh caw of a bird awakened her to the fact that they were standing in the middle of open lawn in plain view of whoever wanted to watch. Her heart hammering, she stiffened and pulled away and walked on.

They reached the back steps of the mansion in silence. Her legs were still rubbery when she turned to face him. "Thanks—"

"Yesterday I checked out a place I own where you can keep your horses until we get this crisis resolved," he interrupted. "The stalls are too small for my Percherons, but they should be fine for your minis. The fence surrounding the pasture is a little too open, though, so I have a couple of workmen putting in an extra bottom rail. It should be ready by this afternoon. As soon as they're finished, I'll take you to inspect it to make sure it satisfies your requirements.''

''Thanks, Jed.'' Discussing business was definitely safer than touching. ''I'm sorry to be so much trouble.''

''You're paying for a safe place in which to keep your animals,'' he reminded her.

The formality of his speech amused her. Apparently he, too, was discomfited by their close contact.

''Unfortunately,'' he continued, ''it's not as convenient as where they are now, but I think it'll work.'' He extended his hand. ''Got time for a cup of coffee?''

It was tempting, oh, so tempting. She sighed. ''I still have animals to feed. Thanks, anyway.''

He dropped his arm, frustrated. ''Do you need a lift home?''

Shaking her head, she retreated a step. ''It's an easy walk. I—I'll see you later.'' She managed a carefree wave before turning back toward her rental house.

There was just the hint of morning breeze as she cut a path through a thicket of brush beneath spindly pine trees to the little house just north of Beaumarais. Her French was rusty, but she remembered enough to understand the name meant beautiful morass. One of Jed's ancestors, it would seem, had had a sense of humor. The label was apt, though, she thought. Caddo Lake was shallow for the most part, little more than swamp in many areas. Tropical cypress trees loomed above the muddy brown waters, their overhanging branches hung with the ragged gray bromeliad. The eerie setting was far more typical of the bayous of Southern Louisiana than the vast plains and open prairies characteristic of much of Texas.

As she stepped through the back door of the modest house that had once belonged to the murdered woman, Gwyn's thoughts wandered from the landscape around her to the episode that had just transpired. Her physical attraction to the tall, gorgeous Texan, an attraction that was clearly reciprocated, was getting harder and harder to resist. But she was beginning to see another aspect of Jed Louis, too, one she didn't like.

How many times had she heard him use the words *private property?*

He'd referred to it when he confronted her over the issue of Tessa Lang's dig, and again when he acknowledged he would have leased his land to Gwyn simply because it was good business even though he didn't like her horses. Then this morning he'd emphasized it in dealing with both the trespassers and the sheriff. He lived in a well-appointed mansion, owned land and houses all over town. Was Jed Louis obsessed with money and possessions? She'd grown up in a family intensely protective of their wealth and the power it gave them—including power over people.

A very pregnant seal point cat wound between her legs, rubbing her soft fur against Gwyn's ankles. It purred loudly, a happy sound, as soothing to Gwyn as the affection of the animal making it.

She went to the pantry and got out a can of cat food, opened it and began scooping the smelly mush into Cleopatra's bowl. Cleo jumped up and began devouring it greedily.

"Hungry, huh? I wonder how many you're eating for."

Putting on the kettle for a cup of instant coffee, Gwyn continued to muse about her landlord. She didn't get the impression he was unwilling to spend money. He owned a late-model Jaguar, though most of the time he drove a new pickup truck. Beaumarais was beautifully maintained. She'd seen a grounds-keeper there almost every time she'd driven by, and Jed employed a full-time housekeeper. Not the life-style of Ebenezer Scrooge. Did that mean he was willing to spend money only on his own comfort?

That didn't quite make sense, either, she decided. After all, he'd hired people to custom-fit a piece of land for her horses—not exactly the actions of a skin-flint. Unless he planned on charging her for the mod-ifications.

AT FOUR O'CLOCK that afternoon, Jed pulled up the narrow driveway on the south side of Frannie's old house. He'd rented it out many times over the past sixteen years, since purchasing it after the bank fore-closed on her unpaid mortgage. He'd repapered, re-painted, upgraded appliances and installed central heating and air-conditioning, amenities the house hadn't had when he lived in it with her. Nevertheless, no matter what he did to the three-bedroom, one-bath residence, or how many different names appeared on the mailbox at the curb, it had always remained "Frannie's house." He wondered sometimes when he showed people through it, if she would have approved of the changes he'd made. Probably, he concluded, though she might balk at his lavishing so much money on a place that was only rented.

He got out of his pickup and walked the mossy brick path from the driveway to the front door. Gwyn opened it before he had a chance to press the button on the right side of the jamb.

"I saw you drive up," she said in response to his startled expression. "Come on in."

He'd changed almost everything except the small entryway. Occupants rarely used the front entrance, so the charcoal-gray slate tile underfoot was in good condition. The raised paneling had a fresh coat of glossy white enamel; the old-fashioned crystal light sconces were still on the walls. Jed had a strange feeling every time he entered by the front door—as if he expected to see Frannie standing there, waiting for him. For the first few years after he'd purchased the house, he'd imaged her frowning in disappointment, the way she used to when he stayed out too late or failed to do his best. In the past couple of years, however, her ghost had met him with a smile, the way she had when he came home after winning an award or achieving some special goal. Today he felt her watching him, her expression curious, questioning, reserving judgment.

"I thought I'd show you where you can move your horses," he told Gwyn as he followed her into the living room.

"They finished the fence?"

"About an hour ago." He almost flinched when something brushed his leg. Looking down, he saw a tan-and-brown Siamese weaving lopsided between his ankles.

"That's Cleopatra. She's pregnant right now and in a very affectionate mood. Usually she's standoffish with strangers."

Jed picked the cat up and cradled her in the crook of his arm. "She's beautiful."

Gwyn smiled. "And temperamental."

Cleo purred as he petted her. "Any problems with sightseers or the sheriff's people today?"

She gave him a wry grin. "Those bouncers you posted at the gates are rather intimidating. Even Fielder's men seem put off by them."

Jed had hired two large gentlemen of his acquaintance to stand sentinel at the gates that gave access to the crime scene. The sheriff had raised Cain about his deputies having to identify themselves to enter the property, but Jed had pointed out he was not restricting access to anyone with a legitimate right to be there. In fact, he was performing a public service by ensuring busybodies didn't distract the investigators.

Jed chuckled and lowered the cat to the floor. "Good. Ready to go?"

"Do you mind if Romeo comes with us?"

Brow cocked, Jed asked, "Romeo?"

"My dog." Gwyn went through the kitchen to the back door and admitted an impeccably groomed, longhaired, tricolor sheepdog. The animal moved cautiously to Jed. He let it sniff a minute, then bent down and petted him enthusiastically.

"Romeo, you're one handsome devil." Jed glanced up at Gwyn. "Is he a collie or a sheltie? He looks too small for one and too big for the other."

"You know something about the breeds." She was pleased. "Actually, he's a purebred sheltie, but he's a throwback."

They rode in his truck in silence for several minutes, Romeo in the back of the crew cab, his mouth hanging open, long tongue dripping on the towel Gwyn had insisted on spreading across the vinyl bench seat.

"What exactly does an animal manager do?" Jed asked.

"I make animals available on a short-term basis for things like advertisements and television commercials, movies, even carnivals and charity drives."

"Do you own all the animals you manage? Your pregnant cat, a dog and miniature horses don't seem like they'd be enough to make a living with."

"They wouldn't be. I also act as an agent for other people's animals. A rancher I know in Colorado has several domesticated deer. Another in West Texas raises llamas. A third one has emus, storks, peacocks and turkeys. If someone needs a flock of sheep for a Little Bo Peep scene on television, they contact me and I find the person who has the requisite number available."

"So you're a middleman…er…woman."

"Exactly. I'm always interested in cultivating new contacts. Would you be interested in having your

Percherons earn you a few extra bucks, maybe in a beer commercial or just for people to admire at a county fair on a weekend?''

"Hmm." He smiled. "Let me think about it."

He turned down a narrow dirt road that wound through low hills and thick stands of untamed forest. When the road forked, he veered to the right.

"The advantage of this place is that it's remote, which means there aren't likely to be any casual rubbernecks. And the disadvantage is that it's remote, which means trespassers aren't likely to be noticed unless you happen to be here at the same time."

"But there is a good gate," she pointed out.

"Gates and locks keep out honest people. They don't seem to inhibit the dishonest."

"Not only handsome, but wise," she quipped, parodying his description of her that morning.

The memory of his arm around her brought a new wave of warmth to her body. Unwilling to fully acknowledge what she was feeling, she cast a sidelong glance at the man on the other side of the console.

He started to open his mouth to speak, then closed it again. "It's just a short walk," he finally said with unusual softness, and opened his door. Romeo bounded across his lap, making him wince.

Jed had unlocked the chain and pushed open the gate by the time she joined him. They walked twenty yards farther down the dirt road until they came to a shed row. As he'd indicated earlier, the corrugated-metal-covered stalls were too small and too low for giant Percherons, but they would be ideal for her small horses. The stalls opened onto a paddock that wasn't as big as the one she had her animals at now, but it was more than adequate for their needs.

She strolled along the fence line, where an extra lower rail had been nailed to the wooden posts, as he'd told her. The job was neatly and professionally done. "This is perfect, Jed."

"Glad it works." There was a note of pride in his reply. "Will you be able to move them tonight?"

"I'd rather wait until the morning, if that's okay. It's better to let them get accustomed to their new surroundings in the daytime, with me around to observe how they're settling in."

He nodded. "If you need any help…I'll be glad to."

Gwyn started to tell him she could handle them quite well by herself. After all, she'd gotten them this far on her own. But the prospect of sharing his company and working side by side with him had an allure she couldn't resist.

"Thanks," she said. "I can always use an extra hand."

"You haven't told me how you got into the animal-handling business," he remarked on the drive back to Frannie's house.

"As much by accident as design," she said. "I've always liked pets, but my folks weren't particularly fond of them. After college, when I was finally on my own, I got a cat and a dog. A friend of mine was a photographer and asked to take some shots of them snuggled up against each other for a contest he wanted to enter. The pictures took first place and an animal food company bought the photos for their advertising. You may have seen the ad campaign. Contented Critters. It was out a few years back.''

''Those were yours?''

''Uh-huh. Well, after that I was asked if I had any more animals for ads and commercials and the next thing I knew I was an animal manager.''

''Where did you go to college?''

She hesitated, then tried to make her reply sound offhanded. ''Vassar.''

He crooked an eyebrow. ''What did you major in there? Anything that prepared you for dog and cat food commercials?''

She'd heard the subtle mocking tone before. Most people seemed to think that someone who'd graduated from a prestigious women's college should be doing more with her life than carting a bunch of animals around the country. Her parents certainly did. What would he say if he found out she came from one of the most distinguished families in the nation, and that she would do anything to maintain her independence from them?

''I took a slew of practical business courses, but my major was less pragmatic. French and Russian lit.''

''Useful, I suppose for training French poodles and Russian wolfhounds.''

Or for being the charming, chosen wife of a politician in the diplomatic corps.

THEY WERE ON the veranda, finishing the chicken-and-pasta casserole June had left for him in the oven, when Romeo, who had parked himself against the low wall, sprang from his snooze and started barking ferociously. Jed and Gwyn jumped to their feet. As she calmed the dog, Jed turned to see Logan Fielder walking around the side of the house.

"Good evening, Sheriff," Jed said, sounding so casual a stranger might mistakenly imagine it was quite ordinary for the man with the star to drop by unannounced at dinnertime. In fact, Jed nearly flinched at the sight of the lawman. This clearly wasn't a social visit, since Fielder was still packing a revolver on his hip.

Eyeing the dog cautiously, the sheriff said, "I need to talk to you, Louis."

"About what?"

"It's private."

Jed didn't respond, except to stare at him.

Fielder belatedly tipped his hat to Gwyn. "Ms. Miller, if you'll excuse us for a few minutes…"

Rather than leave, as he no doubt expected, she settled into her cushioned Adirondack chair. "Since this is Mr. Louis's home, Sheriff, I think I'll let him decide if I should stay or go. If he has no objection, I'd just as soon hang around."

Jed looked at her, his eyebrows raised. He sucked in his cheeks in surprise at her audacity, but the beatific smile he tossed her way said she'd just gone up a notch in his estimation.

In contrast, Fielder's weather-beaten face turned dark red, while his dusty gray eyes nearly bulged out of his head. The irate scowl he cast at her was nothing short of demonic. Nobody talked back to Logan Fielder. Slowly letting the pent-up air out of his lungs, he continued to glare at her for a minute, then turned to Jed.

"The day Granger went missing—I want you to tell me exactly where you were."

"I told you that nineteen years ago." Jed refused to flinch under the lawman's bullying tactics. He'd learned a lot since he was almost eighteen. "My answer hasn't changed."

"Tell me again."

Jed barely managed to keep his hands from tightening into fists. He met the man's hard stare. "Read your notes."

Teeth set, Fielder let several heartbeats go by before he said, "I have. By your own account and everyone else's, you were the last person to see the Granger woman alive—"

His heart beginning to pound with indignation, Jed interrupted before Fielder could go any further.

"Hold it right there, Sheriff. Frannie Granger wasn't 'the Granger woman.' She was my foster mother, the person who brought me up after my own mother died. She's the victim in this case. Treat her with the dignity and respect she deserves."

Logan Fielder worked his jaw for several seconds. "Noted," he finally muttered. "Now, the day she disappeared, where did you go, who were you with, who did you see and who saw you? They're questions you better have answers to if you expect to establish an alibi. I didn't push you real hard back then because I didn't know she was dead, murdered. I know it now, and by God I'm going to get some answers."

Gwyn's insides clenched and her stomach turned to acid. She realized scare tactics and intimidation by innuendo were standard interrogation tools, but she wondered if the sheriff didn't also have a personal agenda in the way he was conducting this investigation. Granted, for some reason, Fielder didn't like Jed Louis, but did he really think one of Uncertain's wealthiest and most prominent—and, presumably, most powerful—citizens murdered his foster mother? Why? Or was he simply looking for a scapegoat on whom to pin the crime?

"Jed," Gwyn said in a voice that surprised her by its apparent calm control, "I suggest you not answer any of the sheriff's questions until you can talk to an attorney and have him present."

Slowly, Jed dragged his eyes from his inquisitor and looked at Gwyn. Though his expression was sober, there was an unmistakable gleam in his eye— just for her.

"I think you're right." Redirecting his attention to Fielder, he said with slow deliberation, "I have nothing to tell you, Sheriff. Now, if you'll excuse us..." He turned his back on his uninvited guest.

"You're making a big mistake, Louis. We could have handled this informally, but you want to play rough. Fine. We can do it your way. The questions won't change whether you answer them here or in an interrogation room downtown. I just thought you might prefer sleeping—" he gazed up at the mansion "—in your own bed than on a rack in the county jail." He took a step toward the path he'd used and turned abruptly. ''I think you're well-advised to get yourself a lawyer, Louis.'' Romeo emitted a menacing growl. ''Make it a real good one, because that's what you're going to need.''

CHAPTER FOUR

GWYN WATCHED Jed after Fielder left. To all outward appearances, he was calm. There were no muttered curses, no imprecations against the sheriff's browbeating tactics. Jed's fork didn't clatter on the plate or his hand shake when he brought it to his mouth, but he ate slowly, quietly, thoughtfully. Beneath the cool facade, she saw a man who was simmering and perhaps just a little afraid.

There was good reason for him to be, Gwyn told herself. The county lawman had all but threatened to charge him with murder. That was enough to chill anyone's bones.

She pointed to an umbrella-shaped tree covered with purple blossoms a few dozen yards beyond the stone wall of the veranda. "What kind of tree is that?"

He raised his head and looked in the direction she was pointing. "Jacaranda. It's in the catalpa family. Originally from Brazil, I think. June's husband, Josiah, is the groundskeeper. He can probably tell you a lot more about it." His tone was mechanical, remote.

"It's beautiful. Is that what I smell, sort of a sweet grape fragrance?"

"Uh-huh."

His mind was somewhere else. She wondered where. None of her business, she tried to convince herself.

"This casserole is delicious," she babbled, hoping small talk might pull him out of his reverie. He gave a vague nod, then seemed to realize he was expected to say something in reply.

"June's an excellent cook," he agreed. "Do you cook?"

She chortled. "I have trouble boiling water without burning it. I'm getting better, though. The other day—"

Obviously not listening to her, he put down his fork and pushed back his chair. "Would you excuse me a minute?"

"Of course. Is there—"

"I'll be right back." He placed his napkin beside his still-full plate and walked toward the French doors at the far end of the patio.

He waited until he was inside the library before he allowed his hands to tighten into hard fists. He'd come close to losing control when Fielder had referred to Frannie with such condescension. Whether it was calculated on the sheriff's part or just the natural disdain he showed for everyone, Jed wasn't sure. It didn't make any difference. Fielder had found a weak spot and Jed had no doubt he would exploit it for all it was worth.

Jed didn't like feeling vulnerable, prey to people's definitions of who and what he was. It gave other people power over him. For too many years, he'd been Helen Louis's illegitimate son, Walter Louis's bastard nephew, Frannie Granger's foster kid. It had taken years to set those labels aside. He'd transformed himself into Jed Louis, prominent landowner and reputable Percheron horse breeder. Then Fielder pulled his chain and he'd reverted to the insecure, defensive teenager of twenty years earlier. Never mind that he was trying to preserve the dignity of the one adult in his life who'd done her best to protect him from others—and sometimes from himself. For a moment he'd slipped, reverted. What would happen if he let himself go completely?

He was grateful for Gwyn's presence during the sheriff's visit. Had she not been there, he might well have reacted differently to the man's questions and blurted out something stupid, something incriminating. She'd stood up to the old bully—or more properly, he thought with a faint smile—sat there like a lady and defied the lawman. Gwyn Miller had a way of inspiring self-control.

The smile faded. That wasn't precisely true. If anything, being with this sophisticated woman with the shiny auburn hair made him want to unleash restraints, not curb them. He'd come dangerously close to kissing her this morning. And this afternoon, when they'd walked side by side, hands almost touching, he'd wanted desperately to reach over and entwine his fingers with hers, feel the warmth of her skin, the softness of her body.

Why hadn't he? He wasn't blind; he'd seen her glances. Gwyn might disagree with him on issues, but it didn't affect their physical attraction. Kissing

Gwyn Miller would be a pleasant thing. He took a deep breath.

So why hadn't he taken the next step? When they were on the lawn, why hadn't he kissed her? Why hadn't he taken her hand in his at the horse paddock, wrapped her in his arms and savored the feel of her body pressed against his? Every time he asked himself those questions, he came up with the same disturbing answer. He was afraid…afraid if he touched her once he wouldn't be able to hold back. Afraid if he tasted one of her kisses it wouldn't quell the hunger. Afraid if he ever made love to her…

He strode to the desk, lifted the handset and punched in a series of numbers. It was picked up on the second ring.

"Hello? Who's there? My daddy can't come to the phone right now 'cause he's in the bathroom."

The juvenile, high-pitched voice immediately dispelled the ache of a moment before.

"Hi, Alanna." He'd dialed Riley's unlisted home number, not his business number, which would have gotten him an answering service. "How's my favorite girl today?"

Alanna was a delightful child, bright and cheerful. Her mother had died giving her birth, but the baby had been blessed with a father who loved her dearly and had done everything in his power to make up for the loss. Raising her by himself couldn't be easy, but Riley was a wonderful dad. A little girl without a mother. The parallel with a little boy without a father was too close for comfort. He forced the image from his mind.

"I got a boo-boo on my finger, Mr. Jed," the four-year-old answered.

"I'm so sorry, sweetheart. I bet your daddy kissed it, though, to make it all better."

"Uh-huh, but he's got to kiss it some more, because it hurts again."

"Well, when he comes out of the bathroom, you have him kiss it for me, too, all right? And would you also ask him to call me at home as soon as he can?"

"Okay. Bye." She slammed down the receiver.

Jed jerked the phone from his ear and chuckled. He turned toward the doors and stopped. Gwyn was standing there on the edge of the early-evening sunlight, her features in shadow, but they weren't so dark he couldn't see and feel her looking at him. For a moment the two of them just stared at each other.

"I'm sorry," she finally said, breaking the silence that was building into discomfort. "I didn't mean to eavesdrop. I just wondered if you were okay."

"I'm fine," he assured her with a crooked smile.

"Perhaps it would be better if I left and gave you privacy."

"No, don't go."

The phone rang.

"Come on in," Jed called out to her, his hand automatically reaching for the receiver.

As expected, it was Riley. "I'm glad you finally got out of the bathroom," he said with a chuckle. "Did you kiss Alanna's boo-boo for me?"

There was a smile in Riley's voice. "Yes, that should do the trick for a while. The next step is a bandage. It's usually good for a day or two. What's up?''

Jed inhaled. ''Our esteemed sheriff was here asking questions.''

''Hmm.'' There was the briefest pause. ''I have to put Alanna to bed, then I'll ask Mrs. Yates to mind her. I'll be over in…give me half an hour, forty-five minutes.''

''That was your neighbor, Riley Gray. He's my attorney,'' Jed told Gwyn after he hung up. ''He'll be over in a little while.'' He moved toward her, or rather, toward the double doors behind her. ''I'm sorry to have spoiled your dinner.''

''Blame it on the party crasher.'' She glanced around. ''So this is the library you're so fond of.''

She couldn't blame him. It was a large room that ran from the front to the back of the house. A wide bay window looked out on the front lawn and the circular driveway. French doors and window panels gave a full-length view of the garden beyond the veranda and the lake in the distance. The two other walls were covered floor to ceiling with dark-stained bookcases. The outside end wall contained a handsomely carved marble fireplace. The polished hardwood floor had several thick Oriental carpets spread across it. The furniture was traditional and conservative, altogether a very masculine room. It suited Jed well; no wonder he liked it.

At his invitation, Gwyn preceded him back to the veranda and the dinner they'd abandoned. Romeo, apparently at home by the low wall, opened one eye briefly, then returned to his contented nap.

"We can at least enjoy dessert. June makes a tantalizing black bottom pie."

"Get thee behind me, Satan," she said, then laughed. "Ah, to hell with it. Bring on the demon chocolate."

Together they cleared the table. She accompanied him as he wheeled the serving cart to the kitchen, which was big and modern with commercial grade worktables and appliances. Not exactly homey, in spite of the houseplants in the windows and on neighboring counters, but it was well suited for entertaining large groups.

He removed a small cream-topped pie from an oversize stainless-steel refrigerator and asked Gwyn to follow him back outside with the glass plates and forks June had left on the counter. Before they sat down, he refilled their water glasses from a covered carafe.

"It's rich," he noted, indicating the pie.

The whipped-cream-and-chocolate dessert was every bit as good as Jed had predicted. At the offer of a second piece, she hesitated, then gave in to temptation.

"They say chocolate has a soothing affect on the nervous system," she noted as she raised her fork. "It may not be true," she admitted, "but the idea at least salves my conscience."

The setting sun gilded the flagstone veranda, drawing out nature's colors in deep relief. Birds twittered as they prepared for the night ahead. The heavy warmth of the day mellowed on a gentle breeze to a refreshing coolness. Conversation waned, but the silence between them was as comfortable now as the soft shadows slowly edging their way across the verdant fields.

When the lights dotting the perimeter of the veranda came on automatically, Jed suggested he make coffee and they go into the library. Once again, she helped clear the table, but when she offered to wash the dishes they'd piled up, he told her that was June's job.

Brows raised, she was momentarily taken aback. The condescension implied in the remark shocked her. Jed was a wealthy man who obviously lived well, but she hadn't expected this arrogance from him.

Apparently sensing the way he'd come across, he said, "June gets very upset if I invade her turf, and she'd flay me alive if she found out I let a guest wash dishes." The tiny smile tickling the corner of his mouth assured her he understood exactly what her reaction had been.

"Do you like Cajun coffee?" he asked.

"I don't know. If that's what you drink, let me try it."

Her wanting to share his tastes inordinately pleased him. "You're on, but you have to promise to be truthful. If you decide you don't care for it, say so, and I'll make a pot of regular."

She held up her hand palm out, three fingers raised. "Scout's honor."

He laughed. "Were you in the Scouts?"

She didn't dare tell him that Millers didn't participate in plebian organizations like the Scouts. "Never got around to it. You?"

"Earned all my merit badges and made Eagle."

He ground a blend of French-roast coffee beans and chicory and boiled it in an enamel pot. She helped him set a tray with large geometrically patterned cups, cream, sugar, spoons and small cloth napkins. He'd just carried it to the library when the doorbell rang.

He put the tray down on a corner of the desk, excused himself and came back a minute later with her neighbor.

"Gwyneth Miller, Riley Gray."

"We've met," she said. "Over the back fence. And his beautiful daughter."

He wasn't exactly Gwyn's image of a lawyer. In the world in which she'd grown up, attorneys wore suits twenty-four hours a day. This man was dressed casually in chinos and a knit shirt. He was a couple of inches shorter than Jed, but was still about six feet tall, exuded the sinewy fitness of a man who took care of himself. Jed was deeply tanned. Riley wasn't any darker, but his complexion was more bronze toned. It took only a moment's glance at his broad handsome features to realize he had a strong Native American heritage.

"Gwyn was just about to sample some of my coffee," Jed announced.

Riley smiled at her. "First time?"

She nodded.

"Brave girl."

"Speaking of brave girls," Jed interposed. "How did Alanna get a boo-boo?"

Riley's face lit up at the mention of his daughter. "A tragedy of the first magnitude, I'm afraid," he said melodramatically. "She sustained a splinter in her finger from the fence when she was out playing this afternoon. We had to perform tweezer surgery. I kissed it, of course, but the anesthetic effect keeps wearing off."

"Maybe she just likes getting kisses," Gwyn suggested.

Riley grinned proudly. "And I'll happily keep giving them."

"Should I send a sympathy card?" Jed asked lightheartedly.

"Not yet. *Sympathy* is a pretty big word for someone not yet five years old."

They settled into easy chairs and sipped the bitter, full-bodied coffee.

"Now," Riley said, "tell me about Logan Fielder's shenanigans."

Jed took a deep breath and related his four run-ins with the sheriff: the morning before, when he'd announced Frannie's gravesite was a crime scene; this morning, when Jed called him to arrest some trespassers; later, when he discovered the guards on the scene; and finally, this evening at dinner, when he showed up asking questions.

"What questions?" Riley asked.

"He wanted me to establish an alibi for the day Frannie disappeared."

"What did you tell him?"

"To read his notes. He asked me the same things nineteen years ago. I shouldn't have to answer them again."

Riley stroked his chin. "It's not a completely unreasonable request. Two decades ago, he was looking into a disappearance with no hard evidence of foul play. Now he has a murder to solve."

"I advised him not to answer any questions, Riley," Gwyn informed him. "I didn't like the sheriff's attitude."

Riley guffawed. "If you're waiting for Logan Fielder to get into a good mood, you're likely to have a crown of snow-white hair first." He tugged on his ear. "Your advice was well-founded, though. The less said to the sheriff or either of his deputies the better."

"Will you come with me when I do get dragged in for questioning?" Jed asked.

"Of course." He paused. "But I have to remind you my specialty is civil, not criminal, law. I can make sure the sheriff isn't too out of line in giving you the third degree, but if he's going to get tough—and knowing Fielder, he probably will—I'd recommend you hire yourself a good defense attorney."

Jed was disappointed that he'd have to confide in someone else, but he respected his friend's honesty. "Is there anyone you can recommend?"

Riley sipped his coffee while he considered a minute. "Dempsey in Jefferson handles criminal matters, but most of them are for assault, robbery and an occasional auto theft. As far as I know he's never been involved in a homicide case. There's a new guy in

Marshall—Kingston or Kingsley. I hear he's taken on a couple of wrongful-death suits, but again that's civil, not criminal. I can ask around...."

"How about Dexter Thorndyke?" Gwyn asked.

The two men stopped in midmotion and stared at her.

"Dexter Thorndyke?" Jed asked incredulously. "*The* Dexter Thorndyke? The guy who defended Trigve Helms against the murder of his fiancée?"

Trigve Helms was a retired Olympian and endorser of athletic equipment for one of the biggest sports manufacturers in the world. Several hours after having a very public argument with his fiancée, McKenna Hasley, the showgirl was found strangled with the tie Trigve had last been seen wearing. The case seemed open-and-shut, despite Trigve's vehement protests of innocence, and public opinion leaned heavily toward his being guilty. It seemed likely he would have been convicted of first-degree murder had Dexter Thorndyke not been brought in at the last minute to defend him. There was still a great deal of controversy over whether the former gold medal winner had actually committed the murder, but the jury had found him not guilty.

When Gwyn nodded, Jed added, "Not a chance."

"You mean you don't want him?"

Jed snorted. "There's no way in creation he'd take my case. Can you imagine the Great Thorn coming all the way from New Orleans to Uncertain, Texas? Give me a break."

"But you would hire him if you could?" she persisted.

He huffed. "Of course I would, but it's not going to happen."

"It won't hurt to ask him."

"I don't even know how to get hold of him," Jed huffed, showing exasperation.

"I do."

She and Jed looked at each other for what felt like an eternity. Finally, Riley got up from his chair. "Gee, I'm going to feel guilty about charging you for this house call and consultation when I wasn't the one who came up with the solution, but I'll just have to swallow my pride."

Jed rose. "You're leaving?"

"No more work for me here, my friend." He closed the short distance to Gwyn, took her hands in his and kissed her in brotherly fashion on the cheek.

"Go for it. Do keep me posted," he said to Jed as he turned toward the door to the hallway. A moment later they heard the front door click shut.

Jed stared at Gwyn long enough to make her fidget.

"I believe we were talking about honesty when Riley arrived." His voice had taken on the hardness she remembered all too well. "Would you care to tell me what's going on? How is it you can call a man like Dexter Thorndyke to take my case?"

Gwyn's knees felt watery. She wanted desperately to collapse into the chair she'd been occupying, but to do so would show weakness, and she had a feeling a subordinate position wasn't the place to be at the moment. Besides, with Jed standing over her she'd have to look up so high she'd get a sore neck.

"Can we sit down?" she asked, in spite of her resolution to be strong.

He gave her a brisk nod and returned to his seat. Eyeing her, he took a sip of his coffee, realized it was cold and placed the cup back on its saucer. She hadn't moved.

He motioned her to the chair behind her. When she finally slipped into it, he asked, "Who are you?"

You would think a man who had just been offered the opportunity to be represented by one of the foremost defense attorneys in the country would be pleased, she complained to herself. Instead, he seemed more miffed than glad.

"I'm waiting," he said when she didn't immediately answer him.

"The name Miller doesn't ring a bell for you. Perhaps you've heard of my father, Wingate Miller."

Oh, yes. The bell chimed this time.

"Senator Wingate Miller of the Miller—"

"—Millions." She let the word out in a sigh of displeasure. It would have been so easy to drop her head, to shrink from what she saw on his face. She managed, however, to maintain eye contact.

"Let me see if I have this straight," he said slowly. "Your father is a prominent member of the United States Senate. You're from one of the wealthiest, most influential families in the nation, and you're living in my rental house next door and playing with animals."

"Not playing with them," she snapped, and jumped to her feet.

Her parents had used terms like that, condescending words that implied she was wasting her time and talents, that she was irresponsible and a disgrace to her heritage. She'd run away from them because she'd had no choice. She wouldn't back away from Jed Louis, because she did. Standing directly in front of him, her feet planted slightly apart, she informed him, "I'm making a living as an animal manager."

He stretched an arm across the back of a couch and met her gaze. "Why?"

"Because of your reaction a moment ago."

Brow furled, he shook his head in utter bewilderment. "What are you talking about?"

She returned to the easy chair and sat down. "You didn't even realize you'd done it. You lowered your voice when you referred to the Miller Millions, like someone praying in church, as if there's something sacred about the Miller family. Believe me, there isn't. I'm not sacred. I'm not holy. I don't want to be spoken of—even behind my back—in whispers. Do you have any idea what it's like to be always held at arm's length?"

He wanted to tell her he did, but from the other side of the church door. To be treated not as sacred but profane, not as holy but a sinner, condemned by his very birth. To be not only whispered about behind his back but to sometimes have it shouted in his face—that he was nothing, nobody, a piece of dirt that was best left in the gutter. Yes, he knew.

"You are special," he said to console, but instead of seeing pleasure in her eyes, he watched her face crumple, as if he'd just insulted her. Rather than bringing them together, his words had driven them apart.

He had a sudden urge to kneel at her feet and tell her she was very special to him, but she didn't want anyone paying court to her or singing her praises. Restlessly, he rose and began pacing the space between her chair and the desk.

"So to conceal your identity, you lied to me," he stated. "Again."

"I didn't lie," she assured him, but there was despair in her voice. "I didn't tell you anything that wasn't true."

He held up a finger to indicate enlightenment. "Ah, yes, of course. I forgot. Telling half-truths is as good as whole truths, and if the listener misinterprets the meaning behind your carefully crafted statements, it's his fault for being so dense."

She clutched the arms of the chair. "I never said that. I've never suggested you're dense."

"Isn't that what you do every time you mislead me?"

"No."

"You have harness horses to pasture," he continued, ignoring her. "But I'm too simpleminded to even imagine they might be miniatures."

"Jed, you don't understand—"

"Someone wants to dig up my land, but I'm too narrow-minded to let them, so it's better to get the authorities to force me to do what's right."

"Please, Jed—"

"Your name is Miller, but I'm too dim-witted to figure out that you might be one of *the* Millers, heir to a legendary fortune. After all, it's a great joke driving a rattletrap Land Rover and slumming in a little rental house, when you could be chauffeured in a Rolls-Royce and build a mansion, if it struck your fancy.''

He was shocked when he turned around to hurl yet another insult in her face and saw the hurt expression in her eyes. Instantly he stopped his pacing. He wanted to reach out for her hand and beg her forgiveness.

''I'm sorry to have caused you so much trouble,'' she said in a voice that was remarkably steady, firm, sincere. ''I shouldn't have interfered. Thank you for dinner.''

She rose with dignity and walked swiftly to the veranda door.

''Gwyn.'' He took a step forward. ''Gwyn, I didn't—''

The door clicked shut behind her. He rushed outside, but she was already moving into the woods, Romeo at her heel. Jed called after her, but she didn't turn around. He followed at a slower pace. At least he could make sure she got home safely. He waited until he saw a light go on inside the house, then he retraced his steps in the dark to Beaumarais.

GWYN CLOSED the door and leaned her back against it. Tears, hot and heavy, threatened to break through. She fought for control, knowing once they started, it would be impossible to restrain them. Part of what Jed said was true. She had purposely misled and deceived him. But, she reminded herself, she didn't owe him the complete truth. She didn't hold back because she was a chronic liar or because she enjoyed deceiving people as Jed claimed. It was self-defense, pure and simple. She hated the distance her name put between her and the people she met, the barrier it put up to ever having a "normal" social relationship.

She'd grown up in a world of fawning isolation, and she'd hated it. Other kids had friends they could talk to, friends who were willing to share secrets. Not Gwyneth Miller of the fabled Miller fortune. She wasn't invited to just drop in at people's homes, and no one ever appeared at the Miller mansion capriciously or unannounced. She felt smothered in politeness and good manners, or hated because she represented what other people didn't have. They didn't know the price of wealth and power.

Jed was wrong, though, if he thought she didn't consider him very bright. In only a few days of close association, she'd found him to be intelligent and honest. Qualities that weren't foremost among Miller bluebloods or their cronies. How would she ever get him to understand her motives?

CHAPTER FIVE

JED RETURNED home from his office in Jefferson around three o'clock the following afternoon. He waved to Josiah, who was trimming a yellow primrose jasmine on the side of the house. June's husband was short, dark and round, and inclined to be as loquacious as she was taciturn. Jed had spent most of the morning reviewing building options on six pieces of commercial property he owned in Marshall. After a business lunch with the president of the chamber of commerce to discuss the upcoming Anglers' Ball, he'd dealt with a feed-store owner who'd recently delivered a batch of improperly cured steam-rolled oats.

Now there was a Mercedes parked in the circular driveway. Jed continued around the side of the house to the detached garage and entered his home through the kitchen door as he usually did. June was mixing something in a bowl that smelled faintly of cinnamon.

''There's a gentleman to see you, sir.'' She nodded to a business card sitting on the corner of the stainless-steel counter.

Jed picked it up and read the embossed print. Dexter Thorndyke, Attorney-at-Law. For a moment, Jed was speechless. After the way he'd treated Gwyn the night before he'd assumed her offer to contact the famous defense lawyer was a dead issue.

"Where is he now?"

"In the sitting room."

"How long has he been waiting?"

June poured the batter into a greased cake tin. "He called a little while ago and asked when you'd be available. I told him I expected you back around three and gave him your number at the office. He arrived here a few minutes later and asked if he could wait. Apparently your secretary told him you'd already left."

Jed looked at his watch. It was 3:10. "I'll take him to the library."

"Will you be wanting anything?"

"Give us a few minutes, then come in and check."

He entered the Victorian sitter. "Mr. Thorndyke, I'm Jed Louis. I'm sorry to have kept you waiting. Thank you for coming."

The prestigious attorney turned from his examination of the contents of a glass cabinet in the corner opposite the room's single window. He was in his late fifties or early sixties, with thinning gray-streaked brown hair. Average in height, neither tall nor short, stout but not obese, he had clear brown eyes that were sharp, intelligent and assessing. His summer-weight tan suit and pale-yellow shirt were complemented by a conservative tie of muted maroon and blue stripes.

"Mr. Louis, I'm pleased to meet you." He held out his hand and clasped Jed's in a firm shake. "You have a beautiful home here. I was just looking at your book collection. One doesn't often see a first edition of Dickens's *David Copperfield* so casually displayed.''

The comment smacked of criticism, but Jed decided to reserve judgment. On its face the observation was, no doubt, true, and he realized it could just as easily be a compliment.

''Let's go to the library,'' Jed offered. ''We'll be more comfortable there.''

He led his guest through the far door directly into the massive room at the north end of the house and waved a hand toward one of two couches in front of the cold fireplace. Thorndyke held back, however, and turned in a full circle.

''I retract what I said,'' he remarked. ''The other room is merely pretty. This is beautiful.''

Jed laughed in spite of himself. ''If you're interested in first editions, I have a much larger collection in here that I'll be glad to show you.''

As if on cue, June appeared in the doorway from the small hall. ''May I get you gentlemen anything?''

Jed turned to his guest. ''Something cold, hot or perhaps stronger?'' They decided on June's home-made lemonade.

''I must tell you, Mr. Thorndyke, I'm surprised you're here, or more correctly, I'm surprised Ms. Miller called you. I'm afraid I wasn't very kind to her last evening.'' Jed pictured the strange commingling of shame and anger on Gwyn's face when she'd told him who she was.

The older man groaned audibly. ''I've known her

since she was born. I watched her grow up and take control of her life. You'll soon learn, if you haven't already, that Gwyneth Miller is a very strong and determined person. She does what's right regardless of what it may cost her.''

''I'm beginning to see that.''

''Your reaction to her yesterday when you found out she was one of *the* Millers isn't uncommon, Mr. Louis. It's what she's been fleeing most of her life.'' More sympathetically, Thorndyke added, ''She's a good woman, Jed. That should be enough for anyone.''

Jed instantly realized why this man was such a formidable advocate. In a few words he'd both reprimanded and encouraged his client, made him ashamed of his treatment of Gwyn and intimated that the breach could be repaired.

June reappeared, served their drinks and left a tray with a crystal pitcher and ice bucket. Apparently satisfied that he'd said enough, the attorney pressed on.

''Gwyn tells me you expect to be charged with the murder of your foster mother.''

Even though the idea had been bouncing around in his head since the sheriff's initial visit, hearing the words spoken out loud sent a shiver down his spine. ''The possibility seems a real one.''

''Why?''

Jed's inclination was to furnish a minimum of detail on his life with Frannie Granger and her abrupt disappearance, but he realized nothing would be gained by holding back. If this man was going to help him he needed as much information as possible.

Jed took the better part of an hour to tell his story. The death of his twenty-three-year-old mother. His being placed under Frannie Granger's foster care. The death of his uncle a few years later and the shock of finding out he had actually inherited Beaumarais. Life with his foster sister, Emerald Monday, and finally his gaining a foster brother who was a juvenile delinquent.

The lawyer listened attentively, asked occasional questions for clarification, but otherwise allowed Jed to ramble on at his own pace.

"Who were Ms. Granger's enemies?" Thorndyke finally asked.

Jed shook his head. "I never knew she had any," he replied sadly. "She was well liked."

"You say she cleaned houses. Servants and housekeepers get to learn confidences. Could she have discovered something about one of her clients that threatened them?"

"If you're suggesting she might have been blackmailing someone, you're way off the mark. Frannie wasn't that kind of person. I don't recall her ever mentioning anything personal about any of her clients, not even on the cleanliness of their houses. She wasn't a gossip, Mr. Thorndyke. She minded her own business. Ask the people around here who knew her. I don't think you'll find anyone who has an unkind word to say about her."

Tracing a finger along one of the bookshelves, his back to Jed, he commented, "There's a flaw in your logic. You realize that, don't you?"

Jed inhaled dejection. "Someone killed her—

therefore she must have had an enemy. Unless it was an accident.''

With an unconvincing shrug, Thorndyke conceded the point. ''People don't normally bury innocent accidents,'' he observed. ''As far as you know, does the sheriff have any other suspects?''

Jed shook his head. ''I'm not aware of any.''

Thorndyke turned around. ''You're suggesting he has a personal animus to you. Why?''

Jed dragged a hand through his hair. ''It goes back to before Frannie's disappearance. My foster brother, Will McClain, had a run-in or two with the law right after he came to live with us. Fielder was a hard-ass deputy back then who wasn't above physical intimidation of suspects. When Frannie found out he'd slapped Will around, she threatened to bring charges of police brutality against him if he ever did it again.''

One brow raised, the lawyer asked, ''Would she have?''

''Oh, yes. Frannie was patient and forgiving, but she didn't make idle threats.''

''How long after her confrontation with Fielder did she disappear?''

Was Thorndyke suggesting Fielder might have had something to do with her untimely end? Remarkably, the notion had never entered Jed's mind. Thinking about it now, he realized it had merit. Logan Fielder had failed to find Frannie's body, even though it was buried only a few hundred yards from her home. Now, all these years later, his incompetence was surfacing and he was trying to pin the murder on Jed.

"Will was with us about four years," Jed responded. "All Frannie's serious problems with him were in the first few months, so I'd say it was two or three years between her showdown with Fielder and her disappearance."

"Could Will have had another run-in with Fielder that resulted in another clash between him and Frannie?"

Jed's brow furled. Why hadn't he thought of this possibility? "Will didn't tell me about any recent incidents with the police...." He let the words trail off.

"Would he have?"

They were as close as brothers by that time, or Jed thought they were. "I think so...unless it had just happened and he didn't have time," he said pensively.

Thorndyke considered him carefully. "Tell me what you're thinking."

Jed lowered his head and studied the sweaty glass in his hand. "Frannie disappeared on Tuesday. We were all worried sick, especially Emmy. Will and I spent most of our time trying to reassure her Frannie would show up, that there would be a perfectly reasonable explanation for her not coming home. The next morning, Wednesday, I insisted we go to school as usual. I guess I was hoping we'd come back in the afternoon and find Frannie there. But when Will and I got home all we found was the note the social workers had left saying they'd taken Emmy. Will panicked. He was convinced they'd be coming for him next and he had no intention of being swallowed up by the system again. He packed up and hightailed it out of there. We didn't really have any time to talk.''

"So it's possible he had another problem with the sheriff and you didn't know about it.''

"It's possible, Mr. Thorndyke, but I really don't think so.''

"Call me Thorny. Was McClain the only reason Frannie and Fielder didn't get along?''

Jed sipped his drink. The ice was nearly melted now. "I don't know, but I can tell you this. The hostility between them was...visceral. They really couldn't stand each other, and by extension he couldn't stand us.''

Jed rose and paced in front of the fireplace. "Fielder couldn't find a trace of Frannie,'' he muttered, as if talking to himself rather than his lawyer. "He came to the school Wednesday morning and questioned Will, Emmy and me separately. That afternoon, Emmy was yanked out of class by Social Services, and Will ran off. With them out of the picture, Fielder zeroed in on me.'' Jed studied the older man, meandered around the room and finally settled into a wingback chair over near the desk. "For the next week, he brought me into the station house just about every day for interrogation. He kept asking me the same questions over and over again, and each time he'd twist what I said to make it sound like something else.''

Which was why Jed was so reluctant to answer questions now—fear of how Fielder would use whatever he said against him.

"Then the newspapers started bugging him," he continued. "Fielder lashed out with a cock-and-bull story that Frannie had simply had enough of us kids and took off. I wrote a letter to the editor saying the idea was stupid and that anyone proposing such a theory was obviously incompetent."

Thorndyke grinned, but said nothing.

"The next time the sheriff tried to pull me in for questioning," Jed continued, "I told him to either arrest me or get off my back."

It was his first real lesson in facing down a bully. Even now, the recollection of his small victory felt good.

"He and I managed to stay out of each other's way for a long time," he continued. "When he stood for reelection a few years later, I publicly opposed him and endorsed the other candidate, and I've consistently supported his opposition in every election since."

Thorndyke nodded. "In your estimation, is he stupid or just incompetent?"

"He's not stupid…or dishonest as far as I can tell. There hasn't been a hint of corruption in the sheriff's department since he's been in office."

"Which means he's either clean or exceptionally good at covering his dirt," Thorny opined. "Might bear investigating."

"As for incompetent," Jed added, "in the case of Frannie's death, he obviously was. After all, he couldn't find her body when it was buried only a few yards over the fence from her property. In other areas, I'd have to say he's been a good sheriff. My opposition to him had been personal, not professional. I know that's something I shouldn't admit—''

''Not in public.'' Thorny rose easily from his chair and wandered again with seeming aimlessness around the room, examining book titles, picking up various objects to study.

''Can I ask you something?'' Jed inquired, and received a nod. ''Why are you here? Surely you didn't interrupt what must be a very busy schedule just to come and see me.''

Thorndyke pinched his pursed lips, his eyes smiling. ''I was in Shreveport on my way to Dallas to see a client there. This wasn't a big detour.''

''And Gwyn knew your itinerary?'' It all seemed too convenient.

''We happened to talk last weekend, so she knew my general schedule. We were lucky things worked out.''

''Does that mean you'll take my case?''

''It's a little premature at the moment, but if push comes to shove and you need me, I'd like to help.'' Thorny twirled the large globe near the windows overlooking the garden, then turned to face his host. He quoted his fee.

Jed was tempted to emit a low whistle, but he maintained a deadpan expression. ''That's acceptable.''

''There are other conditions.''

Jed waited.

''You have to remain absolutely mute in public about this case. Make no comments about the sheriff, his people, the progress of the investigation or anyone involved in it. Give no interviews to the press. I'll issue all public statements. Is that acceptable?''

Jed nodded.

''Has the sheriff scheduled a formal interview with you?''

''No, but I'm sure it's only a matter of—''

''Should he contact you, refuse to answer any of his questions, even the most innocent-sounding ones.'' He removed a card from his inside jacket pocket and handed it to his client. ''Call anytime, day or night, even if it's only with questions. You don't strike me as the impetuous, volatile type, Mr. Louis. Don't disappoint me. Sheriff Fielder will try very hard to provoke you into making statements he can use against you. Don't give him the ammunition he wants.''

The relief Jed felt in having the famous attorney available to take his case was tempered by his strict gag order. Was it standard procedure on his part, or did the Great Thorn seriously think Jed Louis was in danger of being convicted of murder?

SHE'D PROMISED herself she wasn't going to rush to answer the phone. Then she picked it up on the first ring.

''Gwyn,'' he said in a voice that was quiet, even solicitous, ''first of all, let me apologize for last night.''

She said nothing, waiting for him to continue.

''Second, thank you for calling Thorndyke. He was just here and—''

Her palms were clammy, but she managed to make

her tone flat and unemotional. "Is he taking your case?"

"Yes, and I really appreciate—"

"Good," she cut him off. "I'm glad things are working out for you. Now, if you'll excuse me, Jed, I have things to do." She hung up.

FEELING DEPRESSED, Jed called his friend. "Think you can put up with a visitor this evening?"

"Anytime," Riley said. "But don't bring Alanna any more sweets. You keep spoiling her."

"I don't imagine she'd like a pickle."

Riley laughed. "Just come on over, my friend. Seeing you is treat enough. As it is, you'll get her all excited, and it'll take me an extra hour to get her calmed down enough to fall asleep."

"Maybe I shouldn't come."

"You are in a funk. We eat at six. Be here."

Dinner turned out to be hot dogs, boiled for Alanna, done on the grill outside for the two adults. Jed had stopped off and bought a large-piece puzzle. While the girl played with it, Jed told Riley about Thorndyke's visit.

"You know who she is, don't you?" Jed asked.

"Senator Wingate Miller's daughter."

Jed exhaled loudly. "How long have you known?"

Riley turned their franks and put buns on to toast. "I had my first clue when she made the offer yesterday. I came back here and did some research on the Internet."

His friend had figured it out by himself, which

only made Jed feel more inept. "She's not very proud of it."

Riley didn't seem shocked by the revelation. "Wealth and politics often have a deleterious effect on human relations," he philosophized.

Riley went inside, retrieved his daughter's hot dogs, a pot of baked beans and a condiment tray from the refrigerator. He brought them outside, fixed Alanna's plate, and the three of them sat at the picnic table nearby.

Jed studied the glass dish of pickles, olives, radishes and raw carrots. "Do you like olives?" he asked the little girl.

"They're okay, I guess." She tried another puzzle piece, which didn't fit.

"I bet you don't know how to eat them."

She looked at him funny. "What do you mean?"

"Well, you can pop them in your mouth like this." He did so. "Or you can make it fun."

She kept her eyes on him, not sure what he was talking about. "How?"

"Give me your hand."

She offered it.

"Now," he said, picking up a pitted black olive, "we take one of these and put it right here." He stuck her index finger in the hole. "You do one."

Giggling, she placed another one on the next finger. "This is fun, Daddy."

Riley scowled at Jed, but there was appreciative humor behind it.

"Well," Jed justified himself, "you said no sweets."

Later, after the little girl had finished eating and run off to play once more with her puzzle, Riley said, "Gwyn's entitled to her privacy, Jed, just as you are. You probably ought to tell her that."

THE CADDO ANGLERS' BALL had begun fifty years earlier as a simple country club fish fry, but it had grown over the years into a weeklong fair to raise money for charities. It started on Sunday afternoon with the actual fish fry and continued every afternoon and evening for a week, bringing visitors from miles around. Tents were set up for concession booths and there was a small assortment of carnival rides and an even bigger choice of traditional competitions, ranging from horseshoes to three-legged races and a watermelon seed spitting contest. The festivities culminated the following Saturday night in the formal grand ball itself.

Unlike his uncle, Jed contributed more than just a token cash donation. He harnessed two of his giant Percherons, hitched them to a vintage buckboard, which he loaded with bales of hay, and spent Sunday afternoon, every evening and all day Saturday giving hayrides. It was one of the most popular activities among kids and adults. This year, however, he had competition.

After the churches let out Sunday morning, most of the people in town migrated to the campground, where they indulged in fried catfish, hush puppies and coleslaw. Rather than get in the long line for the greasy foods, Jed went to where he'd had his crew set up his wagon and team. Across the wide aisle, in a smaller corral, was a scaled-down open brougham. Hitched to it were eight miniature horses. Diligently checking the harnesses was Gwyn Miller.

The sight of her in tight jeans bending over the diminutive palominos caught his breath. His libido stuttered when the tassels on the sleeves of her red western shirt brushed against her breasts. He would have called out her name, but he couldn't seem to get any sounds through his open mouth. Sensing he was staring at her, she turned her head and glanced up from under the brim of her cowboy hat. She straightened and looked at him but didn't say a word.

She ran her thumbs along the waistband of her jeans, smoothing out the shirt. Jed continued to gape. The fabric fit snugly, tapering down from her breasts to her narrow waist. The jeans rounded her hips to distraction. Without realizing it, he swallowed hard.

"Gwyn, how nice to see you," he said inanely, wondering if she was going to give him the cold shoulder. "I didn't know you were participating in this."

She tossed him a casual glance, not exactly hail-fellow-well-met, but she didn't tell him to get lost, either.

"I'm a sucker for charities."

"Um, I didn't know you had a brougham."

She smirked. "What did you think I harnessed them to?"

Chuckling, he was about to admit his thickhead-edness, when he heard the familiar voice behind him.

"Daddy, look. They're baby horses."

Gwyn instantly broke into a broad smile. "Hello, Riley. Hey, Alanna, I like your hat."

Jed turned to see his friend and four-year-old daughter approaching the fence. Alanna wore a flat-brimmed Mexican-style blue hat with little red puff-balls dangling from the rim.

The girl couldn't take her eyes away from the animals.

"Are they going to be real big like Mr. Jed's?"

"No," Gwyn chuckled mildly. "This is as big as they get."

"It is?" She studied them with a kind of longing. "Can I touch them?"

Gwyn held out her hand. "Come on. Let me introduce you."

Jed watched from the fence line as Gwyn escorted the child and her father to the harnessed miniatures and identified each of them by name, then let Alanna pet every one of them.

"That's it, nice and gentle." She guided the child's hand along the neck of the front horses. "They're very friendly, but you have to remember you're a stranger, so you don't want to do anything to scare them. Would you like to go for a ride in the coach?"

Alanna jumped up and down. "Can I, Daddy? Can I? Please?"

Gwyn smiled at Riley, who took obvious pleasure in his daughter's delight. "You can come with us." She looked over at Jed, who had a foot resting on the lower rail of the fence. "Would you like to join us? There's room."

He shook his head. ''Thanks, but I have to see to my team. Maybe another time.''

Jed watched them climb into the carriage, observed her raise her leg and bounce up onto the box in front and take up the reins. Smiling, he waved to Alanna, whose face was glowing with happiness. Gwyn clicked her tongue and set off down the path to the trail that had been mapped out on the edge of the campground, among the trees and along the shore of the lake.

It took determination for him to focus on the animals rather than the woman driving them. The team was handsome and well matched. They were clearly well trained, too, for they responded precisely to her direction. He'd driven teams often enough to know that keeping eight horses in balance wasn't a simple task. Had she trained the horses herself? Seeing the way she took to Riley's daughter, he knew she had the patience and temperament to make a good parent and a good teacher.

Why was this beautiful woman not married with a house full of kids? For that matter, why wasn't he? In spite of the tragedies and rejections in his life, he'd always wanted a family, but he'd never found a woman he could trust with his secrets or who wasn't distracted by his wealth.

The bridle path wasn't very long. They were back within fifteen minutes, Alanna giggling and chattering with delight. By then, he'd marshaled a full load of older kids for the hayride, which took twice as long.

Over the next few hours, he and Gwyn saw each

other in passing and waved to each other, but it wasn't until late in the afternoon that they were both ready for a break, as were their horses. While she assured the kids she'd be giving more rides after the animals had a chance to rest, Jed went to the concession stand and bought two very large berry-berry ice slushes.

Back at her corral, he handed her one. She pushed up her cowboy hat and wiped her brow. "Mmm. A man after my own heart."

"Let's go sit in the shade," he suggested, his eyes settling on her tongue as it licked the soft ice.

They walked over to a bench that had just been vacated under a large oak tree. For a minute they crunched ice and let out long relaxing sighs.

"Gwyn, I'm sorry about the things I said the other night. It was wrong of me and very ungrateful. I hope you'll forgive me."

Her pique had long since faded. She understood his anger, his feeling of betrayal. "It wasn't completely your fault," she acknowledged. "I misled you. You had every right to resent it."

"That doesn't justify my hurting you," he said.

Her face softened. She reached over and placed her hand on his. "It's in the past, Jed. Let's forget about it."

He held on to her hand, massaging the knuckles gently. Their eyes met. They stared at each other in silence for several heartbeats. He was about to draw closer, to bring his lips to hers, when she asked in a quiet, concerned voice, "Have you told anyone who I am?"

He pulled back, unsettled, frustrated. Was that the reason for her granting forgiveness, to buy his silence?

Irritation took the calmness from his tone. "Riley figured it out, but I haven't told anyone, and I won't."

She waited a minute, aware of his displeasure. "It's important to me."

He let out a huff. "Obviously. Do you mind telling me why?"

"Sometime, maybe," she said, "but not now."

He inhaled. "Fair enough. As I said, it's your business."

More silence.

"I like your horses."

Startled, she looked at him, surprise on her face.

"I mean the kids really seem to get a kick out of them," he qualified.

She chuckled. "Minis aren't quite as intimidating to their little bodies as regular-size horses."

They had turned without realizing it to face each other on the bench. "If you haven't already made plans, Gwyn, will you come with me to the ball on Saturday evening? I'm not the world's greatest dancer, but I promise to do my best not to step on your toes."

"I'd like that."

He grinned. "Going to the ball with me or my not stepping on your toes?"

She laughed, that full throaty sound he'd only heard once from her. It resonated inside him, churning up that libido again. "I'm greedy," she told him, grinning widely. "I want both."

CHAPTER SIX

JED ARRIVED at Gwyn's house the evening of the ball at seven o'clock precisely. It wasn't dark yet, but shadows were lengthening, casting tone and texture in sharp relief. He walked to the front door and rang the bell. While he waited for her to open, he noted the newly planted pink-and-white impatients in the flower bed bordering the walk. Frannie used to grow them there as well, only she favored the red-and-pink varieties.

He tried to dismiss the bittersweet memories by concentrating on the woman who lived here now. Gwyn wasn't just another date for another social gala, though he couldn't say exactly how or why she was different. She was a beautiful woman, but he'd been out with beautiful women before. Good company, but he'd enjoyed good company, too. An enigma? A challenge? She was both—and more.

He was about to press the button a second time, when the door flew open.

The woman standing before him took his breath away. She had been tantalizing him all week in western attire, but in a teal satin evening gown with a single strand of pearls circling her neck and shiny gold teardrops dripping from her ears, she was a knockout. Her sleek auburn hair had always been braided in a single thick rope down her back. Now it was piled high on her head in a complex series of swirls that was regal, yet seemed to invite mischief.

She was more than a knockout, Jed told himself as he stared with his mouth hanging open. A goddess who was raising his body temperature to indecent. levels.

Grinning at him, she picked up her flat evening purse from the table by the door and gazed up at him, "Thank you," she said softly.

He blinked and stood by while she checked to make sure she had her key. "For what?" he asked when she closed the door behind her.

She raised a hand and gently patted him on the cheek. "For the look in your eyes."

Desire, painful and sweet, rocketed through him. He offered her his arm. "The word *beautiful* comes to mind," he murmured in her ear, "but it's much too weak."

"Charmer," she accused him with a breezy chuckle that had the effect of aged whiskey running through his veins.

She tucked her hand inside his elbow as he escorted her to his Jaguar, parked in the driveway. Her fingers slipped easily into his as she sank into the leather seat on the passenger side. He was about to close the door, when she lifted her lashes to him.

"You look very handsome tonight, Mr. Louis." A soft throaty laugh bubbled out of her when he nearly blushed.

The Anglers' Ball was held every year in the Uncertain Legion Hall. In years past it had been outdoors, under a tent top, but dancing in the East Texas humidity tended to leave men sweaty and women glowing, their elaborate hairdos wilting. It was even worse when it rained, as it often did this time of year. Long evening gowns ended up trimmed in reddish mud and shiny oxfords came away looking like construction boots.

The cavernous tin building didn't have a utilitarian appearance this evening. Potted palms had been carefully placed to soften its sharp edges, and colored spotlights were directed into the open rafters, from which hanging plants were strategically suspended. Tiny round tables, hardly big enough for two people to sit at, were set with white linen, globed candles and four chairs. They were arranged around a freshly waxed portable parquet dance floor in the center of the room. A small orchestra specializing in the big-band sound was set up on risers in one corner.

"Oh, this is charming," Gwyn exclaimed, taking in the scene.

Ladies wore a variety of evening ensembles, some simple and elegant, others elaborate and pretentious. The men were more uniformly attired in black tuxedos, starched white shirts and black bow ties, though there were a few mavericks sporting plaid cummerbunds and gaudily irreverent ties. As far as Gwyn was concerned, none was more strikingly handsome than the man at her side, and judging from the glances the other women in the hall cast his way, her opinion was shared.

A self-consciously jovial female shriek of laughter rose above the din from a far corner.

"Amanda's here," Jed commented dryly without bothering to seek out the source of the commotion.

"Who's Amanda?"

He snorted. "You'll meet her later, I'm sure."

"Good evening, Jed," a mature male voice said from behind them.

They turned together to see a tall gentleman of about sixty. His dark hair was sprinkled with gray at the temples, as was his pencil-thin mustache. The president of the local bank. Gwyn had met him when she transferred her accounts there from Denver. He'd greeted Jed, but his attention was focused exclusively on Gwyn.

"Ms. Miller, how good to see you again." He smiled unctuously. "I saw you giving the children rides in your carriage the other evening. I think everybody in town has fallen in love with those miniature horses—as well as their enchanting owner."

"Except maybe Logan Fielder," Jed noted, but with a chuckle.

Jennings sneered. "Logan doesn't love anyone or anything. I'd hardly use him as a criterion of success." He beckoned to a tall, slender woman talking to an older woman a few feet away. "My dear, come say hello to Jed and his date. This is Gwyn Miller. My wife, Catherine," he said to Gwyn.

Catherine Jennings carried herself with a class and sophistication Gwyn instantly recognized. She was wearing a low-cut cream-colored evening gown accented with tiny seed pearls. The bodice molded itself to her full figure and curved down her rounded hips. Her makeup was expertly applied, bringing out the brilliant blue of her eyes while distracting from the delicate crows' feet beside them. At first glance Gwyn would have thought her at least ten years younger than her husband, but closer consideration suggested their age difference was probably not more than a year or two.

"Ms. Miller." Catherine held out her hand in a manner that reminded Gwyn uncomfortably of her mother. Friendly, but with just a hint of condescension.

"Please call me Gwyn. What lovely jewelry."

Catherine Jennings wore a matching necklace and bracelet—a tree motif within a circle of gold. The trunks of the trees were white freshwater pearls with delicate emerald chips leafing out the branches. It was a beautiful, if old-fashioned, set.

"It's absolutely exquisite," Gwyn continued. "I don't think I've ever seen anything like it."

The older woman's aloofness softened perceptibly. "Part of a family heirloom," she announced proudly. "I don't wear them very often, as you can imagine."

"No, indeed," Gwyn agreed. "Such a prize is worthy only of special occasions."

"You must come by one day and tell me all about your animals. They sound delightful."

Gwyn recognized the tone. The invitation was closer to the granting of an audience.

"I'd like that," she agreed diplomatically. She suspected the older woman realized Gwyn had no intention of complying.

Catherine turned to Jed. "Amanda's here."

"Yes, I know. I'm sure I'll see her later. Oh, there's Riley waving at us. If you'll excuse us, Catherine, we need to get to our table." Ray had already moved over to another couple and was busy in conversation.

Beating Catherine to the punch, Gwyn put out her hand like a limp paw. "It's been so nice to meet you, Mrs. Jennings."

"Do enjoy yourself," Catherine said, barely touching the tips of Gwyn's fingers.

After greeting several other people and introducing Gwyn, Jed led the way to their reserved table. She felt a moment of relief at seeing the friendly, familiar face of Riley Gray. He immediately climbed to his feet, shook Jed's hand perfunctorily and gave Gwyn another brotherly peck on the cheek.

"So you hired the Great Thorn after all," he muttered with a twinkle in his eye. Gwyn suspected Jed had told him all about his meeting with the famous attorney, though he had yet to tell her about it, and she refused to ask.

"The Great Thorn?" inquired the woman sitting at the table. Her eyes had gone wide. "Are you referring to Dexter Thorndyke?"

"Excuse my bad manners," Riley said. "Blair, you know Jed, of course." They exchanged greetings. Riley placed his hand at the small of Gwyn's back. "This is Gwyn Miller. She owns the miniature horses I was telling you about—that were such a success with the kids all week. This is Blair Dunning," he said to Gwyn.

Blair nodded pleasantly, a gracious and assessing smile on her face. She was a striking woman with straw-blond hair pulled back in a sleek bun at her nape. Gwyn judged her to be about thirty. There was curiosity, too, in her hazel eyes. Jed held Gwyn's chair and the three of them sat down.

"Is it true?" Blair asked Jed. "You've hired Dexter Thorndyke?"

Gwyn caught Jed's eye. She didn't want to talk about this or her part in getting the Great Thorn.

"He's agreed to help, if needed," Jed replied.

The orchestra started up a 1940s foxtrot.

"I ought to explain," Riley chimed in, apparently unaware of the silent communication. "Blair is an assistant district attorney in Marshall."

Jed rose quickly, came around the back of Gwyn's chair and leaned over her ear. "Shall we dance?"

She turned her head and smiled gratefully at him. They proceeded to the dance floor.

"Do you think Riley told her I was the one who called Thorny?" Gwyn asked.

"Nope," he said as he whirled her around. "He knows how to keep confidences."

Riley and Blair had followed them to the dance floor. Gwyn observed them. Blair's full-length black silk dress was slit up both sides, revealing long slender legs. It hugged her feminine curves in front and was cut very low in back. A striking woman, and in the same profession as Riley. They made an attractive couple. Gwyn liked Riley. She wanted to like his date, as well.

She and Jed spoke sparingly during the first few

dances, which were upbeat and fast paced. Then the tempo changed and the orchestra segued into the lyrical harmonies of ''Sentimental Journey'' and ''Stardust.'' He leaned his chin against her temple and inhaled the floral scent of her hair and the feminine allure of her skin. They could have carried on a conversation very privately now, but they fell silent. The melancholy refrains of the hauntingly beautiful music seemed to trigger a yearning in his soul.

He wasn't surprised that Gwyn was a good dancer. She glided across the floor, accepting his lead, anticipating his steps, as if she were a part of him. A perfect partner. Then perfection shifted from deliciously pleasant to downright erotic. She didn't drape herself on him the way some women did. She molded her body to his, the warmth of her breast penetrating the starch of his shirt, disrupting all thought, while the sway of her hips sent signals to other areas of his anatomy.

Applause greeted the musicians at the end of the sweet medley from another time. Gwyn gazed up at Jed and smiled—a little sadly, it seemed to him—as if she had been reading his mood and sharing his thoughts. The band announced a short break, and people started vacating the dance floor.

''There's a photographer here taking portraits,'' Blair said when they returned to the table. ''Riley and I are going. Coming with us? The proceeds go to the charity fund.''

Jed grabbed Gwyn's right hand, which was still warm from his touch. ''Shall we?'' Did he see hesitation in her glance?

"Sure," she said cheerfully. "It's all for a good cause."

"Hello, Jed," came a seductive female voice from behind them as they stood in line awaiting their turns. "I wondered if you'd be here tonight."

It seemed to Gwyn he began his response even before turning to see who it was.

"I've been here every year for the past fifteen," he said, a broad smile on his face. "Wouldn't miss it for the world."

Gwyn shifted around to see a bleached blonde in her midthirties, wearing a slinky, skintight chartreuse-and-lavender dress that ended a couple of inches above her knees. It took a moment for Gwyn to realize this was Catherine's daughter. The older woman exuded a certain grace and style. This younger version flaunted voluptuous sex.

"You must be Amanda Jennings." Gwyn extended her hand. "I've heard so much about you." She caught the amused expression on Jed's face. It almost made her want to giggle. "I'm Gwyn Miller."

The woman's face went from delight at being recognized to wariness. "The lady with the little horses," she said, taking the offered hand.

"Did you do anything at the fairgrounds this week? I don't remember seeing you there. And I'm sure I would have noticed you."

Jed had to fight to keep a straight face.

"Uh, I was out of town," Amanda stammered.

Riley and Blair, who were just ahead of them in the line, had turned.

"Hi, Amanda," Riley said casually. "I don't think we've met," he said as he held out his hand to the man standing beside her.

He had the looks of a movie star. Not quite six feet tall, he was deeply tanned, with baby-blue eyes, perfect white teeth and a come-hither smile. He sported a gold stud in his left ear. Judging from his stance and proportions, Gwyn decided he was probably a body builder.

"Armand Duvalier." He extended his right hand, revealing a heavy gold bracelet.

Introductions completed, they moved up with the line.

The poses were all the same, of course. The subjects standing next to each other in a little alcove of potted palms, behind them a cardboard sky of blue and white. Jed wrapped his arm around Gwyn's narrow waist and rested his hand on her opposite hip. She stood modestly in place, her hands by her sides. At a word from the photographer, they looked at each other. Before they quite realized they'd made eye contact, the flash went off.

By the time they joined Riley and Blair at the punch bowl, the band had resumed playing. They watched people while they sipped from their cups.

"Tell us about Amanda," Blair said. "Who is she? How do you know her?"

"Ray and Catherine Jennings's daughter," Riley explained. "We all went to school together. She's just returning home after her last divorce."

"Last?" Gwyn couldn't help asking, though on consideration, it didn't surprise her.

Jed smirked and looked at Riley. "Is this number three or four?"

Riley wrinkled his brow. "Three, I think, unless I've lost count. She's taken back her maiden name this time."

"Any kids?" Gwyn wanted to know.

"No, thank God," Riley responded.

"So you were in high school with her," Blair commented. "That must have been exciting."

Jed chortled. "Riley'll tell you she was the femme fatale of Uncertain High."

Gwyn could easily picture Amanda twenty years earlier in designer jeans, schoolbooks tucked below her generous, braless breasts, her eyelids shadowed in green. Had she and Jed been an item? Amanda Jennings struck her as the type of woman who could easily attract men, who enjoyed them but didn't keep them. Which her divorce record seemed to confirm. Or was it that she lost interest in the men first? Didn't make much difference.

They danced for another hour or so, the last number being a torturously slow rendition of "Smoke Gets in Your Eyes."

The night air was comfortably warm and slightly damp when they bade farewell to friends and acquaintances. At Gwyn's suggestion, Jed left the air-conditioning off, and they opened the car windows for the short drive back to her house.

"It's been a wonderful evening, Jed. Thank you for inviting me."

"You're the one who made it wonderful."

He waited to see if she would reach over and put

her hand on his. She didn't. He turned the corner onto the highway. The breeze should be cooling him, but it didn't seem to be having that effect.

"We've been dancing for hours," she commented when he finally pulled up in her driveway. "Yet I don't feel tired."

"Me, neither." He escorted her along the walk to her front porch. "Your glider looks awfully inviting." He took out his handkerchief and dusted the seat. "Would you care to join me?"

They sat side by side, not quite close enough to easily hold hands, but it wouldn't have taken much of a shift for either of them to change that. They swung in silence, listening to the night sounds. Crickets. Bull frogs. A nightingale. An owl.

"You handled Amanda and her mother very well this evening."

She snickered. "They were too easy, no challenge. Are you and the Jenningses good friends?"

"I wouldn't call us close," he answered. "He was the trustee for my uncle's estate, so after Frannie disappeared he was in a position to persuade Social Services to let me stay on at Frannie's place until I graduated. Otherwise I might have disappeared like my foster sister, Emmy."

Gwyn drew in her cheeks for a second before saying, "That was good of him."

Jed emitted a soft chuckle, an acknowledgment of her sarcasm. "I know he's not exactly a paragon of virtue, but he was a friend when the world around me seemed to be falling apart. For that, I'll always be grateful to him. He's been an excellent business adviser, too. He got me started investing in real estate, for example.''

''And Catherine?''

He grinned. ''The queen mother? She's really not so bad once you get to know her.''

''As long as you know how to hold your teacup.''

He slanted her an amused grin. ''Ouch.''

Gwyn ran her tongue across her teeth, embarrassed at having shown her ungracious side. ''Sorry, but I've had enough society women to last me a lifetime.''

It was the perfect opening for him to ask her about herself; what it was like to be a descendant of an old New England family and heiress to one of the world's great fortunes. Why she was so determined to keep her identity secret. Riley was right, of course—she was entitled to her privacy. Besides, he didn't want to bring up a subject that would spoil the rapport they were finally developing. Rapport he didn't want to lose.

''I guess it's time for me to come clean,'' she said in a muted voice that jolted him nevertheless. ''You've been patient, Jed, more patient than I deserve really.''

''Privacy is important to you,'' he said. ''I understand that.''

''It is, I think, for most people, but when you grow up in a fishbowl it becomes almost sacred. Do you want something cold to drink?'' She made a move to get up. ''I have—''

''I'm fine,'' he said, recognizing delaying tactics.

"You want me to keep talking," she concluded, not without humor.

"I like the mellow sound of your voice. It fits in with the velvet softness of the night."

She grinned over at him, a twinkle beneath an uplifted brow.

With a little kick she increased the speed of the swing, not merely for the pure pleasure of it, he realized, but out of nervousness.

"What do you know about the Millers of New England?" she asked.

"That they're bluebloods who can trace their ancestors back to the *Mayflower* and beyond."

"Everyone came over in something sometime, Jed. Except maybe the Native Americans, who walked over from Siberia. What else?"

"That they're very rich."

"What else?"

"Let's see. They served in the Revolutionary War."

"Only toward the end, when they could finally read the handwriting on the wall. Until then, they'd been procrown, but you won't find that mentioned in the history books. It's a deep, dark family secret."

"Well, at least they eventually saw the light," he noted, but she seemed to take no consolation from the comment.

"Did you know they supported the South in the first year of the Civil War?"

That caught him by surprise. "Really? Why?"

"Do you know how the Millers made their millions?"

"Didn't they own cotton mills?" Making the connection, he let the words trail off.

She smiled at him. "Think of something?"

"That's why they were pro-South."

"The fortune my great-great-grandfather made was from exploiting immigrant labor in northern sweatshops that were producing everything from sail-cloth to calico out of cotton grown in the South by slaves."

"Ah." He studied her. "On the other hand, your family has done a lot of good with the money since then—charitable foundations, scholarship funds, endowments to the arts and sciences. That's a part of your heritage you can be proud of."

"And I am proud of that aspect of it, Jed."

"But..."

"Power and money corrupt."

"Seems to me I've heard something like that before."

She smiled.

"And you're saying that your family is now corrupt," he ventured. "Is that it?"

"Do you follow politics?"

"No more than I have to."

She laughed this time. "Smart. It's a dirty business."

"I suppose it always has been. Politics, it seems to me, is a matter of compromise, and one definition of *compromise* is that neither side gets what it wants. Which means you have a lot of dissatisfied people."

"Politics," she corrected him, "is the art of convincing the other guy to compromise, often by persuasion, sometimes by intimidation, usually by manipulation.''

She sounded very disillusioned, but on that particular subject, he was inclined to be cynical, as well.

''And that's what your father does. Gwyn, this isn't exactly earth-shattering news. I've never gone along with the media's infatuation with power moguls or believed the hype about fairy-tale kingdoms.''

Gwyn blew out a breath in frustration. How could she make him understand what she was getting at?

''When I was twenty-one, I was engaged to the son of a prominent statesman. He was almost twenty years my senior, but he had great political potential, as my father pointed out. My mother arranged everything—the big church wedding, the reception to follow and, of course, the select guest list of the politically correct people to attend. A week before the wedding, I came to my senses. I didn't love him. He didn't love me. We got along well enough. He had charm, education, sophistication, but he also had a reputation for enjoying female companionship. I wasn't convinced his being married to me would change that. I talked to my mother about it. Her response was that it wasn't important, as long as he was discreet. My father had kept a mistress for years, but my mother didn't care. She hadn't been completely faithful, either.''

Gwyn had finally managed to shock Jed. ''Your mother told you that?''

She nodded. ''A week before the wedding I broke the engagement. My parents were furious. After all, there was that mountain of presents to be returned with abject apologies. Then, of course, there was the bigger issue. I was throwing away an opportunity for social prestige and political clout. Combined with the Miller fortune, my marriage would have given them—my parents—incredible national and international leverage and power. They saw me as an object, Jed, not a person. A pawn, not a thinking, feeling human being."

He said the only words that were appropriate under the circumstances. "I'm sorry."

"That was thirteen years ago," she said in a detached manner that didn't quite mask the pain. "I packed my bags, got in the Land Rover, which I'd bought on my own, and left the ancestral manor. I've been self-supporting ever since."

"Did they cut you off? Disinherit you?"

"I disinherited them," she said with a determination he couldn't help but admire.

Tearing oneself away from roots that went so deep couldn't have been easy, even in an atmosphere as hostile and perverted as the one she described. The temptation to bend and compromise must have been enormous, yet she'd held fast.

"Every year I contribute the earnings from my trust to charity."

"But you could reclaim the principle at any time."

Was he simply confirming a fact, asking a question or calling her a hypocrite? Maybe a little of all three.

"I can," she agreed, "but I won't." She saw the skepticism in his eyes. "I can still be heir to the

Miller fortune, too, Jed. All I have to do is go to my parents and give them my soul.''

No, she wouldn't sacrifice her soul for money. Could she give her heart for love?

Impulsively, he did what he'd been wanting to do all evening. He reached over and skimmed his fingers along her nape, up to the base of her voluminous hair. She turned only slightly, and it seemed to him a little stiffly, yet it was enough to confirm her trust. Slowly he lifted one amber comb from her hair. The luxuriant auburn waves didn't tumble as he'd hoped until he'd removed the second comb. Then they cascaded down in thick tresses, covering his hand with silky warmth that had him burning with need and desire.

With slow, deliberate care, he inched closer to her across the swing seat and brought his other hand up to cradle her chin between his fingers. Their eyes met. Her lips were slightly parted. Acknowledgment, anticipation and an invitation he couldn't resist.

Their breaths mingled as he drew her against him, their eyes wide-open, transfixed on each other. He touched his lips to hers, softly, tenderly. Her arms slipped under his, and she gave herself over to the growing passion of his unhurried kiss.

CHAPTER SEVEN

THE KISS was lingering and luxurious. Gwyn found herself frustrated by the brittle front of his tuxedo shirt as she skimmed her hand across his chest. She should be feeling hard muscle under warm flesh, not coolly damp starch. She raised her hand to his cheek. The stubble of his dense beard rasped like sandpaper under her fingers. The heat of his skin made the sensation not unpleasant, but it definitely left her wanting more. She concentrated on his mouth, on the lips that were soft yet firm, coaxing and dangerously persuasive. He probed her mouth, searching, exploring. Shock waves rippled through her when their tongues met.

He tasted of fire and need and longing. She savored the hunger, the slow, raw melding of passion and restraint. He wanted her, but she discerned hesitation, too, as if he were apprehensive. Of her or of himself? Afraid she would back away or that he would go too far? The tension throbbed in the way he held her, close, intimately. His thigh against hers. One hand behind the column of her neck while the other stroked her chest, her breast. His touch was an exploration, an inquiry, not a demand, and it drove her heart to pounding wildly. She sensed that he still had the power to back away. It should please her, but it didn't. She wanted him wildly reckless about her, overwhelmed by passion, not sweetly in control. Realization that at that moment she was totally under his spell frightened her. His tender embrace also made her feel like a woman cherished, not possessed, a woman respected, not used.

He broke off the kiss as slowly as he had initiated it, his lips nibbling hers as he gently pulled away. Her breathing came in little puffs, and she realized, as they looked into each other's eyes that his did, too.

"Gwyneth." The single word was like a prayer, a sacred hymn. He'd never used her full name before. She'd never heard it spoken with such devotion.

She stroked his cheek, wary of the sensations and the longing whirling inside her. Her experience with men was limited. Intellectually she knew intimacy had the power to captivate and possess, but emotionally it had always left her with a vague feeling of inadequacy, of letting down and being let down. Then Jed Louis kissed her and she felt defenseless in his arms. Maybe vulnerability was what had been missing with the others.

She pulled her hand away, fearful of what might lie ahead, shaken by the temptation to surrender. Climbing to her feet, she took a step forward, establishing separation before she turned back.

"It's been a wonderful evening, Jed—"

"But it's getting late." She sensed frustration and disappointment in the way he finished the predictable sentence, but there was acceptance, too.

Better this little dashing of hopes, she thought, than bigger ones.

He rose lazily to his feet, the tautness in the line of his mouth unrelenting as he approached her.

''Thank you for coming with me tonight.'' He placed his hands on the edges of her shoulders and leaned forward to plant a tender kiss on her lips. ''We'll have to go dancing more often.''

With the feel of his touch imprinted on her skin and her heart still tumbling, she murmured, ''I'd like that.''

She watched as he walked to his car, got in and started the engine. He waved as he backed out of the driveway. ''Good night,'' he called as he turned onto the road to Beaumarais.

ON MONDAY MORNING, after stopping off at Haddad's Animal Emporium for a couple of fifty-pound sacks of oats and sweet feed, Gwyn decided to stop in at the Caddo Kitchen for a quick cup of coffee. Four men, who looked as if they might be retired and hanging out to pass the time, occupied a booth in the corner by the window. Six women sat around a table in the middle of the room. One had an infant in her arms; another was gently rocking a stroller with her foot. Cassie stood over them, a coffeepot in her hand, an expression of rapt attention on her face. Her hair seemed an even brighter shade of orange-red than it had been last time—if that was possible.

Gwyn slipped onto one of the stools at the counter and waited for the waitress to notice her.

"I never read that trash," one of the women was saying with obvious distaste.

"Oh, you should," a second woman advised her, apparently unoffended by the first woman's put-down. "Of course, some of it is silly. Spaceships and men from Mars. As if we didn't have our hands full with the ones we already have here." She huffed mischievously. "I don't believe a word of that stuff, but it's fun to read. Then there're the real interesting stories about all those free-loving movie stars."

"And the stuff those politicians who are always preaching family values do," another woman chimed in with a giggle.

"So who's this Norman Hollis guy?" a fourth woman asked. "I can't remember ever hearing the name."

"He writes as Simon Sezz," Cassie explained as she topped off a cup. "Came in this morning for coffee and a Danish. Didn't want it heated up in the microwave, either. Had Jake stick it in the bake oven for two minutes. Said microwaves toughened the dough."

An older woman in a muumuu, who sat at the end of the table, snorted. "Anyone who would eat one of those plastic-wrapped things wouldn't know dough from dirt." Judging from the woman's bulk, she made everything from scratch and did a lot of sampling in the process.

"They're not that bad," Cassie assured her. "Especially if you're in a hurry. With a pat of butter melted on top they're actually pretty good."

"So what's this Hollis character doing here, anyway?" number three asked impatiently.

"Cassie, I think you have a customer," said the woman at the other end of the table, who until then had remained silent. She nodded toward the counter.

Cassie looked up. "Oh, hi, Gwyn. I was so caught up with this reporter being here that I didn't see you come in." She walked behind the end of the counter. "What'll you have, hon? Not a Danish, I hope. We're all out. The guy who was in a little while ago ate the last two."

Gwyn chuckled. "Just coffee, thanks. Who's this reporter you're talking about?"

Cassie placed a thick mug in front of Gwyn and filled it with steaming coffee from a fresh pot she'd removed from under the dip spout of the coffeemaker. "He's from the *National Tabloid,* you know, that tells-it-all rag that comes out every week."

An uncomfortable feeling churned in Gwyn's stomach. She'd never heard of good news being published in one of those scandal sheets. "What's he doing in Uncertain?"

"Here to cover Frannie Granger's murder. Says he's fixing to talk to everyone in town."

The knot in Gwyn's insides grew tighter.

One of the ladies at the table chortled. "In Uncertain that shouldn't take long."

More seriously Cassie said, "Claims he's already interviewed the sheriff."

"Can't imagine Logan telling him much," the woman holding the baby commented.

"You never know," someone else piped up. "Logan's pretty good at beating his own drum when he has a mind to.''

"How long's this reporter planning to be here?" Gwyn asked.

Cassie shrugged. "Says he'll be hanging around for a while, but wouldn't say exactly how long. He's staying at the Kit and Caboodle Cottages."

"Why would he or anyone else outside Uncertain care about Frannie Granger?" one of the older women asked. Gwyn had the same question in her mind. "I mean, I liked Frannie, but she wasn't some famous celebrity or anything."

"She will be by the time Simon Sezz gets finished with her," Cassie noted. "Maybe it's just the intrigue of a nearly twenty-year-old murder."

"Jed Louis is the only one of her foster kids still around."

"I'm sure that reporter will make something of that," said the stroller woman. "Think he'll try to interview him?"

The skinny woman at the end of the table cackled. "Easier to get blood from a turnip. Jed Louis can be very tight-lipped and discreet when it comes to his own affairs."

There were several snickers.

"That may be so," said the mother holding the infant, "but it's going to be hard finding anyone who'll say a mean word against him."

"I wouldn't be so sure," the big woman commented. "He didn't get to be a successful business-man and own half the county by being a nice guy. Success makes enemies."

"I never heard of him cheating anyone," Cassie contributed.

"That's 'cause most people don't like to admit they've been hoodwinked or outmaneuvered," came the reply. "Give them half a chance, though, and the dirt'll come out."

A couple of heads nodded thoughtfully.

"Well, however he does business now," Cassie insisted, "has nothing to do with Frannie getting killed."

"People don't change," the skinny woman observed. "He used to have a pretty bad temper, got mixed up with the police—"

"When he was a kid and Will McClain was around," the mother holding the infant chimed in. "McClain was the one who got him into trouble, as I recall."

"That may be. But the record's still there."

"At least he didn't run off," Cassie argued.

"Because he had Ray Jennings to protect him. When you're fixin' to inherit a place like Beaumarais and a whole bunch of money, it's easy to find people willing to come to your rescue."

"He's helped a lot of people in this town, too."

"Ray?" the woman holding the baby asked in amazement.

"Not Ray, silly. I bet the only reason our playboy banker helped Jed was that he was the trustee for his uncle's estate and wanted to stay on Jed's good side. He's made big bucks on Louis's investments. No, I'm talking about Jed. When my Harry got laid off last year, Jed was the one who gave him part-time work until he could find another full-time job.''

''You don't really think he could have killed her, do you?'' the mother with the stroller asked.

The woman in the muumuu shrugged her heavy shoulders. ''People with money get away with a lot of things.''

''But not Jed,'' the other woman objected.

Cassie caught the concern in Gwyn's eyes. ''You should have seen him at the ball the other night,'' she observed to the others. ''I've always thought tuxedos did something for a man, but what that man does for a tuxedo is downright sinful.''

A little shiver of excitement shot through Gwyn at the memory of him holding her in his arms. ''You were there?'' she blurted out. ''I don't remember seeing you.''

Cassie looked at her and laughed good-naturedly. ''No reason you should have, hon. I was busy keeping the service bars stocked with ice and clean glasses. Maybe someday Hank and me can spring a hundred bucks a person to go to a charity dance, but not this year.'' There was no bitterness in the remark, Gwyn noted. Just an acceptance of the way things were. On the other hand, Gwyn remembered the waitress mentioning having a couple of kids. No dance could make up for that.

''I saw you, though,'' Cassie continued. ''I really liked that dress you were wearing. The way Jed kept looking at you, I reckon he did, too.''

Remaining at the counter, Gwyn found herself drawn into conversation with all the women, but after a refill of coffee she didn't ask for, she excused herself and left. She had to let Jed know he was about to be tried in the court of public opinion.

THE *NATIONAL TABLOID* came out on Thursdays.

Gwyn bought two copies of the rag first thing Thursday morning and carried them to Beaumarais. By now, June regarded her and Romeo as regular visitors and showed them immediately into the breakfast room. While the dog settled in the corner by the window, head resting contentedly on his paws, his people read the article in silence over coffee and bran muffins.

"He's good with words," Jed commented dryly.

"A thief with words, you mean," she retorted. "He steals truth and mangles it. Is anything he says factually incorrect?"

"He's too smart for that. No, the facts are all accurate—as far as they go." He scanned the article again. "He accomplishes one thing, though."

Gwyn couldn't see anything redeeming about the twisted syntax. "What's that?"

"Simon Sezz confirms that Fielder's mind is made up." Jed quoted from a paragraph on the third page: "'Sheriff Logan Fielder informed this reporter that his only suspect at this time is Jed Louis. Mr. Louis is the man who inherited Beaumarais, one of the few and best preserved antebellum plantation mansions in East Texas. Asked why the prominent landowner and reputable Percheron horse breeder was his prime suspect, Logan Fielder replied that it was a matter of elimination. Of Granger's three foster children, Louis is the only one left.'"

Jed winced as if in pain. "He makes it sound like Emmy and Will are dead."

Gwyn bit her lip. "Is it possible they are?"

Blinking slowly, Jed shook his head in denial. Gwyn wasn't sure whether it was in rejection of the premise or that it might actually be true. "I told you what happened to them. Social Services kidnapped Emmy, and Will ran off."

But did it end there? she wondered. Could whoever killed Frannie have found them and killed them, too? How else explain why they never contacted Jed? The supposition raised more questions—like, why kill them at all? And why then not kill Jed, as well? It didn't make sense.

Unless Jed was the killer. Fielder's logic, that Jed was the lone survivor and therefore must be the murderer, was a frightening premise.

"Phone call, Mr. Jed," June announced from the doorway. Gwyn hadn't even heard it ring in the background. "Mr. Thorndyke."

Jed reached behind him to the small table within arm's reach and picked up the muted instrument. He spoke for only a minute before hanging up.

"Thorny's passing through on his way back to Shreveport. He's coming for lunch. Care to join us?"

She was a little surprised by the invitation. This couldn't be a purely social visit. Discussions between attorney and client were usually very private. "If he'll let me. Did he say what he wanted?"

"No, but I think it's pretty obvious." He held up

the newspaper, which he'd laid neatly folded beside his plate.

Gwyn considered for only a moment. "I still have animals to feed. What time will he be here?"

"Noon."

Gwyn looked at her watch. "That should give me enough time to get my chores done."

There was a slight hesitation before Jed added, "I have a feeling I'm going to need your moral support."

Did he know what she'd been thinking? "I'll try to get here a few minutes before twelve."

JED FOUND HIMSELF watching the way Gwyn and Thorny greeted each other. She'd given up her old life, yet there was a comfortable familiarity between them, as if he were a favorite uncle. Thorny expressed no concern about her sitting in on the lunch meeting.

They ate on the veranda, a seafood salad with pita bread. Thorny had turned down the offer of beer or wine, so they all opted for iced tea, which June served in copious amounts.

After the obligatory pleasantries, Thorny got to the point of his visit. "Any idea who called Hollis?"

It was a question Jed had been mulling over. Unfortunately, he'd been unable to come up with any candidates.

"None," he said. "Since the sheriff gave him an interview, I thought maybe he had, but even Fielder isn't that low. I would think a journalist, especially the muckraking kind, is the last person he'd want breathing down his neck and second-guessing him."

"It's not Fielder. I checked," Thorny declared between bites of chilled lobster.

"How do you know?" Gwyn inquired.

"Simple. I asked him."

"And he answered?" The very notion of getting any information out of his archenemy astounded Jed.

The attorney stuck his tongue in his cheek as he examined a marinated scallop on the tip of his fork. "He's not very happy with the situation. At the moment his opinion of the press is even lower than his opinion of lawyers."

Gwyn's smile was perfunctory while she waited for him to elaborate. Which he did after the effective use of a pause.

"Seems the so-called interview he gave Hollis was more like a lecture about minding his own business, but Hollis managed to trick him into saying just enough to get a story. I'll give you odds there won't be any more interviews, or even statements, by Sheriff Logan Fielder to Simon Sezz or anyone else."

Gwyn speared a cherry tomato. "That's a relief."

"Not necessarily," Thorny corrected her.

"But—"

"It means Fielder is likely to be more reluctant than ever to give out information," Thorny told her. "Makes my job harder."

Gwyn remembered Jed's reaction to the article— that he had clear proof now that Fielder was out to get him.

"But he has to tell you what evidence he has, doesn't he?" Jed asked.

After swallowing, Thorny responded. "There are several layers of information in any case. The sheriff knows what he must give me, but there's always plenty more he's under no obligation to divulge. He has to pass on evidence he's uncovered, but he doesn't have to share his interpretation of it. Lawmen and D.A.'s often do that to get a feel for how the defense will use the information. The same goes for speculation that has no concrete basis in fact."

"It sounds like a game of bluff," Jed commented, none too happily.

Thorny took a generous slug of his tea and rested back against the wrought-iron chair. There was a hint of amusement in the curve of his lips, but seriousness underlay it.

"Jed, you deal in real estate. Do you always tell a prospective buyer everything you know about a piece of property? And don't you mention speculation and rumor that could potentially increase the future value of the property in question?"

"I don't withhold critical information," Jed objected. "And I don't lie."

"Neither will Fielder or the D.A.'s office," Thorny responded evenly. "But as a result of Hollis's insinuating himself into the situation, they're not going to give us the details they might have otherwise."

"There is one major difference," Jed noted. "Real estate is free trade. Both parties go into it of their own free will and can withdraw at any time. Being accused of murder is not the same thing.''

''Agreed. The best we can hope for is that both sides play by the rules. I understand your dislike of the sheriff, Jed, and I have to admit it isn't without some justification, but I think Logan Fielder will obey the law.''

Jed was about to say he didn't find that a great consolation, when June saved him from making the cynical remark by moving in to clear their dishes and serve dessert.

''The main reason I came,'' Thorndyke said halfway through his lime sherbet, ''is to remind you not to say anything to Hollis or any other reporter. Unless you have total trust in the discretion of the person you're talking to, keep your mouth shut about Frannie's disappearance or the murder investigation.''

He looked at Gwyn. ''That goes for both of you. I assure you, it won't be easy. Hollis is an old tiger at this game. He'll do anything and everything to get a rise out of you, including bribe your friends for statements. Your best defense against his kind of guttersnipe is to utter absolutely nothing beyond 'no comment' and use even that statement sparingly.''

Jed took a mighty breath and expelled it harshly, frustration as strong as anger in his reaction. They wrapped up their lunch talking about other things, including the Anglers' Ball and the success of Gwyn's horses with the children.

''You always were good with kids,'' Thorny told her.

It could have been his imagination, but Jed thought he heard regret in the apparently casual statement, as if he were mildly chastising her for not being married and settled down with a family of her own.

Jed and Gwyn turned back to the wide front door after seeing Thorny's car down the drive to the public road. "Can I ask you something?"

"Sure." She glanced up at him, realizing it wasn't a casual question.

"You said you broke off relations with your family, with the high-profile Washington set. So, how come you've kept in contact with Thorndyke?"

His hand went to the small of her back as he pushed the door open and allowed her to precede him into the mansion.

"Fair question." Without thinking, she turned automatically down the narrow corridor to the library. They were both comfortable there.

"I told you about my engagement." She leaned on the arm of the couch, her hands folded under her breasts. The stance should have been off-putting. Instead, it only made him more aware of the feel of her under his hand the evening before.

"When I announced that I was calling off the wedding," she continued, "only two people stood up for me. Clarice Quincy, my roommate from college, and Dexter Thorndyke. He and my father go back a long way. They went to law school and passed the bar together and formed a partnership until Dad got a foothold in politics. When Thorny sided with me and opposed my parents in the matter of my marriage, however, they severed their ties with him, too."

So her rebellion had cost her a family and destroyed a friendship. All his life he'd wanted a family, and here Gwyn had thrown one away.

"Do you miss them—your parents and old friends?"

"I miss the idea of them. It would have been nice to have a mom and dad to go home to once in a while, to call on the phone on Sundays and holidays, friends I could drop by and see. But that life never existed for me, Jed, so I guess I really haven't lost anything."

She pushed away from the couch and walked toward the cold fireplace. It needed a big spray of flowers with a grow lamp on it. Yellow mums or maybe white ones with pink centers.

"I have a mother who was never a mommy. We never baked brownies. She never dressed me up for Halloween to go trick or treating. My father wasn't a daddy. He didn't carry me on his shoulders or take me to the circus. The three of us never went on a picnic or flew kites." It all sounded so pitiful, but he'd asked for the truth. She had been pitiful. She wouldn't be again. "So there's no one to miss."

"Do you ever go back?" he asked.

"I did once—about a year after I left. It was a waste of time. They were as frigid as ever, colder because I had embarrassed them. Oh, they would have let me return—if I'd accepted their authority. I told them very politely I wouldn't do that and left. I haven't been back since. I never will."

"It must have been hard giving up the life of luxury."

Anger flared and was quickly replaced with the cold ashes of desolation. She'd hoped he'd understand, but he didn't. Like everyone else, he saw only the wealth and privilege of the life she'd left.

"I made my choices. I don't regret them."

CHAPTER EIGHT

LIKE FRAYED COTTON threads the mist drifted lazily from tree to tree. Wispy tendrils swirled over the dark still waters. Despite Jed's flannel shirt, Gwyn shivered in the cool damp air as they set out in the flat-bottomed boat from the low wooden dock. Night smells, earthy decay overlaid with the sweet scent of blossoms hovered in the damp air. Overhead, gray cobwebs of Spanish moss hung in ghostly splendor from outstretched branches.

Slipping the oar into the brown stream, Jed maneuvered among the knobby knees of cypress roots toward the main channel of the lake. Behind him, Gwyn watched his broad shoulders sway in smooth, powerful thrusts as he plied his single paddle into the murky water, its rhythmic whoosh alone breaking the hovering, hollow silence of the eerie swamp.

The ghostly white cloud over and around them diffused the predawn light, isolating the two of them in a timeless realm of peaceful quietude. Gwyn quickly lost all sense of direction and didn't care. Jed knew the way.

"Almost there," he said softly, the sonorous depth of his voice blending into the surreal miasma.

He continued to arch and dig, bend and stroke to

a music only he heard, yet she could feel it pulsing, experience the idyllic harmony of man and nature, male and female. Thrust, flow, withdraw. Thrust, flow, withdraw. An eternal cadence. A timeless beat.

"This is beautiful," she said in a reverential whisper. "It's like the rest of the world has ceased to exist."

"For now it has."

She could hear the smile in his voice. Contentment. This is where he came to be alone, to think, to recharge his energies. Not the morning room, with its long-distance view of nature. Not the library, where wisdom secreted itself between the covers of books. But here, in this simple, sepia-and-gray world of primeval creation. Here, where nothing else existed, a man could rediscover himself. He'd brought her here, to his place of solitude.

In a drifting clearing of the fog, she spied an egret standing motionless on its spindly legs, aloof on its watery perch. Nearby, a turtle splashed from a flat rock into the muddy morass. Somewhere overhead, out of sight, a crow ruffled its feathers and cawed.

"Here we are," Jed said and stowed the oar.

"How can you tell?" she asked on a muted laugh.

"Swamp rats know the swamp," he answered.

She caught his eye and held it when he turned. "Is that what you are, a swamp rat?"

A smile curled the edges of his mouth. "Parttime." He stood and stepped easily onto a jutting rock.

Rising, she asked playfully, "And the rest of the time?"

He extended his hand to her. "Sometimes I'm just a man." Humility and pride resonated in his words. Incompatible emotions overlaying each other in all their complexity.

She couldn't define the sensation she felt when his hand clasped hers. It was warm and strong, as she knew it would be. She found comfort in the way her fingers fit neatly into his. But there was more. An erotic vitality whipped through her in the way he drew her to him. His firm, reassuring touch offered a promise of fulfillment. He lent her balance as she stepped from the tiny floating craft to firmament.

"Are you cold?" Arm spanning her shoulders, he guided her along a tiny spit of land to the stand of pines beyond the cypress.

"I was," she acknowledged, and snuggled into his embrace, "but not now."

He touched his lips to the top of her head, inhaling the scent of her. "I'm glad."

The pines were spindly, totems with their heads in the clouds. The green undergrowth was lush with dewy ferns and tear-dropped sumac. As the vague surreal light brightened, sounds began to creep into consciousness. A scurrying here, a fluttering there. Calls and alerts were exchanged among other species. Danger. Man.

"We'll have a good view from this spot." Jed led her up a short hill, into a denser layer of mist that encircled them, swallowed them up.

The warmth of his hand still holding hers contrasted with the sharp coolness of moist air entering her lungs. Suddenly, the fog lay like a frothy carpet below them, and the sun, previously unseen, glowed red above an endless sea of white. A few stars emitted final twinkles and disappeared into the glowing blue.

Jed pulled her to his side as they watched the sun rise. Another promise. Another day. No words were spoken. None were necessary.

THEY WOULD HAVE relaxed on the veranda to eat the fish they caught later that morning if the clear morning sky hadn't turned dismally gray. It was raining now, so they sat in the morning room and watched sheets of water ribbon down the windowpanes. It cast the world outside in wavy streaks, the dull pitter-patter rumbling like a muted snare drum.

"Thank you, June." Jed grinned at the platter of sautéed bass and crappie, neatly garnished with spiced apples and young sprigs of rosemary from Josiah's garden. "There's nothing like fresh-caught fish," he told Gwyn.

They said little during the meal, content in each other's company. Gwyn's attention was not on the food in front of her, however, but the man on the other side of the table. They'd passed their solitary morning largely in silence. Strange, she thought, that it would make them feel closer.

They were finishing up small portions of blueberry cobbler when June brought the latest edition of the *National Tabloid*. Jed pushed his plate aside, took another sip of iced tea and picked up the paper. He was relieved to see a story different from the last issue slashed above the masthead, the outing of some celebrity. But not to be missed was the feature headline under the Simon Sezz byline.

He ripped open the paper to page three, his face hard with anger. Suddenly a growl erupted from his throat, and with one impulsive sweep of his arm, he fisted the newspaper and slammed it onto the table. China crashed to the ceramic-tiled floor.

Gwyn's head shot up. Shocked and momentarily frightened by this unexpected violence from a man who was always in such exemplary control, she watched him fight to regain that composure.

"Jed," she murmured unobtrusively, "what is it?"

Drawing in a deep breath, he carefully straightened the paper and handed it across the table to her. June appeared in the doorway.

"I'm sorry, June. A little accident," he said.

June withdrew and reappeared a few seconds later with dustpan and brush.

Jed took them from her. "I'll clean it up."

"It's all right, Mr. Jed." She grabbed a cloth from the serving cart and started to bend down over a puddle of tea, but he took her elbow.

"Let me do it," he said softly, and lifted the cloth from her hands. "I'll take care of it."

A baffled expression creased June's dark face. Cleaning up was her job, and she was offended at not being allowed to do it.

"The lunch was absolutely delicious," Gwyn noted to divert her. "There's an art to cooking fish, and you've obviously mastered it." Compliments usually worked, especially the well-deserved variety.

"Thank you, miss. It's very simple, really. When you think they need one more minute, they're done." She looked over, appalled that her boss was on his hands and knees picking up broken glass. She made a move toward him, but Gwyn caught her gently by the arm.

"We'll be fine. I promise," she confided.

June stared at Gwyn for a moment, nodded solemnly and quietly left the room.

While Jed carefully gathered the shattered pieces, Gwyn read the cutline. "Wealthy East Texas landowner refuses to explain role in foster mother's murder."

Gwyn shared Jed's outrage. She also recognized that it was typical tabloid hyperbole that walked the fine line between truth and liability. The words didn't actually accuse him of being involved in the crime, but the innuendo was clear. Yet she wondered why this particular article should so enrage him. She opened the paper.

"Jed Louis, illegitimate son of Helen Louis—"

Gwyn stopped reading. Illegitimate. He hadn't told her that. He'd said only that his father was dead.

Whether he'd been born in or out of wedlock, however, wasn't the point. She'd promised no more secrets. She thought he had, too, even if the words had never been spoken. What other secrets was he keeping?

Without even realizing she was doing it, she looked down at the man soaking up spilled tea. Did he find it symbolic that he was on his hands and knees? With a shake of her head, she resumed her reading: "—is the only one of Frannie Granger's three foster children to still reside in the quaint little town of Uncertain, Texas. His foster siblings, Emerald Monday and Will McClain, vanished within two days of Frannie's sudden disappearance. We now know she was murdered. Were they? No trace of them has ever been found."

Gwyn sank into her wicker chair and closed her eyes, wishing she could shut out this ugliness, but the technique never worked in the past, and it wasn't working now. She found her place and read on.

"There was good reason for Jed Louis to hang around, of course—Beaumarais, a beautiful antebellum manor on Caddo Lake. He inherited it from his uncle, Walter Louis, the estate's last legitimate heir." The second twist of the knife. "That's not to say the strikingly handsome bachelor has been idle. As the men of the town will tell you, he's made big bucks buying and selling real estate and breeding Percheron horses, the enormous draft animals that are about the size of the famous Clydesdales of Budweiser beer fame. And the local ladies will remind you, Jed Louis has developed quite a name for himself spreading his largesse."

Gwyn secretly smiled. She could agree with the scandalmonger about one thing: Jed's looks. The size of his horses was accurate, too.

"The big house on the hill and the money that the Louis name attracts, also brings power in this quiet East Texas community. When Sheriff Logan Fielder tried recently to interview the wealthy landowner about his whereabouts at the time of Frannie

Granger's death, Louis flatly refused to answer his questions and ordered the lawman off his property.''

The last statement was untrue. Where had Hollis gotten that part of his story? She doubted Fielder would have told him about their brief meeting, if only because it showed him to be weak. More likely, the sheriff had recounted his visit to one of his deputies, who then passed it on. She didn't imagine Fielder would be pleased by this misstatement, either. Not that there was much he could do about it. By itself, the comment was too insignificant and open to varying interpretations to warrant legal action.

Referring to Jed, Simon Sezz went on, ''He then hired the famous—some would say infamous, after the notorious Trigve Helms murder case—Dexter Thorndyke to represent him. The Great Thorn, as prosecutors are inclined to refer to the high-priced attorney, has reportedly issued a gag order on his client. One wonders why an innocent man would refuse to answer perfectly legitimate questions about the woman who virtually brought him up, and whom he claims to have loved deeply. But then, legitimacy isn't Jed Louis's strong suit.''

Gwyn dropped the paper on the table in a mood of abject disgust. Jed had finished cleaning up the mess and was wiping his hands on his cloth napkin.

''Where did he hear about the gag order?'' she asked quietly.

''I imagine Thorny issues them to all his clients. Hollis has called here several times asking questions, requesting interviews. June or I have consistently said 'No comment.'"

He settled again in his chair and leveled his eyes on hers. "You're upset with me," he commented contritely.

She gazed out the multipaned window at the water drops streaking down the glass like so many teardrops.

"You accused me of lying to you," she intoned flatly, "when I didn't tell you everything—about the horses, about my identity. You've done the same thing, Jed."

"I'm a bastard, Gwyn. That's not something I'm proud of."

"We're not responsible for who our parents are, remember?" she reminded him.

"You know, I would have expected you to be more understanding," he retorted, anger creeping in behind the humiliation of his confession. "You walked away from a family, from an identity, because you were ashamed of it. Why won't you extend the same courtesy to me?"

"It's not the same, and you did lie to me, Jed. You told me your father was dead."

"He is. Remember I told you about my mother coming here to see my uncle when I was about four?"

Gwyn didn't answer.

"My mother had just received word that my father had been killed in a car accident. She thought, she hoped, that with him out of the picture permanently, her brother would take her back. We waited in the sitting room for what must have been an hour. Most of the time, she was bubbling over with nostalgic stories about living there. She'd run her hands across the back of the settee and the fiddleback chairs or hold the delicate figurines to show me.

Jed's jaws worked as he fought for control. "When we fled the house, she was in tears. I wanted to ask her what the word *whore* meant, but I was afraid to. Much later I found out."

Closing her eyes, Gwyn muttered, "I'm sorry." She understood now why that one room had remained unchanged. It held memories of his mother.

He ignored her. "My mother was seventeen when she had an affair with a gambler ten years her senior. She loved him, or thought she did, but he didn't love her." He lowered his eyes and stared at his hands as he laced and released his fingers.

Gwyn turned to face him. "Jed—"

"When she told him she was pregnant with his kid, the guy bolted. He never came back to see her—or me."

Gwyn sensed it would be a mistake to interrupt him now. She didn't know how long he'd kept this shame locked inside him. Too long. Had he ever spoken to anyone about it?

"The reason I was sent to Frannie after my mother died suddenly of an aneurysm—she was twenty-three years old, I was six—was that her brother, Walter, my dear uncle, didn't want to have anything to do with a bastard nephew. He never came to see me, though I lived right next door. He died a few years later."

Gwyn remembered Jed saying Walter was a sanctimonious skinflint. The irony was unmistakable.

"Yet he left you Beaumarais," she reminded him.

Jed let out a low, bitter snort. "Because there was no one else. I'm the last Louis."

Now he was about to be humiliated again by having his illegitimacy broadcast. No doubt, older members of the community knew of it, but it had certainly never been mentioned to her, and she suspected they'd all but dismissed it as irrelevant. They accepted Jed Louis because he'd earned their respect. Which was all that mattered—except to him.

Was this why he acquired land and horses? His comments about private property made sense now. She understood, too, why her helping the archaeologist Tessa Lang disturb his land had so angered him.

GWYN RETURNED to her house to find a message on her answering machine. The publicity director of a western-wear company was looking for animals to use in a commercial they were planning for a new line of women's jeans. She called the man back and they talked for nearly an hour, discussing various approaches. He wanted something exotic, not the usual horse, not even her cute miniatures. Mules were out. Elephants? Their rough skin would send the wrong message. They finally settled on llamas. He needed them in three days.

That sent her scrambling. She'd have to go to West Texas herself to select the llamas from the herd of the rancher who owned them, then arrange for transportation. What about her animals here? The dog could go with her, but not the horses, and she didn't want to take Cleopatra, her pregnant cat. Would Jed feed the horses? She'd check. Feed the cat, as well? He'd probably do it, but she had another idea. She picked up the phone.

"I wonder if I could ask a favor of you," she said after the polite preliminaries were taken care of. "I have to go out of town for a few days. I'll see if Jed can feed my horses, but I was wondering if Alanna might like to keep my cat during that time."

"Oh, Gwyn, Alanna would love it. Actually, I've been wanting to get her a pet, but—"

Gwyn felt a wave of relief. "I have to warn you, though, Cleo is pregnant."

"Uh-oh." But there was humor, not concern, in the remark. "Do you expect her have the kittens while you're gone?"

"Probably not. She's not due till late next week."

"But things happen." Gwyn could picture a broad smile on his face.

"I've noticed."

"Not to worry. As I recall, cats have been having kittens all by themselves for some time now."

"I doubt you'll have any trouble, but I'll leave you the name of the vet—"

"When can I bring Alanna over?" He sounded as excited as she imagined his daughter would be.

"Why don't you come by after work—"

"We'll be there about five-thirty."

Gwyn hung up with a grin on her face.

JED DROVE to his office in Jefferson. No appointments today, which was why he'd been able to take

Gwyn out to see the sunrise and share a leisurely lunch—leisurely until he'd read the paper. He had no doubt his employees would have seen it. The first article had whetted their appetites. This latest installment would have them salivating. He didn't think any of them would bring up the subject to his face. He'd always frowned on gossip and made clear private lives were just that. But he knew they would be talking among themselves. Human nature. The question was how they would see him now.

He'd invited Gwyn back for dinner this evening, and she'd accepted. He'd kissed her this morning after sunrise, before they'd returned to his swamp boat and fished for an hour. The way she'd snuggled against him told him that if conditions had been different, they might have made love then and there. But dew-dropped wetlands, like fog-shrouded English moors, were hardly the places for lovemaking.

He'd asked June to prepare a light supper, something that wouldn't demand attention. June, ever discreet, had said nothing to suggest she knew she was catering a tryst, but he didn't miss the tiny smirk on her face as she ruminated over what to prepare.

It was after six by the time he returned to Beaumarais. Gwyn wasn't due over until seven. He went upstairs and changed from his business clothes to casual chinos and a sage-green Polo shirt. What would she be wearing? he wondered as he pulled off dark socks, replaced them with white ones and donned casual Adidas.

He went to the kitchen to see what June had left.

Chicken enchiladas. There was a note on the film covering the ovenproof serving dish to heat them for half an hour at 350 degrees.

Maybe Gwyn would wear jeans like this morning. A clinging blouse? Or maybe a simple dress. Easier to slip out of, he reasoned with a grin.

He turned on the oven and set it to the proper temperature.

Or perhaps she would wear loose-flowing slacks, the kind he'd seen in the fashion magazines at his barber's.

The morning room was already set. June had even put a candle in the middle of the table. *Definitely have to give that woman a raise,* he told himself. Returning to the kitchen, he placed their main course in the oven.

Of course, Gwyn could always surprise him by wearing cutoffs and a T-shirt. He liked the picture, but she wouldn't dress that way for dinner. Even at home. He'd never seen her legs, he realized, but he didn't have to to know they'd be perfect. And smooth. He imagined himself running a hand along her thigh....

He jumped and his heart buffeted when he heard a tap on glass. He looked over, to see Gwyn standing on the other side of the kitchen window with a Cheshire-cat grin on her face. Did she know what he'd just been thinking? Of course not. She couldn't...could she?

He motioned for her to come in and glanced at the clock over the sink. Right on time.

She was wearing chinos, too, with a dark-green

blouse that wasn't giving his heart much of a chance to settle down. And she was bubbling. Because they were going to spend an evening alone? His spirits soared but then leveled off when the gleam in her eyes told him she was happy about something else.

"Good news?"

She explained about the call she'd received from the jeans manufacturer offering her a good-size contract.

"You have to go out of town?" He couldn't keep the disappointment from his voice.

"Just for a few days. Romeo's coming with me, and I've arranged for Riley and his daughter to take care of Cleopatra. I was wondering…if you'd…be willing to feed my horses while I'm away. It's all right if you can't," she rushed on. "I talked to the vet. He can board them for me for the three days—"

"No need to do that," he said over his shoulder as he removed their dinner from the oven and placed it on the stainless-steel counter. "Besides, boarding a dozen horses would be terribly expensive." He faced her with a smile. "Just let me know what they eat and when, and I'll be glad to take care of them."

"You're sure?" He could hear the relief in her voice.

He wrapped an arm around her shoulders and drew her to his side. Bending his head, he whispered in her ear, "I'm sure."

She turned her head and gazed up at him. The words *I'm sure, too* were on the tip of her tongue, but they never got a chance to come out before his lips sealed them in. He shifted his stance, placed himself squarely in front of her and completed the kiss. Her hands slid behind his back and joined there. Her arms bracketed his lower rib cage like a vise.

Keeping his eyes open, he studied the way her lashes fluttered and closed as he deepened the kiss. He resolved not to let her leaving tomorrow interfere with tonight. It disturbed him, though, that she seemed so eager to get away.

Dinner was filled with laughter. She told stories about her animals and some of the antics they'd pulled—always at the most inopportune time, of course.

"I had a sponsor who wanted to use a dachshund in a hot dog commercial," she explained between mouthfuls of spicy chicken enchilada. "Seemed easy enough. So I bought a pedigreed dachshund and took him to the studio. Would you believe the little rascal was such a nervous wreck in front of the camera that he wouldn't stop shaking?"

Jed laughed. "Well, I guess if I was going to be the subject of dinner, I'd shake, too. So what did you do?"

"Bought another dog, except I tested this one out first to make sure he wasn't the panicky type."

"Double the expense."

"Actually, it worked very well. We used Old Shaky, as he came to be called, for an antacid commercial. In fact, I made more on that contract than I did on the one for hot dogs."

"And Old Shaky?" Jed asked.

She smiled broadly, pleased that he would ask. Most people laughed at the story but never asked about the dog. "I'm happy to say he's retired now, living with an elderly couple in Kansas City."

"Does he still shake?"

"Whenever a door slams or a stranger comes near him. But in between times, he seems perfectly content."

"More wine?" Jed asked as he wrapped his hand around the neck of a bottle of zinfandel and splashed a few extra drops in both their glasses. "I thought we might go dancing after dinner."

"Oh, where?" She really didn't want to leave the house.

"It's a place nearby called the veranda."

"Hmm. Sounds lovely."

They finished eating, piled their dishes onto the serving cart and wheeled it into the kitchen. Back in the library, Jed turned on a CD player and hit the switch that piped the music outside. He led her there.

A tango came on. He grabbed her right hand stiffly in his left, pressed his cheek against hers and paced her across the flagstone patio. Quickly they reversed and stepped livelily to the Latin beat. He held her in a dip, whirled her around, then once more pressed his body to hers. They laughed when the music ended.

The kiss, when it came, was not like the one earlier in the day. This was not a kiss of affection but of passion. A message of desperate longing, of unbearable need and a fumbling trace of frustration. He gathered her closer, recklessly assaulting her senses. At first he thought he tasted panic, but the resistance passed so quickly he couldn't be sure. Her lips felt hot as they opened to the beckon of his tongue. His blood heated, raced, pooled. His arousal was complete, intense, unbearable.

He spread his feet, lowered his hands and molded her bottom. In response her arms rose and spanned the broadness of his back and wallowed in the heat of his skin beneath the cotton shirt. She groaned when he withdrew his mouth from hers. He pressed his forehead to hers, noses touching, their eyes locked.

"Would you like a tour of the upstairs?"

Desire and a hint of apprehension whirled and danced in her eyes. "That would be very nice."

He extended his lips to make quick contact with hers. His hand clutching hers, he led her through the library, pausing only long enough to flick off the stereo, then proceeded to the main hall.

Smiling, he spun her toward him, bent, caught her behind the knees and gathered her easily into his arms. She clasped her hands behind his neck and practically giggled.

He turned to the right at the head of the stairs to dark-stained double doors. With hardly a shift in his carriage, he depressed the handle and threw the door open.

Her eyes widened as she looked around. "I'm impressed."

It wasn't at all what she had expected, though on reconsideration, she wasn't sure what she thought she'd find. The room was high ceilinged, with molded cornices and elaborate woodwork around the doors. Built-in shutters were folded back from the sash windows, and heavy drapes bracketed a pair of narrow French doors leading out onto small balconies overlooking the lake. But it was the bed, a massive four-poster, that dominated the space.

Jed put her down and watched as she approached it. "It's original," he said. "One of the few pieces my uncle kept. He sold off most of the antiques over the years. But he was especially fond of this."

"How beautiful." Gwyn's taste generally ran to the simple rather than the ornate, but this massive piece of furniture felt absolutely right in this room.

Jed's hands reached around her waist from behind.

"But much too big for one person," he whispered in her ear.

She tilted her head toward his. "Hmm. I can see how it might be."

The heat of his body against her, the warmth of his arms caging her, had her breath slowing and deepening, her heartbeat racing. He nibbled her ear and she felt herself toppling into a world that had no dimensions, only limitations. His hand crept up and cupped her breast. Her nipples hardened.

"I want to make love to you," he murmured in her ear. "Will you make love with me, Gwyneth?"

Her name in his mouth, on his lips, melted through her. She turned in his arms and gazed up. There had never been any doubt that her body wanted this man, and now she knew her heart did, as well.

"I have to leave in the morning," she reminded him.

"In that case—" he began relieving the gold but-

The Harlequin Reader Service® — Here's how it works:

Accepting your 2 free books and gift places you under no obligation to buy anything. You may keep the books and gift and return the shipping statement marked "cancel." If you do not cancel, about a month later we'll send you 6 additional novels and bill you just $3.80 each in the U.S., or $4.21 each in Canada, plus 25¢ shipping & handling per book and applicable taxes if any.* That's the complete price and — compared to cover prices of $4.50 each in the U.S. and $5.25 each in Canada — it's quite a bargain! You may cancel at any time, but if you choose to continue, every month we'll send you 6 more books, which you may either purchase at the discount price or return to us and cancel your subscription.

*Terms and prices subject to change without notice. Sales tax applicable in N.Y. Canadian residents will be charged applicable provincial taxes and GST.

If offer card is missing write to: Harlequin Reader Service, 3010 Walden Ave., P.O. Box 1867, Buffalo NY 14240-1867

BUSINESS REPLY MAIL

FIRST-CLASS MAIL   PERMIT NO. 717   BUFFALO, NY

POSTAGE WILL BE PAID BY ADDRESSEE

HARLEQUIN READER SERVICE
3010 WALDEN AVE
PO BOX 1867
BUFFALO NY 14240-9952

NO POSTAGE
NECESSARY
IF MAILED
IN THE
UNITED STATES

tons of her blouse ''—we don't want to waste any time.''

She tugged at his Polo shirt, pulled it above his waist, then insinuated her hands beneath the cotton to the warm hardness of tight muscle. Her eyelids drooped as she snaked her way up his belly, along the sprinkling of hair to the firm ridgeline of his chest. His small nipples were peaked and pointy. He sucked in air when she ran the tips of her fingers around them.

He slipped her blouse off her shoulders, exposing her satiny bra. He bit his lip at the warm feel of her breasts. He brought his fingers to the front clasp, unhooked it and brushed the material aside. She let the garment fall to the floor. He tore off his shirt, then bent once more, gathered her up in his arms and carried her to the bed.

CHAPTER NINE

GWYN WAS gone three days. Not a long time, Jed told himself, unless you were falling in love with her. He didn't use those words, of course. He wasn't ready to acknowledge the level of emotion and commitment they implied, but he couldn't deny feeling something that went beyond the desire for another night of incredible sex. Incredible was an understatement.

He smiled at the picture that had arrived that morning in the mail, the one taken at the Anglers' Ball. The photographer had captured the gleam in her eye as she gazed up at him. She looked so perfect standing beside him. He could still remember the feel of his hand on the small of her back and later, the smooth texture of her skin and its warmth against and around him.

She wasn't on the pill, and he'd been very careful to use protection, but that caution in no way inhibited their touching, tasting, teasing each other's bodies. He took immense delight in scaling the walls of her initial shyness, watching her eyes widen and glaze as he trailed his fingers along her skin, assailing the edges of her senses.

The second time they made love she'd dedicated

herself to exploring his body. She'd made his heart pound, his breathing take on a long, slow labored ache, as she toured the surface of his skin, cupped and pressed, finding erogenous zones he didn't even know existed, then mercilessly exploited them.

They agreed on the third excursion that they still had much to learn about and from each other. As he'd settled into her warmth and she wrapped her legs around his hips, he'd been tempted to suggest they spend the rest of their lives continuing the adventure. When he extended his arms beside her breasts, boxing her in, she'd draped her hands on his shoulders and looked up at him with smiling, wondrous eyes. But in their depths he'd seen the hesitation. *Don't say it yet. I'm not ready for the next step.*

He wasn't yet, either, and he'd been grateful to her for her warning. Nevertheless, her wisdom also left him with a gnawing tug of guilt. He wanted this woman in his bed, and he'd been willing to say anything to keep her there. He'd never considered himself obsessed or even capable of so all-consuming a physical desire, a need, but he was becoming obsessed with Gwyneth Miller. He wasn't indifferent to the allure of sex, but he'd never felt dominated by it. Until he met her. He knew now nothing he'd ever felt before compared with what he experienced that night with Gwyn.

Now he couldn't get her out of his head. All day long he asked himself where exactly she was, what she was doing, who she was doing it with. Jealousy was an emotion he'd never fully understood, yet here it was tapping at his psyche. He wanted her, and the possibility of not being able to make love to her again was driving him crazy.

She called Wednesday afternoon to confirm she was on her way back from Dallas. After June left for the day, he sat by the bay window in the library, watching, waiting, annoyed that he couldn't concentrate on anything but her. It was his greatest pleasure. The sun was casting long shadows when he saw her cranky Land Rover roll past his driveway. He jumped up, strode out the French doors onto the patio and from there ran along the path to her back door.

Romeo was the first to greet him with a friendly whimper and wagging tail. Absently he petted the frisky sheltie, all the time staring at the rear end of the woman dragging a suitcase from the back seat of the vehicle. He walked up behind her, arched over her and placed his hand beside hers on the luggage. Reflexes had her backing up, only to bump into him, her back against his chest, her hips caged by his. He inhaled the unforgettable scent of woman and floral shampoo. With a little mew of excitement, she stopped.

"Miss Gwyn, Miss Gwyn," came an ecstatic child's voice. They both turned, to see Alanna racing toward them from her house. "They're here. They're here."

Rather than take the gate a few yards away, the four-year-old tried to scale the low chain-link fence. Alarmed that she might fall and hurt herself, Jed rushed forward and lifted her over it.

"The kittens?" Gwyn asked with open-faced excitement at the child and then at Jed.

He smiled broadly and nodded.

"They was borned last night when I was sleeping," Alanna prattled. "I came here with Daddy to feed Cleo this morning, and there they were. Six of them." The girl was bubbling.

"Six?" Gwyn asked a little startled. "The vet said she probably wouldn't have more than three or four. Six?" She got out her key and opened the back door.

There, in a corner of the kitchen was the newspaper-lined box she'd prepared before she left, and in it was Cleo, stretched out on her side, her new progeny snuggled against her. The cat eyed her guardedly but didn't object while Gwyn examined each one.

"That's my favorite," Alanna declared when Gwyn picked up the last of the litter.

What made that kitten special was hard to tell. They were all perfect, all had the characteristic markings and coloring of purebred seal points, but obviously something about that particular one especially appealed to the little girl. Gwyn found a piece of pink ribbon and tied it loosely around the kitten's neck. She'd offer it to the child if Riley approved. She petted the proud mother, who purred when her tiny offspring sought her milk. "They're all so adorable," she remarked.

Alanna bounced up. "Daddy's home."

The adults hadn't even heard his car, but a minute later the tall dark figure of Riley stood in the doorway. "Cute, aren't they?" he said by way of greeting.

They talked about the surprise they'd had that morning.

"No bother at all," Riley insisted when Gwyn apologized for the inconvenience. "I'm glad it happened. Every little girl needs to enjoy a litter of kittens."

A few minutes later father and daughter departed for home, Alanna promising to return in the morning. Waving goodbye, Gwyn and Jed went outside to unpack her Rover. Their bodies bumped when they both reached for the same piece of luggage. He steadied her at arm's length and contemplated the weariness tugging at the corners of her mouth, the fatigue sagging her shoulders. But the glow in her eyes was vibrant and inviting.

"Welcome home," he murmured into her silken hair.

She looked up at him, a come-hither expression playing on her face.

Blood rushed to his nether regions. Their eyes met and suddenly their mouths joined with a wantonness that had them both gasping for air.

"I've missed you," he said softly, his forehead glued to hers, their breaths mingling.

"Me, too."

"Good trip?"

"Really good."

She reached inside the car and snagged an oblong makeup case. "The llamas were an overwhelming success. The sponsor wants to use them as a symbol of their new line. They're going to bring me a lot more business."

"Congratulations." He meant it, but he also couldn't help asking, "Does that mean you'll be going away again?"

"Probably, but that's the way this business works." She stepped inside the house.

Jed didn't wait until the door was closed to pull her into his arms once more. He kissed her slowly, intensely, with a hungry need that had her pulse skipping.

"Mmm," she sighed. "It's good to be back."

He tipped her chin up. "Let's get you unpacked, then there's dinner at my place. June left another of her carefree meals."

"God bless her. She deserves a raise."

He smirked. "I already gave her one."

She grinned, pleased their minds thought alike.

"The house has been awfully empty without you."

Tongue in cheek, she said, "Yeah, I missed the old place, too."

He took her hands, held them by her sides and backed her against the kitchen counter, his hips hemming her in. "Only the house?" he asked, one brow raised precipitously.

The feel of him against her sent electric waves of lustful desire shimmering through her. "Well, I did think about its owner a few times."

"Only a few?" He sounded disappointed. "And what did you think about him?"

"I wondered if he might give me another tour of his upstairs. It was so dark the other night I didn't get to see too much of it."

"Upstairs?" He dotted kisses along her forehead. "A private tour?" He skimmed his mouth along her collarbone. "There are secrets in Beaumarais." He nuzzled the soft skin between shoulder and neck. "Hidden recesses I haven't shown you yet."

Secrets at Beaumarais. The phrase sent adrenaline pumping through her. Or maybe it was the way he curled his tongue along the lobe of her ear. She sucked in air and held it. "I'd love to learn more about your secrets."

"Shall we begin?" He brought his mouth to hers and captured it. A teasing, coaxing tangling of tongues, filled with temptation, implying greed.

"I need to shower first." She was panting from his siege on her senses. "I'm all grungy."

The gleam in his eye said he hadn't noticed or didn't care.

"You can shower over at my place while dinner is heating in the oven," he suggested. "I'll wash your back."

The thought of his hands on her skin had her knees going weak. She gripped the edge of the counter behind her. "You will, huh?"

Gently, he began kneading the muscles at the base of her neck. His hands whispered down her chest just far enough to make both of them aware how close he was to the tips of her breasts, before he moved up again. "Might even work in a bit of massage therapy," he murmured.

She needed to concentrate to keep her eyes open and focused. It would have been so easy to lose herself in the ecstasy of his touch. She stroked his cheek. "I didn't know you were a therapist."

He cocked his brows. His lips curling into a devilish grin, he brushed back a wispy strand of her vagrant hair. "I can see you still have a lot to learn about me."

She tilted her head into his hand. "So much to discover." She dragged a fingernail along his jaw. "This could develop into a challenging quest."

His eyes continued to smile into hers as he kissed the tip of her nose. "Just might. I'm a very complex person, you know."

"Are you?" She slid her hand down the front of his pants and watched his eyes widen. "Seems to me you're pretty straight forward."

"Um," he groaned on an indrawn breath, "maybe we should stay right here."

She laughed and pushed him away. "Nope. I'm a lousy cook, remember."

"Hmm." He reached for her, but she ducked to the side. "I've never tasted your cooking."

She picked up her cosmetic case and carried it to the bedroom. "Be thankful." He followed with her suitcase. Instead of unpacking, however, she grabbed some clean clothes from the closet and her chest of drawers and rolled them up hastily. "Ready?"

He arched an arm over her shoulders. "Willing and able."

As they strolled hand in hand through the piney woods to the stately home on the hill, a phrase kept echoing through Gwyn's mind. *Secrets at Beaumarais.*

JED HAD RESOLVED not to let articles in the *National Tabloid* get to him, but that Thursday morning it took an exceptional amount of willpower to keep his cool.

"Simon Sezz has an interview with Amanda Jennings," he noted as he passed the paper across the breakfast table to Gwyn.

Nothing in the scandal sheet was going to be complimentary, Gwyn realized, but interviews from "friends" felt like a stab in the back. She accepted the paper, neatly folded to the article about the recent events in Uncertain.

"I remember the day poor Frannie disappeared," Amanda was quoted as saying. "She was such a nice, friendly lady. Everybody loved her." Gwyn frowned, suspecting that if the perky flirt ever thought of Frannie as "poor," it was with condescension rather than affection.

"Jed didn't come to school that day. He was always so conscientious, got straight As, and he was the best basketball player on the team. That was the only time I ever remember him being absent."

Simon Sezz went on to explain that Amanda Jennings and Jed Louis had gone to school together and been in the same homeroom their senior year at Uncertain High, the year Frannie Granger was murdered. He also didn't miss an opportunity to remind his readers that the dead woman's body had been buried right over her property line on a corner of Beaumarais.

"I found out the reason he ditched that day," Amanda continued in her interview, "was that he'd had a terrible fight with his foster mother."

"About what?" the interviewer asked.

"I don't rightly know. But I did hear Will and Jed talk about Jed storming out of the house after accusing Frannie of ruining his life and swearing to get even."

Gwyn rested her hands on the edge of the table, the paper spread between them, and glanced over at Jed, who appeared to be working the *Uncertain Times* crossword puzzle.

"How much of what she says is true and how much of it's hype?" she asked.

Deliberately, he poured coffee from a carafe into her cup and his own. "It's all true," he acknowledged. "I did cut classes that day."

No need to ask the obvious question. He'd tell her what had happened when he was ready. She continued reading the article, but it said nothing that hadn't already been covered.

June was clearing the table of the breakfast of bagels, cream cheese and jam, coffee and juice when Jed beckoned Gwyn to join him in the library. Once there, he walked over to the stereo and inserted a CD. A moment later the sweet melodic strains of Brahms's "Double Concerto for Violin and Cello" filled the room. It was beautiful music that Gwyn knew well. She wasn't particularly surprised at his liking it, having examined his collection of CDs, tapes and old records. His tastes were eclectic. A few Broadway show albums, some rock-and-roll and a curious emphasis on country-and-western and classical music.

She sat on the couch by the fireplace and remembered she wanted to get a floral arrangement for the hearth. She'd pick one up today. At the moment, however, her attention was drawn to the man resting his arm on the mantel.

"Right after I came to live with Frannie, she wanted me to take music lessons. Piano. I was six years old, in first grade, the perfect time for a child to learn."

Gwyn watched his face and wondered what thoughts were going through his mind. His mother had just died suddenly and without warning. His uncle had rejected him and now he was in the care of a woman he'd never met. It must have been a very sad and confusing time for him. Alone. Forced to live with a stranger, and told he had to take piano lessons.

"I liked music. My mother usually had the radio on, mostly rock-and-roll, occasionally a little jazz. Except on Sunday morning. Then she'd tune in to Wheeling, West Virginia, and we'd listen to what she referred to as hillbilly music—what we now call bluegrass. That was my favorite."

There was a childish pleasure in the way he related this. Apparently, all his memories weren't sad ones, after all. Gwyn bit the inside of her mouth as she contemplated the scene: mother and child enjoying the Americanized version of Irish and Scottish reels and jigs. Spirited banjos, guitars and wailing fiddles.

"I was excited about the idea of being able to make my own music. There was just one problem." He chuckled softly with a hint of mischief in his eyes. "I hated the piano. Not the instrument. Trying to play it. What absolutely fascinated me, what I really wanted to learn, was the violin.''

He paced in front of the fireplace.

''That created a bit of a problem, though. Frannie had an old spinet I could have practiced on, and one of her clients had agreed to give me lessons in exchange for housecleaning. But Frannie not only didn't own a violin, the nearest teacher was in Marshall, and he wanted cash. Undaunted, Frannie found me an old fiddle in a pawnshop, took on another client and drove me over to Marshall every week for lessons. The hour I was torturing the strings, she did her weekly grocery shopping.''

Gwyn smiled, imagining that his playing must have sounded a little like someone dragging fingernails against a blackboard. ''What about practicing at home?'' she asked. ''Where did you go?''

He smirked. ''Whenever the weather allowed, to the dock by the lake. I think even the fish fled.''

Chuckling at the memory, he took a step toward the couch as if he were going to sit down, but restlessness had him pacing.

''I stuck with it and over the next ten years got pretty good—good enough that in my senior year I was offered an opportunity to go to the Juilliard School of Music in New York.''

Gwyn would have expected pride in the statement. Instead, she found discontent.

''Naturally, I wanted to go,'' he continued, ''but when I asked Frannie to sign the consent form as my legal guardian, she refused.''

''Why would she deny you the opportunity to attend so prestigious a school, Jed? I don't understand.''

He drew himself up, apparently undecided if he still wanted to sit down or pace. He compromised by resting an elbow on the mantel again.

''Her logic was that very few musicians made names for themselves,'' he explained, ''or even earned a decent living—especially in classical music. I was a fairly good fiddler, she admitted, but even she could tell I wasn't great, and Juilliard wasn't going to make me great.''

''Sounds pretty harsh,'' Gwyn ventured.

Jed managed a crooked smile. ''Frannie could be blunt when circumstances called for it. She didn't believe in mincing words, especially when it came to right and wrong.''

''And she didn't think Juilliard was the right thing for you?''

He shook his head. ''She wanted me to treat music as a hobby, not a profession. As far as she was concerned, I should be working toward a well-paying occupation.'' He stopped and looked at Gwyn. ''I reminded her that with my uncle's inheritance coming to me in a little over three years when I turned twenty-one, I didn't need to earn a living.'' He shook his head. ''It was the wrong thing to say, and she let me have it with both barrels. I had a obligation, she insisted, to be self-supporting and self-sufficient, not live off the money someone else had earned.''

''Tough lady,'' Gwyn commented, ''and smart.''

''Yeah, well, I didn't see it that way. You may

have noticed I'm a little thin-skinned about my paternity.''

She gave him a confirming nod.

"Instead of interpreting her remark as an incentive, I took it as a reminder that my birth certificate says Unknown where my father's name should be."

Something he would have to live with all his life. "So if she didn't think you had the makings of a great concert violinist, what did she want you to do?" Gwyn asked.

"I'd been offered an athletic scholarship to the University of Texas. She wanted me to accept it and major in something practical."

Gwyn thought of the many *useful* things she'd wanted to do that her parents had rejected. She would never have to earn a living, they'd explained, sometimes patiently, more often with exasperation. There was no need for her to study medicine, architecture or engineering. Her role was not to be a scientist but an artist, to be a model of culture. Studying languages, as long as they were the politically correct ones, could advance her future husband's diplomatic career. Being fluent in the nuances of painting and sculpture likewise—so long as she didn't dirty her hands actually *doing* those things.

"So you wanted to go to Juilliard and Frannie wouldn't let you," Gwyn prompted.

He pulled away from the fireplace and started pacing again; this time there was anger rather than hurt in his expression. Gwyn waited.

"I won't tell you I wasn't furious at her for not signing the paper. I was. We'd had arguments before.'' He gave a mirthless laugh. ''They were earth-shattering problems to me at the time. It wasn't until much later that I realized it was typical teenage stuff. I was almost eighteen by then and feeling very independent. I bristled when she'd ask me where I was going, who I was going to be with, what time I'd be home. I was living in her house and knew I had to follow her rules, but I resented them.''

He stopped in midstride and turned to Gwyn, an ironic grin on his face. ''Guess what we argued about most?''

''School? College?''

''Nope. Amanda Jennings.''

''Amanda? Why?''

This time he chuckled with amusement. ''She was the head cheerleader in high school and really knew how to strut her assets. I'm not just talking about her pom-poms. Believe me, there was never any question she liked men, liked teasing them and leading them on. She'd bat her eyes and brush up against a guy and he'd turn into a slobbering idiot. Then she'd walk calmly away with a smirk on her face.''

Gwyn's boarding-school days had been so different. She'd been a wallflower at the arranged dances she'd been allowed to attend. Carefully nurtured poise kept her from babbling or stuttering in an uncomfortable situation, which was exactly how she'd felt when a dance partner took her in his arms. Her demure silence and inability to act spontaneously had earned her a reputation as an ice maiden. Memory of the image still gnawed.

''I think I can tell why Frannie didn't like her.''

"Frannie was no fool," Jed insisted. "She could see Amanda was playing me better than I played the fiddle. I wasn't alone. Amanda worked her claws into Will and Riley, as well."

Gwyn easily pictured the scene. Clarice, her roommate in college, was one of those convivial party girls who seemed to know instinctively what men wanted and how to handle them. Gwyn had envied the striking redhead's easy rapport with the opposite sex. Their personalities were so different they shouldn't have gotten along at all. Instead, they'd become the best of friends and still were.

"Did the three of you fight over her?" Gwyn asked.

Jed rocked his head, obviously amused. "Let's just say we came close a couple of times." He crossed one ankle over the other. "But I think secretly we knew we were being used. It's rare, but sometimes even testosterone-crazed males can use their big heads."

Gwyn chuckled. "So what happened, as they say, on the morning in question."

He grew somber. "We were running late. I didn't even have time for breakfast. I asked Frannie again to sign the admission form, but she still refused, and I lost my temper. Amanda overheard Will and me talking about our fight the following morning. Her version is essentially correct. I accused Frannie of ruining my life."

Gwen glanced at the paper she'd brought with her. "It also says you threatened her. Did you?"

"No," he snapped, his face slightly distorted,

color rising. He lowered his voice. "I would never have threatened Frannie, and I would never, ever have harmed her. Gwyn, that woman had been my mother for twelve years, twice as long as my real mom. Sure we argued sometimes. How many kids don't disagree with their parents, especially during their teenage years?"

Gwyn doubted he could understand how she envied him. She'd never wrangled with her parents, never been allowed to, until there was no room left for argument. How often she'd wished she could stand up to them, challenge them, make them justify their imperious demands, say something herself that would convince them to change their minds. But she hadn't. She'd never even sought compromise; she'd simply acquiesced. In the end it had left her no options.

"I can't remember my exact words," Jed admitted, "but they were something to the effect that I would show her."

"What did you mean?"

He hesitated then spoke. "I don't think I meant anything specific by it. It was just one of those things you yell at somebody when you're mad. I admit I toyed with the idea of forging her name on the application. I figured once I got accepted to Juilliard, she would keep quiet. Besides, I was going to be eighteen in a couple of months. By then, it wouldn't matter. I wouldn't need her permission."

"Is that what you did? Forge her name?"

He shook his head. "No. I could never have faced

her when she found out, and of course she would
have.''

He paced the worn Oriental rug. "After our fight,
I went down to the dock. I was steaming, but I at
least had the smarts not to do anything in the heat
of the moment.''

"Not many people have that kind of wisdom. Especially not teenagers."

He agreed. "And that's what makes Amanda's
statement so damning." He took a deep breath. "I
had a real problem with my temper after I first went
to live with Frannie."

"Which is understandable," Gwyn said sympathetically. "You'd been through a lot."

"Anyway," Jed continued without dwelling on it,
"Frannie taught me to cool off before I acted." He
settled at last into the chair across from Gwyn. "I
don't deny I was enraged when she refused to give
me her permission. Deep down inside, though, I
knew she was right. I wasn't a great violinist. I was
mediocre good, and that was all I was ever going to
be." He inhaled deeply and let it out slowly. "The
truth, Gwyn, is that by the time I stomped out of the
house that morning, I was no longer mad at Frannie.
I was mad at myself." He paused, his face glum. "In
the heat of the moment I did something I've been
ashamed of for nineteen years. I insulted her."

He pictured the pained expression on her face
when he reminded her that they were poor. *I'm doing
the best I can,* was all she'd had to counter with.
Few people could say that with any degree of hon-

esty. Frannie could, but there was humiliation in her acknowledgment.

"She'd been good to me, Gwyn, good to all of us. She worked hard, and in return all I did was complain because I had to share a room with Will."

"You loved her very much. She knew that." When Jed didn't look convinced, she added, "Kids often say things they don't mean, or say them in a way they don't intend."

Too painfully, she remembered her parting conversation with her mother in which she accused the socially perfect woman of being a selfish, arrogant phony who hid behind glamour and posturing. "Hide what?" her mother had demanded in that snugly superior tone that until then had been enough to intimidate. "Hide the fact," Gwyn had answered back, "that you don't have a soul."

Claudia Miller's eyes had grown big with amazement, and for an insane moment, Gwyn thought she saw admiration for her cutting words, but a pained expression quickly followed. To this day Gwyn didn't know if her mother had actually been offended by the barb or was just putting on another of her performances. In any event, Gwyn had refused to back down. Not this time. Not ever again. *Goodbye, Mother.*

"I'm sure she understood you were upset and didn't mean it," she told Jed, but he didn't look consoled. "Where did you go?"

"I took my swamp boat and went fishing."

To the piney woods he'd taken her to last week,

she thought. She could picture a confused teenager going there to sulk and try to sort things out.

"Emmy and Will barely made the school bus. I had my own car and usually drove in. Seniors didn't have to be at school as early as the others, especially in those last few weeks of the term. I stomped down to the boat dock. I remember Frannie calling after me, but I ignored her."

Gwyn knew nothing would ever relieve him of the pain of that parting. Words of consolation were useless and might be perceived as patronizing. "Did you hear her car drive away?" she asked.

He thought about it for a minute. "I don't think so." He didn't sound sure. "But it would have been a noise that's so familiar it doesn't register when you hear it."

"So you don't know if she left her place and came back later, perhaps with her murderer, or met him there after you went out in your boat."

Dejected, he shook his head. "I wish I did."

Gwyn rose and went behind his chair and massaged the taut muscles of his neck. "I'd like you to come with me over to the house, Jed. There's something I want to show you."

He turned his head and looked up, curious, her breasts so close that it was difficult for him to concentrate. "About Frannie?"

"About me."

CHAPTER TEN

"YOU SAID you stayed in Frannie's house after she disappeared. By yourself?" Gwyn asked as they strolled the path between Beaumarais and Frannie's old place. The air was calm and sweet.

He nodded. "The authorities didn't quite know what to do with me. I was two months shy of eighteen, so theoretically I wasn't an adult, but I was due to graduate in six weeks and pulling me out of school would have cost me a diploma."

They walked into the bright sunshine. "Remember, too," he continued, "we didn't really know what had happened to Frannie. We never received a ransom note, so it didn't seem likely someone had kidnapped her, yet with her clothes and car still there, it seemed pretty clear she hadn't left voluntarily. I guess we all knew she was dead, but no one wanted to say it."

"The uncertainty must have been terrible."

If he noticed the unintended pun on the name of the town, he didn't acknowledge it. They reached the back door of the house. Romeo, tail wagging, trotted up to greet them, eager to be petted. Jed scratched behind the sheltie's ears.

She opened the door but ordered the dog to stay

on the enclosed porch. Romeo and Cleopatra had always gotten along very well, and Gwyn didn't think he would do any harm to the kittens, but there was no sense in tempting fate. Animosity between the two species was a far older instinct than amity.

The morning sun angled into the screened area, filling it with a golden light. She crossed the tiled floor and entered the house proper. Cleopatra, resting contentedly on her side in the newspaper-lined box, purred loudly enough to be heard across the room. The gargling stopped when Jed raised his hand to pet her, but then resumed with even greater intensity.

Except for the dishwasher Jed had installed next to the sink several years ago, the kitchen was almost exactly as it had been when Frannie left it nineteen years ago. An unexpected wave of emotions—melancholy, anger—rippled through him. Whoever murdered Frannie hadn't just taken a single life. He'd robbed peace from many more. Where was Emmy? Where was Will? Were they alive, safe? Had they been able to find happiness? Would he ever see them again? Questions he had pondered many times.

Gwyn glanced at Jed as she closed the door behind them. She didn't know exactly what was going through his mind, but she was sure it had something to do with his foster mother and was painful. She wondered if the sadness that seemed to be a permanent part of him would ever be lifted.

"How long did you stay here by yourself?" she asked as she set about feeding Cleopatra and relining her box with clean newspaper. The kittens' eyes were open now. As she worked, she tried to imagine what it had been like for Jed—alone in the house that had once been happy, always listening for a familiar voice, a greeting that would end the feeling of abandonment.

His face retained a blank faraway look for a second before he answered. "About six weeks. Long enough to graduate. I passed my final exams by the skin of my teeth, escorted Amanda to the senior prom—" he smirked "—and disappointed her by not taking her to the Shady Lane Motel in Marshall for a night of mad sex."

It shouldn't matter now. It was nearly two decades ago. But Gwyn was glad he'd rejected the sexy blonde.

"So you never went to Juilliard."

"Actually, I did. I turned eighteen shortly after graduation, submitted the application myself and went to New York City. I was there exactly two weeks and came back. Frannie was right. It wasn't where I belonged."

He leaned against the counter next to the refrigerator. The muted light spilling in from the window over the sink opposite him cast his tall frame in sensuous relief.

"It must have been a terrible disappointment."

"Hmm," he mumbled, "but not a surprise. We don't always know when we're good at something, but I think we know when we're bad. My counselor there held out hope that I might develop a talent for composition, but I wasn't interested in that aspect of music."

Gwyn propped herself against the kitchen table. "What did you do?"

"Came back to Uncertain. Whether Ray had also figured out I wasn't going to make it in the Big Apple, I don't know, but he definitely believed in hedging bets. He'd insisted before I left that I accept the basketball scholarship to the University of Texas, saying I could always reject it later. I didn't feel comfortable doing it, but I was glad later he talked me into it. I packed up all my worldly goods and headed west to Austin."

"Did you give up music altogether?" she asked.

He shook his head. "Not completely. I joined a country-and-western band. Between a full load of courses and playing basketball, I didn't have much spare time on my hands, but I managed a few gigs here and there, enough to keep me in pocket money."

"Do you still play?"

"The fiddle's up in the music room, but it's been a long time since I've touched it."

"I'd like to hear you sometime."

He grinned. "Maybe."

She smiled back. After a moment she asked, "By the way, did you major in something practical in college?"

He let out a soft chuckle. "Biology, and soon found out it was as difficult to get rich as a biologist as it is as a musician." He ran a hand through his thick black hair and grinned ironically. "But I'd taken Frannie's dictum to heart and was determined to earn my own way. Ray offered to give me an allowance from my uncle's estate, which he managed, but I insisted on working full-time during the summers, so Ray gave me a job at the bank. That's when he got me hooked on real estate and mortgage banking.''

''Sounds like he really was a good adviser.''

Jed nodded. ''He was.''

Gwyn wondered if Jed realized it had been in Ray's own self-interest to befriend the lonely heir. She suspected he did, but that it didn't matter, and perhaps it didn't. She knew from experience what it was like to be suddenly alone, unsure of oneself and the world around you.

She smiled sympathetically. ''You're very fortunate to have had him then.''

She'd never had such a mentor in high school, someone she could confide in, someone she could count on for sound advice and encouragement. On the few occasions when she did try to share her thoughts and aspirations with a friend, her confidences inevitably reached her parents, who made it clear that her goals and aspirations were inappropriate for a person of her station. The lesson wasn't hard to learn. Trust no one. Keep your own council. You're on your own.

The mood in the kitchen had grown unexpectedly somber.

''So what is this great surprise you want me to see?'' he asked, looking around eagerly.

The lightheartedness he was trying to engender didn't seem to convey itself. The serious expression remained on her face.

"I grew up with manipulation and half truths, Jed, not to mention outright lies," she told him. "My parents defended themselves on the few occasions I questioned them by saying they were only protecting me. After all, there were opportunists out there, willing to say or do anything to get my money. Which no doubt was true—at the time. What my parents didn't seem able to comprehend was that by using deception and dishonesty, they made themselves deceptive and dishonest, too."

Jed understood her words—at least on the surface. What he couldn't figure out was their significance.

Gwyn pushed away from the table and tilted her head. "Follow me."

Moving from the kitchen into the living room, she entered what had been Emmy's bedroom. Standing aside, she nodded toward the corner between the two windows. There, grouped with a straight-backed chair and a music stand, was a cello.

Jed froze in the doorway, his eyes wide. "You play?"

She grinned. "Like you, I loved the violin—until I discovered the cello. My mother wasn't particularly pleased with my choice." She smirked and nearly giggled. "A lady doesn't spread her legs."

Jed's laugh was spontaneous and filled with impish mirth. "It depends upon where and when."

He walked over and reverently examined the instrument that gleamed in the soft light of the shadowy room. "It's magnificent, Gwyn." And expensive, he noted.

"My uncle gave it to me for my thirteenth birthday when he realized I was serious about it. It's my prize possession, the only thing of real value I took with me when I left home, except for the Land Rover, of course.''

Jed plucked a string and closed his eyes as he listened to the reverberation of its deep, mysterious tone. "Beautiful." He took in the sight of her, still standing beside the doorway. There was a shy glow about her, an almost childlike pride, but he also sensed the guardedness of a mature woman.

"I don't want any more secrets between us, Jed. No hidden agendas, no white lies or half truths.''

The unshed tears glazing her eyes tore at him, heated his blood, made him want to protect her from ever being hurt again. He placed his hand just below her ear and felt the measured throb of her heartbeat under the soft, delicate skin. Slowly, he brought his lips down to hers and gently made sweet contact.

"Will you play for me?'' he asked with a quiet smile.

The request pleased her and sent a warm feeling shimmering through her. "Maybe one day.''

He was disappointed, but he didn't press her. He had no idea how much or how well she played, and he didn't want to embarrass her into doing something she wasn't comfortable with. He understood the need to make music, and how very private that pleasure could be.

He took her elbow and guided her to the foot of the twin bed, where they sat side by side, facing the instrument. The room was small. The only other furniture was a dresser.

"Did you want to be a professional musician?" he asked.

She stretched out her arms, trapping her hands between her knees. "Among other things, but none of my ambitions was ever *suitable*. Being a dilettante was perfectly acceptable and preferable for a young lady in my mother's circle. Being a professional at anything, other than a refined lady and model wife, was not."

"Sounds frustrating."

She nodded sadly. "Several of my mother's friends had genuine talents and skills that went beyond those of being the perfect hostess, but they were forced to hide them under bushel baskets of hothouse roses." She sighed. "Maybe that's why many of them were alcoholics and hypochondriacs."

The waste had Jed shaking his head. "So when you left home and struck out on your own, did you pursue a musical career?"

"It was too late." She reached over and rested a hand on his thigh. "It wasn't important to me to be a soloist. I probably could have gotten jobs in various orchestras, but the fire of ambition had burned out, smothered. I love music," she insisted, "but I have no desire to *perform* for other people. Maybe... someday..."

He took her hand in his and brought it up to his mouth and pressed his lips to it. "Someday what?"

She closed her eyes and savored the feel of his touch, the closeness of his body. "Maybe someday we can play the double concerto together."

Still holding her hand, he shifted around and

peered into her eyes. "I'd like that, making music with you. A duet of melodies that intertwine and wrap around each other, that complement and complete each other."

He brought his lips to hers, touched them, then pulled away. She wanted more, but instead of being encouraged by her receptiveness, he seemed to withdraw.

"Jed, what is it?"

He rose and began pacing the narrow space at the foot of the bed, raking a hand across his face like a man waking up, sobering.

"I care for you, Gwyn," he muttered, "in a way I've never cared for any woman. I want you in my life and in my bed. I want to spend the rest of my life making love and music with you."

She gazed up at him. "Are you saying you love me, Jed?"

An unfamiliar tension invaded his body as he turned and studied her—the woman of his dreams, if he allowed himself to dream.

"Because if you are—" she carried the conviction of one who has made a bold decision "—you should know I think I'm in love with you, too."

"No," he cried, and instantly saw the hurt in her eyes just before she lowered them. Color tiptoed up her neck. He sat once more beside her, lifted a hand and tilted her head up enough to capture her glistening gaze. "I do love you, Gwyn, but I can't ask you to love me in return."

"I didn't know I needed your permission." Her voice was husky now, filled with an anger born of humiliation. She'd offered him her love, and he'd rejected it.

He gathered her in his arms. The contradiction between his words and his gestures confused her, until she allowed herself to be guided by her feelings. Impulsively she wrapped her arms around him and pressed her cheek to his chest.

"I can't make a commitment to you, Gwyn, not while there's a murder charge hanging over my head, and I have no right to ask you to wait for things to get better. Maybe they never will. Fielder might yet find something that proves I killed Frannie."

She pulled away enough to look up into his brooding eyes. "But you didn't."

Was it a statement or a question? The ambiguity cut into him like a rusty knife. "You don't know that," he said.

Her smile, a little sad, yet remarkably reassuring, broke through incipient tears. "I do know it, Jed. I know it in my mind. More important, I know it in my heart. You couldn't possibly have killed her."

Thoughts of death and murder scattered like wispy puffs of smoke when his lips met hers. This time he didn't retreat but plunged forward, deepening the kiss.

Unsteady, unsure, he rose to his feet and half turned from her. "It's wrong for me to lead you on, Gwyn," he insisted. "I—"

"Wrong?" Gwyn blinked. "It doesn't feel wrong. It didn't last night. It doesn't now."

"Do you think truth and justice always win out?" Frustration, longing, the memory of what it was like to hold her in his arms, to make her a part of him in the most intimate union a man and a woman can share, flared into anger. "Fielder's convinced I killed Frannie and buried her on property I knew would one day be mine. When Tessa Lang asked to dig on my property, I refused her so adamantly she had to get a court order forcing me to allow it. How do you think that looks?"

"It's circumstantial evidence. It doesn't prove a thing," she insisted.

"And how do we know there won't be more circumstantial evidence turning up that's even more damning."

There are secrets at Beaumarais.

"If you're trying to scare me, Jed, you're not doing a very good job. You didn't kill your foster mother. There is no proof that can be uncovered to the contrary."

"That we know of. And what don't we know, Gwyn? Can we even be sure Fielder or that journalist won't manufacture something…"

"That's why you have one of the best criminal attorneys in the country," she interjected forcefully, maybe because he really was frightening her now. It wasn't unknown for police departments to plant evidence. Sometimes it was for expediency, sometimes because they sincerely thought they had the guilty party but didn't have a strong enough case. She didn't know Sheriff Logan Fielder very well, except that he did seem utterly convinced Jed was guilty. Was he prejudiced enough to railroad him?

"Thorny isn't going to let them get away with anything. He's the best."

Jed exhaled and seemed to wilt. "I know that, and I'm very grateful to you for getting him for me—"

"Damn it," she sputtered, "I didn't do it for your gratitude—"

"Shh," he murmured, and put a finger to her lips. "I know, sweetheart." He bracketed her slender neck between his hands. "But we have to be practical and realistic. Until this is settled, I can't let you get involved with me—"

She shot to her feet, almost knocking him down. "Don't tell me what and who I can get involved with, Jed." Her voice was shrill with anger. "That's not your decision, it's mine."

"Gwyn—" he pleaded softly.

She moved away from him, took a step toward her cello, paused and, on a deep breath, spun around in the confined space and looked down at him.

"All the years I was growing up, Jed, I was told what to think, how to feel, what was appropriate, what was not, whom I could and should associate with, whom I could not. Well, those days are over."

He remained on the edge of the bed, his elbow resting back on the mattress. There was fire in her eyes, which he liked, and sadness in her message, which tore at him. He realized for the first time how unhappy her young life must have been, ordered around like a servant, cosseted in fine clothes and cold, sterile luxury. He comprehended something else, too. He'd been more fortunate than she had—in spite of her pedigree. He might be illegitimate and rejected by his only blood relation, but he'd been cared for by a kind woman who'd genuinely loved him, who'd valued him as a person, not a trophy.

"Nobody," Gwyn announced forcefully, "is going to run my life for me. Not parent or friend…or lover. If you don't want me—"

"Gwyn," he interrupted, and surged to his feet, "I don't want to change you. I love you just the way you are. And I don't want to run your life." He took one small step and stood only inches from her. He looked straight into her eyes. "I love you for your strength and independence, for your drive and compassion."

She bit her lip, and he drew her into a warm embrace. "What I'm trying to say," he murmured in her ear as he stroked her back, "is that I have nothing to offer you. Until this murder is cleared up and I'm free of suspicion, I'm a liability to you."

She squeezed herself tightly to him. "Just love me, Jed," she whispered against his chest. "That's all I ask of you. Just love me."

"IT SEEMS TO ME," Gwyn said that evening, after they'd finished dinner and were sitting on the veranda watching the last streaks of sunlight burnish the tops of distant cypress trees in a dusty golden glow, "that even if the good sheriff's mind—"

"You use the term lightly, I assume," Jed interjected.

"Even if the good sheriff's mind," she repeated with feigned annoyance at the interruption, "is made up, it doesn't mean we can't explore the alternatives."

"Elementary, my dear Watson. We just check the Yellow Pages under *Murderers.*"

She arched back in her seat and slanted him an irritated scowl. "There shouldn't be too many candidates for murderer in a town this size."

Gwyn gloried in the prospect of working with him on a real puzzle, one that mattered. That is, she would have enjoyed it if his life hadn't been at stake. What were the chances of his knowing the murderer? And what would his reaction be when he discovered who it was? Suppose it turned out to be one of his foster siblings?

She gave herself a mental shake. It wouldn't be. It couldn't be. She'd heard him talk about Emerald Monday and Will McClain often enough to know they couldn't have done violence to Frannie Granger. In fact, she'd heard enough about the dead woman to wish she had met her. A simple, hardworking woman who had a heart of gold—and stainless steel, if what Jed said about her was true.

Jed shook his head. "I don't see how Frannie could have been a threat to anyone. She did her job and minded her business. I never knew her to gossip, so even if she had learned something unpleasant about one of her clients, for example, she wouldn't have gone spreading rumors."

"Maybe she knew something but didn't realize it, or someone thought she knew something."

"Like what?" Jed asked unconvinced. "This is a

small town. It was even smaller then. There weren't many secrets.''

There are secrets at Beaumarais. ''How about infidelity?''

Jed pursed his lips. ''Sal Borden, the guy who owned the real estate agency back then, was routinely unfaithful to his wife. But everybody knew it, including his wife. Mike Garfield, the barber, ran high-stakes card games and craps shoots at his place on Saturday nights, but as I recall the previous sheriff even participated in them from time to time. And Billy LaDieu, who owned the feed store, was reputed to have a still in the back room. But those were all open secrets, Gwyn. I can't imagine what Frannie could possibly have found out that would be a threat to anyone, especially when she was the soul of discretion herself.''

''Jed, there had to be a reason she was killed. What was it?''

He shook his head in frustration. ''She wasn't a live-in servant who might hear all sorts of private conversations. She was a day cleaner. Most of her clients weren't even home when she cleaned their houses, at least not after they got to know and trust her. Many of them would put the key under a doormat or in a flowerpot and leave a check or even cash for her to pick up when she was finished. Some people didn't even bother to lock their doors back then.''

''Is there anyone she would have talked to if she had come upon something that made her uncomfortable?''

Jed shrugged. ''Maybe. Her best friend was Joleen

Berber, a nurse who worked in a geriatric center in Marshall."

"Is she still around?"

He nodded. "Lives over on White Lane. I used to bump into her from time to time, but I haven't seen much of her lately. She's retired now. Keeps pretty much to herself."

"Would Frannie have confided in her?"

Jed rubbed his jaw. "I don't know. As I said, Frannie didn't gossip, but Joleen did. Whether Joleen could keep a real confidence I can't say. She came by the house quite a bit, but I really didn't have much to do with her."

"Perhaps we can talk to her and find out if she knows anything."

"It's a thought. She was the first person I called when Frannie didn't come home. I thought she might be over there, but Joleen hadn't seen her. She got pretty upset and started phoning around on her own. That's probably how Social Services got wind of Frannie's being missing and why they came and took Emmy away."

Gwyn stretched out her legs. "For the time being we seem to be stuck on motive. What about opportunity?"

Jed seemed to brighten marginally. "I know who didn't do it—other than me, of course. Emmy and Will went to school that morning. They were just rushing out the front door to catch the bus when I stormed out the back."

Gwyn aligned her face thoughtfully. "Okay, that eliminates them, but I never really thought they did it, anyway, and apparently neither does Fielder. He must have checked their alibis at the time. So who else?''

Jed closed his eyes in concentration. ''I don't know. Frannie's first job that morning was at the Jenningses', but if I remember right, the sheriff asked Catherine about it, and she said Frannie never showed up.''

Gwyn got up and began to pace. ''Maybe we're going at this all wrong. Why does it have to be someone she knew or who knew her?''

''A random killing?'' he asked skeptically. ''If that's what it was, Gwyn, there'll never be a solution—not after all this time.'' And I'll always be a suspect, he thought despondently.

''You're right.'' Gwyn sighed. ''Let's forget about that. Do we know what she died of?''

''All Thorny's been able to find out is that she had a fractured skull. That indicates violence.''

She fixed him with raised eyebrows. ''Or an accident.''

He gave it a moment's consideration. ''I don't buy it, Gwyn. If it was an accident, why not call for help and explain what happened? Why bury her?''

''Suppose the person with her didn't feel safe calling the police.''

He thought for a moment. ''Somebody with a criminal record, you mean?''

She nodded. ''Was there anyone in town like that in those days?''

''Burt Hawkins's son, Carlyle, went to prison for a couple of years for car theft and writing bad checks, but I think he was still there when Frannie disappeared. Besides, he wasn't violent. A little stupid, maybe, but not violent. He's been dead for six years."

Jed stopped to think. "A few drunks in town were familiar with the inside of the jail, but...wait. There was someone. What was his name? He worked as a handyman when he was sober. Frannie hired him to enclose the north end of the back porch to make a separate bedroom for Will. What was the guy's name?" Jed paced, then raised a finger. "Hank Belmonte. He was probably about thirty-five or forty at the time, but could have passed for sixty after one of his all-night binges. Spent most Saturday nights in the jail. He started the job, then Frannie disappeared. He never came back."

"Was he violent?" Gwyn asked.

"I don't remember ever hearing about him getting into a fight with anyone...although there was one incident when he threw a chair through the window of Catfish Corner because the owner refused to serve him and asked him to leave."

"And he was working for Frannie when she disappeared?" Gwyn asked.

Jed's face took on that faraway look again. "I wonder what ever happened to him."

CHAPTER ELEVEN

JED DROVE down a country road under a dense canopy of oak, elm and sycamore trees to a house several miles outside Uncertain.

"Tell me about Joleen Berber," Gwyn prompted as they glided by a relaxing pastoral scene of heavy-uddered cows grazing in a sweet green meadow.

"Not much to tell," he responded, "or at least not much I know about her. She was a nurse who worked in a geriatric center in Marshall, and I think did volunteer work at a street shelter." He climbed a gentle hill. "She was a couple of years older than Frannie, which means she must be close to seventy now. Never married. She and Frannie were best friends for as long as I remember. Joleen stopped by our house almost every afternoon, supposedly for a cup of tea but really to gab. Joleen did most of the yakkin'. A regular chatterbox." He chuckled. "She seemed to know everything about everybody."

"A gossip," Gwyn concluded, but not unkindly.

He grinned. "In spades."

He pulled up in front of a place that wasn't much bigger than Frannie's. White clapboard with shrubs and a neatly trimmed lawn, but no flower beds, the kind of nondescript residence one tended to characterize as a house rather than a home. Jed switched off the engine. Gwyn noticed that the wide picture window to the left of the front door and the single sash to the right were covered with foil.

"It looks rather foreboding," she commented before they got out of the car.

Jed frowned. "I haven't seen much of Joleen the past few years. She used to be a ball of energy, full of jokes and laughter, but she became rather reclusive after Frannie disappeared."

They stepped out into the humid air and walked up the chipped concrete path to a little wrought-iron-railed stoop. The chalky, white-paneled door had an unused look about it and Gwyn would have thought the house vacant, except for the aging Ford Escort sitting in the carport at the end of a narrow driveway. Jed pushed the button on the right side of the door-jamb.

The woman who answered a minute later was of average height, with watery blue eyes and steel-gray hair coiled atop her head. She had a stocky build and her shapeless, drab brown dress made her appear dumpy. Her plump face also had an unhealthy pasty look about it.

"Hello, Joleen," Jed began.

She didn't open the screen door separating them. "What do you want?" Her voice held a raspy, querulous tone.

"I'm sure you've heard they found Frannie," he said with quiet sympathy.

The old woman closed her eyes briefly. "She's dead. Murdered."

"I just wanted to come and tell you how sorry I am. I know how close the two of you were. Even after all these years, this news must be very difficult for you."

She pinched her lips together.

"Do you think we can come in?" he asked politely. "I'd like to ask you a few questions about her."

Rather than answer, the woman shifted her gaze to Gwyn.

"Oh, I'm sorry. Joleen, this is my friend, Gwyneth Miller," Jed announced. "She's renting Frannie's house."

"Forgive us for dropping in on you like this," Gwyn said politely, "but you may have heard that Sheriff Fielder thinks Jed had something to do with Mrs. Granger's disappearance."

"That's nonsense," Joleen snapped.

"My sentiments exactly," Gwyn agreed. "We're hoping you might remember something that will shed light on what happened, something to help us convince Fielder to look elsewhere for whoever killed her."

"I can't help you," the old woman declared. "I don't know who killed her."

"We just want to talk to you for a minute or two," Jed assured her. "Then we'll go."

Joleen heaved a sigh. The prospect didn't seem to please her, but she unlatched the screen door and walked away from it.

They stepped into a dark and shabby living room that smelled of stale cigarette smoke. Gwyn had to resist the urge to tear the foil off the picture window above the couch. On the other hand, the light of day might make the place look even worse. She and Jed waited until their hostess had taken her seat in an overstuffed chair, then they sat on the worn couch.

"I understand you were her best friend," Gwyn said sympathetically. "It must have been terrible to have someone you're so close to just disappear without a trace or explanation."

Joleen's heavy face seemed to sink further. "I knew she had to be dead."

"How's that?" Jed asked.

She glared at him. "It's the only way she could have vanished like she did—without a word."

"I didn't realize you thought that," he commented. "At the time you seemed intent on finding her."

She picked up the cigarette that was smoldering in an ashtray overflowing with curled butts. "If I'd said anything I would have had Fielder and his people on my back." She pulled a drag on her cigarette and let the smoke out through her nose. "But I knew. Deep down inside, I knew."

The room remained silent for what seemed a very long time. Finally, tamping out her butt, Joleen looked at Jed. "I don't know what you think I can tell you."

"I was a teenager, Joleen, focused on myself, school, music. You knew her better than anyone," Jed reminded her. "You would have noticed if she was having problems, or if she had plans to go away."

"Where would she have gone?" Joleen scoffed as she used a butane lighter to light up again. "And why? Her whole life revolved around you kids."

"From what I've heard," Gwyn contributed, "the sheriff thought at the time that she'd just sneaked off to be by herself."

Joleen scrunched up her lips and shook her head in disgust. "Logan Fielder is an ass." She took a deep drag and watched the smoke she expelled form a cloud over her head. "He was then. He is now." She settled back in the chair and closed her eyes. A tone of impotent rage rang in her voice when she spoke. "He wouldn't listen to me. Why, I asked, would Frannie go off without any of her clothes? And how could she get away when her car was still sitting in the driveway? Stupid. That's what he is." She puffed angrily. "Even when Frannie didn't come back after several weeks, he still wouldn't admit something bad must have happened to her."

Confusion knit Gwyn's brow. "But why would he cover up a serious crime?"

"He claimed there was no proof that a crime had been committed," Jed informed her.

Joleen carelessly brushed away ashes that had fallen on her dress. "Male vanity. That's all it was. He'd just been elected sheriff and he didn't want an unsolved case on his record, so he tried to pretend nothing happened." She ground out her butt. "He knew better, though."

Jed raised an eyebrow. "What do you mean?"

Joleen narrowed her eyes and tightened her mouth into a wrinkled scowl. "He questioned everybody in town, didn't he? Took statements, didn't he?'' She tapped out another cigarette from her half-empty pack. ''He knew what happened to her, I tell you. He just wouldn't admit it.''

''Knew she was dead?'' Gwyn couldn't hide the shock in her voice.

''He's an ass.''

''Could he have had something to do with her disappearance?'' Gwyn asked.

Both Jed and Joleen stared at her as if she'd just said something idiotic—or brilliant.

''What are you suggesting?'' Jed asked.

''Wouldn't you expect a new sheriff to jump on a crime like this? His first big case—''

''I told you,'' Joleen interrupted with exasperation. She picked up her lighter. ''He couldn't solve it, so he just swept it under the rug.'' But there was a hint of doubt in the declaration.

''Tell me what you remember about that day and the days leading up to it,'' Jed urged.

Joleen tightened her mouth. ''Frannie was there Monday afternoon when I stopped by after work for tea. Everything was fine.''

''What did you discuss?'' Jed asked. ''I never paid much attention when the two of you had your heads together.''

''Nothing special. They'd just added a new wing onto the geriatric center where I worked. We were getting more new patients and I told Frannie about some of them. I never worried about discussing my patients with her because I knew she'd never repeat anything. It was nice to have someone like her to talk to. After she... There was no one I could trust the way I did her,'' she added with quiet sadness, then seemed to catch herself. ''I could always count on Frannie.''

''Did she mention us?'' Jed asked, suddenly curious.

Joleen actually chuckled. It was a rusty, not particularly pleasant sound. ''All the time. She told me about the fights you used to get into with Will. Then the two of y'all would go to school and you'd—'' she pointed at Jed ''—get into more fights defending him. Didn't make much sense. I thought it was a mistake taking in that troublemaker, but she insisted he was a good kid.'' She looked at Jed. ''They ever find him after he run off?''

He shook his head. ''I never heard from him or from Emmy.''

''Emerald,'' she said wistfully. ''They shouldn't have done what they did to sweet Emmy. It wasn't right taking her away like that before they even knew what happened to her Mom Fran.''

''Did you try to find out where they placed her?'' Jed suddenly asked.

She grunted. ''Those Social Services people can be tighter with information than a doctor is with a buck.''

''I guess Frannie had her hands full with her three foster children,'' Gwyn offered.

Joleen gazed at Jed and smiled. ''Y'all were a trial. That's for sure.''

''Did Frannie ever talk about getting away?'' Gwyn asked.

Joleen shook her head. "Frannie was happy. She worked her butt off, had to pinch pennies, but get away? How? She had no money, and she would never have left the kids. They were her whole life. Emerald couldn't have been more a part of her if she'd been her own flesh and blood."

Joleen peered at Jed. "She was proud of you. Said you had what it took to make something of yourself."

Jed fidgeted, uncomfortable with the compliment.

"Was Frannie seeing anyone?" Gwyn asked.

"You mean a man?" The older woman wagged her head. "I told her she ought to find herself another husband, but she said her life was already full. Said she'd had one good man and reckoned that was more than most women got."

"What did she mean?" Jed asked.

Joleen snorted. "When you clean other people's houses on a regular basis you get to see plenty more than the dirt on the floor. She saw what a lot of married couples went through."

"Did she talk about them?"

Joleen waved the question aside. "Not by name, but I knew who her clients were, so it wasn't hard to figure out." She snickered. "Like Lottie Mickels. Everyone knows about the reputation traveling salesmen have for playing around. Nobody talks about their wives. Harry Mickels was gone a good deal of the time selling insurance or whatever. He was hardly out of the driveway before Lottie was entertaining her gentlemen friends."

"And Frannie knew about this?" Gwyn asked.

Joleen smiled. "She changed the bedsheets and did the laundry."

"Who were her other clients? Do you happen to remember?"

"Of course I remember." There was umbrage in her retort. "I'm not doddering."

"Sorry," Gwyn replied sincerely, "I didn't mean to imply anything. I just wondered if you knew who all her other clients were."

Only slightly mollified, Joleen nevertheless replied. "Sure I knew who they were." She rattled off a list of names. Jed added a few and together they identified the days of the week when Frannie went to their houses to clean.

"So on that Tuesday," Gwyn ventured, "she would have cleaned the Jenningses' home, then Reverend Briggs's and Mrs. Colby's. In that order."

Joleen's mind seemed to have wandered off.

"She changed the order once in a while," Jed commented, "if one of them asked her to. Mrs. Colby was ninety-two and a shut-in, so it didn't make any difference when Frannie showed up, and the Reverend Briggs or his wife occasionally had meetings at their house right after lunch and would ask Frannie to come in the morning, but that didn't happen very often."

A cuckoo clock in another room chimed, reminding them they'd been there over an hour.

"Was the order changed that day?"

Jed paused to consider. "Not according to Catherine Jennings or the Briggses. But she never showed up at either place."

Gwyn addressed Joleen. "Can you think of anything Frannie said in the days or weeks leading up to her disappearance that might give us a clue who murdered her or why? Anything unusual or troubling her?"

The old woman shook her head unhappily. "She seemed thoughtful…preoccupied the last time I saw her. Something was bothering her, but when I asked her what it was she claimed she was just annoyed at the mess Hank Belmonte was making."

Jed and Gwyn exchanged glances.

"Is that the way you remember it?" Gwyn asked him.

"Frannie liked things neat and orderly," he confirmed. "Hank wasn't particularly well organized…left tools about, scraps of lumber—"

"If he was so unreliable, why did she hire him?"

"He was a good carpenter when he was sober," he explained. "The secret was to not pay him a penny until he was finished. Otherwise he'd go off on a bender and might not return for a month."

"He wanted money," Joleen blurted, then retreated again into silence.

"I remember now," Jed added. "He asked Frannie for his pay to date that Monday night. She refused, told him he'd get paid when the job was done and not before. He claimed he was so broke he didn't have enough money for food. She said he was perfectly welcome to stay and have dinner with us."

"Did he?" Gwyn asked.

Jed laughed. "Nope. I guess he wasn't that hungry—or that broke."

"Frannie had his number," Joleen said with a chuckle that deteriorated into a cough.

Gwyn thought a moment before turning to Jed. "You said that was on Monday night. Did he show up for work on Tuesday?"

Jed's eyes shifted as he pondered, his expression distant. "No," he replied slowly, "he didn't, now that you mention it. The job wasn't completed until months later, after the bank repossessed the house and had a licensed contractor finish the job."

"I told Fielder about Hank," Joleen said peevishly. "But he just dismissed it as a coincidence, said Belmonte likely just went off on one of his binges. 'Without money?' I asked. But Fielder wasn't interested in looking for him. Said he'd come back when he sobered up."

"Did he show up again?" Gwyn asked.

Joleen shook her head. "I haven't seen or heard of him since."

"WHAT ARE you thinking?" Jed asked as they drove back to Beaumarais in his Jaguar. The air-conditioning hummed softly in the background.

Gwyn tapped her finger on the tip of the armrest. "I'm thinking there are probably more people in this town who might have had a motive to kill Frannie than we thought."

He twisted his hands around the leather steering wheel. "I can't imagine her being a threat to anyone, Gwyn. Even if she might have known, for example, that Lottie Mickels was playing around on her husband, apparently half the town did, too. And she wouldn't have said anything to Harry or anybody else. Besides, killing her after the cat was out of the bag wouldn't have accomplished anything." He looked over at her critically. "And if you're suggesting that she might have tried to blackmail one of the lovers, forget it. Frannie just wasn't that way."

Gwyn gazed out at the forest of green gliding by. It looked so peaceful and quiet. Thinking about murder seemed a desecration of its pristine beauty, except the cycle of birth and death...and violence was going on there, too.

"Suppose it wasn't just private immorality she'd discovered," she said at last.

Jed's brow furled. "Sorry, you've lost me."

"Lottie's infidelity was sort of a closed loop. It involved only Lottie, her husband and her lover. Their business, no one else's. But what if Frannie found out about something going on that had wider repercussions and affected innocent people?"

"Such as?"

"I don't know." She shrugged. "Maybe this Reverend Briggs was stealing church funds—"

Jed laughed. "I'll have to introduce you to Horace Briggs. Not a chance."

"I'm not accusing him specifically, Jed," she said, annoyed that he was dismissing her idea so quickly. "I'm just using it as an example. Suppose she discovered something like that. Would she make it public?"

He glanced over, saw she was serious, faced forward and stroked his chin. "I see what you're getting at." He considered the matter for a minute. "Frannie had a strong sense of right and wrong, but she also believed in forgiveness. I'd say she'd confront the offender first, give him or her a certain amount of time to make restitution—''

''And if he didn't, she'd go to the authorities,'' Gwyn finished for him.

He nodded vaguely and turned into the driveway. He stopped in front of the mansion and faced her. ''Do you think that's what happened?''

''I don't know, but I think it's a possibility we've got to consider.''

''You're suggesting she confronted someone, and rather than face exposure, that person killed her and buried her.'' It sounded far-fetched, preposterous.

''We know,'' Gwyn said defensively, ''she was killed, and we know she was buried here on Beaumarais. Can you think of any other reason why?''

They released their seat belts but didn't get out.

''You hypothesized the other day,'' Jed reminded her, ''that it might have been an accident and that the person with her was afraid of being blamed, so he buried her. Still think it's possible?''

She took in his profile. ''Don't you?''

He glanced over with a scowl. ''Stop answering questions with a question.''

She quirked a facetious grin at him. ''Why?''

They both laughed, exited the vehicle and went into the house.

''Seriously, though, do you think Hank Belmonte might have done it?'' he asked after closing the door behind them.

Gwyn pondered the question a moment before answering. "You were acquainted with the guy, so you'd be in a better position to answer that, but it seems to me the circumstantial case against him is at least as strong as it is against you, maybe stronger."

"I'll grant you that Hank Belmonte might have had means and opportunity, Gwyn." He steered her toward the library. "But I have to question his motive. Hank wasn't a violent man, and he wasn't a thief. I don't know what psychological hang-ups drove him to drink, but I never felt he was a dangerous person."

"What about the incident at Catfish Corner?" she asked.

June appeared. "Is there anything I can get y'all?"

Gwyn sighed and grinned. "Something cold to drink would be wonderful."

Jed nodded agreement. "You wouldn't happen to have any of your lemon-tea, would you?"

June smiled. "I just made a fresh pitcher."

"Hank had a temper tantrum at the Corner," Jed resumed after June left the room. "He was drunk, which was why Gus Ferguson threw him out of the place."

Gwyn settled on the couch and crossed her legs. "So he was capable of violence when he was drinking."

Jed absently pawed through the correspondence June had piled on his desk. Mostly bills and junk mail. "We're all capable of violence from time to time. One incident doesn't establish a pattern."

"But Frannie had refused his request for the money he had coming to him—"

"Until he finished the job," Jed interjected uncomfortably. "Hank knew the rules. He was just testing her, and she called his bluff about going hungry."

"I'm not questioning the propriety of what she did, Jed. It was a wise decision. But from Belmonte's perspective, you can see it could have been the reason for his having a fight with her. We don't know he intended to kill her. Maybe in the heat of emotion he pushed her and she fell. He panicked…"

Jed had to concede the possibility, though he obviously didn't agree with it. "It would explain why he took off and never came back. God, Gwyn, I'd hate to think Frannie died because of a few bucks of booze money."

She rose, walked around the side of the desk and placed her hand on his. "If that's the way things happened, it wasn't over money—it was over a principle. I think Frannie would tell you that's a good thing to die for."

He faced her and looked deeply into her eyes. "You really can find silver linings, can't you."

She grinned. "It comes from being born with a silver spoon in my mouth."

"I like the taste of your mouth," he muttered, and skimmed his lips over hers.

She clasped her hands behind his neck. "You do, huh?"

A discreet cough announced they weren't alone.

With a soft chuckle, Jed buzzed her nose as she slid her hands down his chest.

"Thank you, June," he said to the housekeeper, who was placing a tray with two glasses, a crystal ice bucket with tongs and a pitcher of cloudy pale-amber beverage—half iced tea and half lemonade—on a side table. There was also a wooden bowl containing corn chips.

"I thought in this heat you might like something salty to go with it," June said, betraying just the hint of a smile.

Gwyn and Jed looked at each other and burst out laughing as June left the room. Gwyn lifted one of the glasses and passed it to Jed. She picked up her own drink and took an appreciative sip. "Maybe Thorny can put pressure on Fielder to try to find Belmonte."

Jed rolled the cold wet glass across his forehead. "Find an alcoholic drifter after nearly twenty years? It doesn't sound very promising. Chances are he's dead by now."

"Maybe." Gwyn reclaimed her seat on the end of the couch. "Or maybe one morning he woke up, decided to get some help and turned his life around. Such things have happened."

Jed shot her an appraising glance. "You know, I hope he did."

She took a long swallow of her drink, idly picked up a chip, but didn't eat it. "What's the story between you and Fielder, Jed? Why is he so hell-bent on pinning this murder on you?"

Jed had wondered when she would get around to asking him that.

CHAPTER TWELVE

"IT'S COMPLICATED." Jed settled into the corner of the couch and extended his long legs, the cold drink dangling from his hand beyond the end of the sofa arm. "We'd never had any problems with the law or any of the people in the sheriff's office until Will McClain came to live with us. He'd had a pretty rough life. I was an orphan, but I wasn't unloved, either by my mother or by Frannie."

But he'd known rejection, Gwyn thought, first by the father he'd never met and later by the uncle who'd shunned him. As sensitive as Jed was about his illegitimacy, it was a mark of the man that he was able to focus on the positive people in his life.

He sipped his lemon-tea. "Will had grown up in a broken home. His parents split up when he was a baby. After that his mother had a string of men, some of whom were abusive. He was a scrawny kid of thirteen when he came to live with us. By then he'd learned to look out for himself. Sometimes that involved physical violence. He had a pretty big chip on his shoulder." Jed smiled with unmistakable fondness for the foster brother he'd lost. "Will McClain didn't shy away from a fight. In fact, he seemed to look for trouble wherever he went, and he wasn't averse to bashing heads when he found it.''

Restlessly, Jed climbed to his feet, wandered over to the side table and topped off his glass. He held up the frosty pitcher in an offer to do the same for Gwyn, but she declined.

''There were incidents in school right after Will came to live with us. A few of the kids tried to pick on him. Will responded in the only way he knew how—by hitting back harder. He gave them a couple of bloody noses, actually.''

Gwyn's high school hadn't been coed but a very exclusive girls' boarding school. The experience hadn't been unpleasant as much as it had been socially limiting. Girls didn't usually get into fisticuffs, though there were occasional catfights. The pain they inflicted was more subtle and tended to cut deeper. Some of the wounds never really healed.

''Okay, I think I get the picture. The usual male adolescent rites of passage.''

Jed chuckled. ''The bullies stayed away from him after that, but the immediate result was the school calling the cops to report Will's 'antisocial' behavior. Fielder was one of the town's two deputies in those days, and he came to 'counsel' Will. Since I'd stuck up for him, I was included in the sessions. Will had been through the process before, so he was able to shrug off the lecture and threats. But it was a new experience for me, and I didn't take to it nearly as serenely.''

''Uh-oh. Don't tell me. You mouthed off and

Fielder threw you in jail. I've been sleeping with a jailbird.'' Her eyes sparkled with delight.

This time Jed laughed. ''Sorry to disappoint you. Fielder—''

''Disappoint? Did I say I was disappointed? Hmm. Remind me to let you make up for it later, though. Anyway, you were saying…''

His mouth hung open for a moment, a smile coming to his eyes before he went on in a serious tone. ''Fielder wasn't above intimidation. He warned us that if we didn't watch our steps he'd call Social Services and have us taken away from Frannie. I blew my stack and told him in rather crude language that I wasn't a ward of Social Services, which he damn well knew, and that I thought it was against the law to threaten people.''

''I don't imagine he liked being talked back to,'' Gwyn commented, remembering the dark glower she'd received when she'd defied him. ''But it hardly seems sufficient reason for a twenty-year-old vendetta against you.''

''Oh, there's more,'' Jed assured her. He finished his drink, put the glass on the tray and sat down again. ''Fielder had just been elected sheriff a month or two before Frannie disappeared. I told you about Emmy being virtually abducted the next day.''

She nodded.

''Riley Gray—his last name was Gray Wolf in those days—was sort of stuck on Emmy. He went charging down to the Social Services office and demanded to know where they'd taken her. They refused to say and he got pretty vocal, so they called

Fielder, who came and arrested him. Riley ended up spending a couple of nights in jail. He was seventeen, Gwyn. All he wanted to know was where they'd taken a girl who'd spent nearly as much time in his house with his mother and sister as she did at home.''

Gwyn shook her head, appalled at the way people treat each other, though it was hardly a new lesson.

"When I found out," Jed continued, "I went to the sheriff's office and begged him to release Riley."

It couldn't have been easy, Gwyn reflected, considering the bad blood that already existed between them, but she also realized Jed wasn't a person to abandon a friend.

"Fielder not only admitted he knew Emmy had been taken, but he hinted he knew where she'd been placed, and he absolutely refused to tell me."

Gwyn's eyes went wide. "That's unconscionable. Did he really know?"

Jed studied his fingers. "Probably not. The people at Social Services are pretty tight-lipped. Unless he had an inside source, which he might have. He infuriated me enough that I took a swing at him, Gwyn. I missed only because Ray Jennings had stopped by to find out what progress the sheriff was making. He managed to step between us and back me off before I actually made contact. Fielder kept his cool. Very quietly he informed me that if I didn't leave his office immediately he'd throw me in the cell with Riley, and that I wouldn't be getting out nearly as soon."

The heat of outrage warmed Gwyn's cheeks. "The man's a sadist."

Jed merely nodded. "Four years later, Fielder was

up for reelection. By then, I'd come into my inheritance, so I had money to spend. I supported his opposition. The other candidate happened to be a woman, and unfortunately, Uncertain wasn't ready yet for a female in that kind of role. But I bankrolled her campaign to the point that Fielder had to go into debt to pay for advertising. I've supported his opponents in every election since.''

''Why have people kept him in office? Or are the elections rigged?''

''No, he's been elected fair and square, and by and large he's been a good sheriff,'' Jed acknowledged. ''At least, I thought he was. Now some of the things Joleen said are beginning to make me wonder.''

''You and Fielder don't like each other,'' Gwyn stated, ''and I guess both of you have pretty good reasons. But is his bitterness so great that he'd intentionally cover up a murder and then try to frame you for it?'' The question was rhetorical, so she didn't give him a chance to answer it. ''Would he have had a motive to kill Frannie?''

Jed took a deep breath in frustration. ''I can't imagine what.''

''Is he married?''

''He was once. His wife and young son were killed in a car accident, but that must be close to twenty-five years ago.''

''And he never remarried?''

''He's pretty much a loner. I've never even seen him with a woman. When he isn't on the job he's usually out fishing by himself on the lake. If he has any close friends, I don't know who they are.''

"Did Frannie clean his house?"

Jed nodded. "On Thursdays, as I recall." He studied the woman with the tantalizing eyes and felt the desire inside him claw for release. There were distinct disadvantages to having a full-time housekeeper, even one who was discreet. "You're thinking Frannie might have found something—"

"It would explain why he wasn't more aggressive in pursuing her disappearance at the time, and why he's going after you now to the exclusion of everyone else."

WHEN THEY were finished eating lunch on the veranda, Jed pulled back Gwyn's hair and draped his arm around her waist. June had left a few minutes earlier, announcing that she was going into Marshall to do some shopping and didn't expect to return for several hours. Jed pointed to the back wing of the mansion. "I told you there were secrets at Beaumarais."

The words sent a tiny chill tumbling down her spine. She cocked an eyebrow inviting elaboration.

"What is now the kitchen, butler's pantry and breakfast nook was once a separate building. It was moved here by barge from Jefferson around 1850."

"It blends in beautifully. You can usually tell when two houses have been joined. Different clapboards, trim, that sort of thing."

"They had a good reason for making it seamless," Jed remarked.

"Oh?"

He grinned. "There's a hidden room between them."

Her breathing went shallow as she stared at him. "I beg your pardon."

"You've heard of the Underground Railroad?"

"Of course."

"Beaumarais was part of it." He said it with pride. "Slavery was legal in Texas before the war. It wasn't widespread, but here along the Louisiana border there were several plantations that employed slaves."

She wanted to laugh at her sense of relief. She couldn't say exactly what she'd expected—a family history of lunacy or serial killers, perhaps. *Secrets* sounded so ominous and sinister. She wrapped her arm around his waist as he led her into the kitchen, past the large work area and refrigerator to the butler's pantry.

"The Louises came originally from New Orleans," he continued. "Some say exiled because of their rabid opposition to the *peculiar* institution, as it was referred to back then. Caddo Lake in those days and in the decades following the war was a natural hiding ground for runaway slaves, cutthroats and pirates." He draped an arm casually over her shoulder. "Beaumarais became a haven for the slaves fleeing plantations to the east. They were hidden in the secret room until they could be moved to the next stop on the route north to Canada."

She turned her head and looked at him, her eyes sparkling with seductive humor. "Can I see it?"

He smiled and whispered, "I thought you'd never ask."

He took her into the butler's pantry, an oblong windowless room, tucked neatly between the kitchen and the formal dining room, which was almost never used anymore.

"A hundred and fifty years ago, kitchens were out-buildings, separate from the main house. That was for two reasons. One was as protection against the constant danger of fire. The other was to keep the living quarters cool."

"Makes sense," she agreed.

"This pantry was where food was delivered for serving in the dining room."

Jed reached over his head to the top of a darkly varnished panel. With an almost imperceptible click, another panel to his right slipped open. He smiled at Gwyn, moved over and pushed the well-oiled door completely open. Jed retrieved a flashlight from a drawer nearby and invited her to step inside.

The wall immediately in front of her wasn't more than four feet away. The room itself was long and narrow, perhaps ten feet from one end to the other— less square footage, she decided, than commonly found in a modest bathroom. In the corner to her right was a rickety washstand with a chipped china bowl and pitcher. On the lower shelf was a wood-covered chamber pot. Single candle sconces were attached to the two short walls.

"They also had a mattress or two on the floor," Jed pointed out.

"How many people stayed in here and for how long?" she asked, already feeling claustrophobic in the confined space.

"Anywhere from one to five, and for periods ranging from overnight to several days, according to the journal I found several years ago in the attic."

In spite of the warm closeness of the room, she shivered. "The alternative must have been pretty horrible to make this seem better."

Turning to Jed, she saw a deep sorrow on his face, as if he could feel the pain of the wandering souls who'd passed days and nights of boredom and fear crouched in this ugly place.

"You have a heritage to be proud of, Jed."

He looked at her, startled by her words.

She smiled and raised a hand to his face. "I'm glad your mother gave you her name. It's a good name, Louis."

She lifted herself on tiptoe and kissed him gently on the mouth. He was about to take her in his arms and further explore the invitation he tasted on her lips, when he noticed a faraway expression in her eyes.

"Jed, this secret space…" She let the words drift as she retreated deeper into thought.

He waited, but after a minute had to call her back to the present. "What is it?"

"This secret hideaway has made me think of something. It might not make sense…." Again she lapsed into distracted silence.

"Tell me," he urged impatiently.

"One of the big questions is why the sheriff and his people didn't find Frannie's body when it was so near, so close by, right?"

"Go on."

"Suppose it wasn't there at the time of the search. Suppose whoever killed her did it somewhere else, or took the body somewhere else, and only later buried it on Beaumarais, after the sheriff had completed his investigation."

"But why here?"

"I can think of a couple of reasons," she said. "One, the estate was not lived on, so there was little chance of the body being discovered."

A cold shudder of understanding rippled down Jed's spine.

"And," he added, "if and when it was discovered, it would be on *my* property."

"I'VE NEVER REALLY given much thought to Frannie's estate," Jed admitted much later that afternoon, as he pulled his maroon Dodge Ram into one of the diagonal parking spaces in front of the Cypress Bank and Trust.

"Did she have any family around here?" Gwyn asked.

"Her parents were both dead. She'd had a younger brother, but he was killed in the Korean War. Her late husband was an only child...so, no, we were all she had."

It sounded like a lonely life, yet from what Jed had told her, Frannie Granger had been a person who accepted what she couldn't change and devoted herself to the children in her care.

"She wasn't a wealthy woman," Jed continued. "The house we lived in is proof of that." He rolled down the windows a crack before switching off the air-conditioning and then the ignition. "We never went hungry, but prime steak wasn't an item on the menu, either."

Gwyn opened her door the same time he did, but neither of them got out immediately. "Why are you interested now? Do you think you'll find a clue to her death there?"

Could the loneliness and the poverty have gotten to the struggling foster mother? Gwyn wondered, not for the first time. The woman saw how the other half lived and the careless ease with which financially secure people spent their money. She'd also been in a position to learn all sorts of private details about her clients. Had she finally succumbed to temptation and tried to use that information to enhance her own fortune, only to make herself the victim of the person she was blackmailing?

Jed shook his head. "Curiosity more than anything, I guess. I know she had a checking account and probably a savings account."

They alighted from the truck and approached the massive doors of the old bank. It was a corner building, built during the twenties when the country was in a boon of prosperity. The neoclassical lines of its two facades, with their stone columns and projecting cornices, lent it a solid, trustworthy appearance. Jed opened one of the double doors and followed Gwyn into air-conditioned comfort.

The interior was as staid and reassuring as the exterior. Four brass chandeliers were suspended from a lofty molded ceiling. The Greco-Roman motif had been continued in the pink marble floor and the face of the long counter across from the entrance. Both were appropriately accented with lighter tones of tan and bold black. Brass grates no longer fronted each teller station, but Gwyn had no doubt they had once been there.

Jed led her around the high, glass-topped counter where patrons made out deposit and withdrawal slips to a short hallway to the right. He opened a frosted glass-paneled door that had President stenciled on it.

Inside, the woman sitting at a timeworn secretary's desk sharply contrasted with the buxom young ladies who worked in the lobby. Gwyn estimated she was in her late sixties. She wore her coarse gray hair in a bun at her nape and half glasses perched on the tip of her nose. The smile she offered Jed was pleasant enough, but it didn't invite familiarity, or even informality.

"Hello, Miss Arbuckle," Jed said respectfully. He introduced Gwyn. The two women nodded to each other.

"What can I do for you, Mr. Louis?"

"I was wondering if Mr. Jennings was in, and if he might have a few minutes for me."

The secretary picked the phone on her desk and announced him. "Go right in," she said with a nod toward the far door.

Ray Jennings opened it before they got there and invited them in with a sweep of his hand. Jed's old friend and mentor had on a gray pinstripe suit that perfectly complemented his silvering hair and gray eyes.

His office in some ways was in a time warp. It

could have come from the set of a 1930s movie, except it was in rich, luxurious color. The heavily carved mahogany desk was nearly black with age, the expensive Oriental carpet, though worn, still sported vivid tones of burgundy, gold and deep blue.

The bank president motioned his visitors to a pair of maroon leather chairs. On the end table between them stood a stained-glass shaded lamp, which Gwyn recognized as a genuine Tiffany.

"I haven't had an opportunity to express my condolences on the confirmation of Frannie Granger's death, Jed," Ray said as he moved behind his desk. "Somehow the ball didn't seem the right place or time. Please let me do so now. I know she meant a great deal to you. Maybe, finally, you can bring this terrible affair to closure."

"She was a good woman." Jed waited for Gwyn to sit, then sat down himself.

Obviously eager to get off the morbid subject, Ray asked simply, "Now, what can I do for you today?" He smiled avariciously. "Another big-bucks business deal?"

"I was wondering about the residual of Frannie's estate."

The bank executive had a poker face, but Gwyn didn't miss the blink behind his wire-rimmed glasses. "Frannie's estate?" He snickered like a man enjoying a ribald joke. "There wasn't any estate, Jed. You of all people should know that. What pitiful savings she had were quickly eaten up by her debts." Realizing his guest wasn't pleased with his choice of words, Ray sobered. "Why, after all these years are you even interested?"

Jed casually crossed an ankle over a knee. "No specific reason. The sheriff's asking a lot of questions that have made me realize there are aspects of Frannie's life I really don't know much about, her finances being one of them."

With a quick lowering of his gaze that suggested he was reliving an old annoyance, Ray said, "Fielder inspected her accounts when she went missing. He didn't find anything unusual or that might give a clue to her whereabouts."

"Now we know why. Nevertheless, I'd like to see the records," Jed informed him.

"There's nothing in them," Ray insisted, then leaned back in his chair and laced his fingers across a middle that had grown more prominent with the years. "I'll let you see them, Jed—though I probably shouldn't—but I don't know what you expect to find."

He picked up the phone and asked his secretary to bring him the Granger folder. "The accounts were retired years ago, of course. When that snooping archaeologist found her bones...well, I had Gladys retrieve the files from our archives. Figured Fielder would be back to review them again."

"Has he?"

"Not yet."

The aging secretary brought in an accordion file, placed it silently on his desk and left. It wasn't very thick. Ray untied the faded cotton string and dumped the meager contents on the green blotter. "I can't let you take any of this with you, but you're welcome to look at the documents here."

Jed rose and stood over the desk while the banker sorted through the papers. Quietly Gwyn came to his side and watched.

"She had a checking and a savings account," Ray explained. "Neither of them ever had very high balances."

Jed studied the statements.

"She had three sources of income," Ray explained. "From Social Services for Emmy and Will. From the Beaumarais estate for you, Jed. And from her earnings as a housemaid. She was enrolled in our new security protection plan, which allowed us to automatically transfer funds from her savings to her checking account if she inadvertently wrote an overdraft."

"Did she?" Gwyn asked curiously.

"No," Ray acknowledged. "She was always very careful with her money, always maintained a positive, if low, balance."

Jed stared at the paper in his hands. "Is that all the support she got for me? Fifty dollars a week? That was hardly enough to feed me."

Ray had the good grace to look embarrassed. "It wasn't an unreasonable amount at the time your uncle made out his will."

"It wasn't generous, either," Jed proclaimed angrily.

Without thinking, Gwyn placed her hand on his in an attempt to calm him.

"Unfortunately, he didn't make any provisions for

increases. As you recall, we suffered serious inflation in the late seventies. What had been an adequate allotment—"

"And you couldn't increase it?"

"Not without a court order," Ray replied defensively, "and Frannie didn't have the money to hire an attorney."

"So she supported me virtually on her own." Jed inhaled deeply, then he picked up his foster mother's final statement. "According to this, her last check was to the grocery store the day before she died."

"What happened to the funds after she disappeared?" Gwyn asked.

"For several months, we used her savings to pay the interest on her mortgage. Social Services had cut off her payments immediately when they removed Emmy and McClain ran away, but I continued to transfer Jed's money into her account. It delayed things for a while, but eventually we were obligated to initiate foreclosure proceedings. As you may know, it's not a quick and easy process. The advantage goes to the debtor. We had to send registered letters—which we knew would be returned—then post public notices of foreclosure."

He paused and almost seemed embarrassed to add, "Frankly, I wasn't too aggressive in pursuing the matter. Her disappearing the way she did was very strange and clearly didn't bode well, but should she have returned, I didn't want her to find her house had been sold out from under her. After several months we repossessed it, but it was more than a year before we actually foreclosed on the property."

"What did you do with it all that time?" Gwyn asked.

"Jed continued to live there until he went off to college, then we rented it out."

"The bank still owned it when I came into my inheritance three years later," Jed told Gwyn. "I bought it from them."

"It was your first plunge into real estate." Ray smiled broadly in self-satisfaction. "I told you you'd do well. You've got a head for business. I could see that from the start."

Jed settled back in his chair. "Who could have killed her, Ray?"

The older man acknowledged his confusion with a regretful shake of his head. "I didn't know her, Jed. She cleaned my house and banked here. I have no idea what went on in her private life. We didn't travel in the same circles."

"Do you remember Hank Belmonte?" Jed asked.

Ray tilted his head to one side in thought, then his eyes lit up. "Belmonte. I'd forgotten about him." His features hardened perceptibly. "A nasty drunk, as I recall."

"He was doing some renovation work at the house at the time Frannie went missing."

"Now that you mention it, I remember. We had to hire a contractor to complete the job." Ray pursed his lips in disapproval. "Do you think he—"

"I don't know," Jed admitted with a shrug. "I'm grasping at straws."

Ray gazed off into space. "I don't remember Belmonte being a particularly big man, but he was strong. It wouldn't have been difficult for him to overpower Frannie. I doubt she weighed more than a hundred pounds. Carrying her the thousand yards or whatever it was through the woods to the spot where she was buried wouldn't have been hard for him.''

"Joleen Berber says she mentioned Belmonte to the sheriff, but Fielder showed no interest in looking for him,'' Jed observed.

"He seems bound and determined to pin this murder on Jed,'' Gwyn pointed out.

Ray stroked his chin, his eyes narrowed in concentration. "Or maybe he did search for him and is just trying to keep it low-key. Logan can be very tight-lipped when he wants to be.''

"If he checked around for him and couldn't find him,'' Gwyn suggested, "he probably would keep it quiet—another failure.''

"True enough.'' The banker straightened and looked forthrightly at his former protégé. "Logan and I get along reasonably well. He might talk to me. Let me see if I can find out anything. I can't imagine him ignoring any lead in what's undoubtedly the biggest case in his career, or at least the biggest one Uncertain's ever seen.''

"Did he or his men search the estate following her murder?'' Gwyn persisted.

Ray frowned. "More than once. As well as the property on the north side of Frannie's place. It was a vacant lot back then and remained that way until Riley Gray bought it a few years ago and built his house.''

"So why wasn't her grave found, since it was so close?" Gwyn asked.

Ray laced his fingers across his stomach. "I've wondered about that myself. I can only speculate, of course. Two theories come to mind. First, the body wasn't there at the time of the investigation and was only moved there later."

Jed's head shot up. "We've considered that. Grisly thought."

"When did they search the premises?" Gwyn asked.

"Hmm, I don't think it was the morning she was reported missing." Ray stroked his chin. "It seems to me it wasn't until the next day. They brought in dogs. You must remember there was no evidence of foul play at the time. Everyone was waiting for her to turn up on her own and explain where she'd been."

Gwyn pursed her lips, unconvinced. "You said you had two theories. What's the second one?"

Ray hesitated. "I'm not even sure this is possible, but I was thinking if Belmonte or whoever killed her scattered camphor balls or something like that over the site, wouldn't the dogs have naturally avoided it?"

CHAPTER THIRTEEN

THE MORNING SUN was draining some of the humidity from the air, but Jed knew it was only being stored for later use. Today would be another of those hot, steamy days when the damp heat penetrated straight to the bones and put them on roast.

Not nearly as hot and steamy as the night he'd spent with Gwyn, he thought, as he gazed at her across the glass-topped table on the veranda. In clinging tank top, with her long auburn hair pulled back casually in a ponytail, she kept his blood stirring whether he was touching her, looking at her or only thinking about her. And she was on his mind constantly. Their lovemaking kept taking on new dimensions, venturing into realms that went beyond physical pleasures, touched his soul and brought him to a level of intense awareness the French called *la petite mort*—the little death. It was strange and wonderful and a contradiction, for he never felt more alive than when he was making love to Gwyneth Miller. They were no longer two separate beings, two individual persons, but one soul, one body, one vessel of joy and rapture.

She offered him the basket of cinnamon rolls. The

smile, the gleam in her eyes, made him want her all the more.

"What's on your agenda for today?" he asked. They'd already gone together to feed their animals. His earlier disdain for her miniatures seemed petty now. They weren't his equines of choice and never would be, but he admired her ability with them. He'd wondered early on if she'd favored the dwarf variety because she was afraid of big horses, but watching her around his huge Percherons quickly disabused him of that notion. She was respectful of the power of his creatures, but not intimidated by them.

She tore off a piece of the sweet bread. "I have calls to make to Dallas and Denver about commercials that are being filmed there. The western-wear company that used the llamas is interested in shooting some more commercials with other animals, so I need to talk to them. Then I need to drive into Tyler and see a man who answered one of my ads. He's apparently interested in purchasing a pair of miniatures for his grandchildren."

"Will you sell your own? What about your coach and carriage?"

"I won't break up my team, but I have contacts who raise minis. I'll see if I can broker a deal."

"That's where the money is," he noted between bites of the pastry. "No inventory to maintain, no operating expenses. What time do you expect to be finished today?"

"I have some other chores to do, as well—pick up feed, get in touch with the farrier. Probably not before five, maybe later."

"I expect to be out all day, too, looking at property in Longview, and I don't reckon I'll be back much before then, either. How about I pick you up at seven and take you to Santiago's for dinner. Do you like chicken mole?" He pronounced the last word in two syllables.

"Why don't you try me?"

He couldn't suppress the grin that swept across his face. "Mmm. I'd like that."

She wanted to sneer, but it came out as an equally erotic grin. "I was talking about food."

"Of course," he intoned, eyebrows lifted. "So was I."

She laughed happily. "You're impossible."

"And you're tantalizing." He reached a hand across the table to cover hers. "More temptation than a man can endure."

Her eyes twinkling, she brushed her fingers over the back of his hand. "Your endurance so far seems to be holding up."

Jed groaned, blinked slowly and was about to toss another comment Gwyn's way, when June appeared, her expression registering anything but amusement.

"Excuse me, sir, but the sheriff is here to see you."

Jed felt a stab of alarm and saw what he assumed to be a similar emotion scatter across Gwyn's face. He was about to tell his housekeeper to show the lawman in, when Fielder appeared in the doorway behind her.

"Louis, I got a bone to pick with you."

June whirled around and faced the visitor. "I told

you to wait in the sitting room,'' she snapped at him. The star on his breast pocket didn't seem to intimidate her in the least.

Before she could give Fielder the tongue-lashing Jed suspected she was about to deliver, he spoke up. ''It's okay this time, June. Thank you.''

The cant of her head clearly indicated she didn't like being dismissed, but she respected her boss. With a huff of disapproval, she walked around the tall man wearing the cream-colored western hat.

''Since this obviously isn't a social call, Sheriff, I won't invite you to join us for coffee. What is it you want to talk to me about?''

''You've been sticking your nose where it doesn't belong.''

Jed leaned back in his wrought-iron chair, apparently unconcerned by the hostile glare from his visitor.

''Would you care to be more specific?''

''You know damn well what I'm talking about. I got a call last night from Jennings, asking what I was doing about investigating Granger's murder and demanding I pull out all the stops to locate Hank Belmonte.''

So Ray had followed through on his promise. ''Sound like perfectly reasonable requests to me. What are you doing?''

The pink of Fielder's face grew a shade deeper. ''None of your goddamned business.''

Jed eased the knife he'd picked up to cut the Danish onto the table, but the movement was so deliberate that it drew attention to itself. ''Sheriff, unless you came with a warrant, you're here as a guest. In that capacity, you'll watch your language. Perhaps you have no respect for women, but I do. I'd ask for an apology from you, but I doubt it would be sincere, so I'll just advise you to choose your words carefully.''

Fielder's complexion now was a glowing red, like that of a man who'd been out in the sun too long and was feeling the pain of his burn. And even if he had been inclined to apologize, his jaw was clamped so tight he probably couldn't have gotten the words out.

''So what are you doing to find Belmonte?'' Jed asked.

The sheriff inhaled deeply before answering. ''I'm not here to answer questions but to ask them.''

''And I've told you I don't answer questions without my lawyer being present.'' Jed leaned once more against the back of the chair. On an exhale, he said, ''Tell me what your problem is, so I can get on with my breakfast.''

''You've been going around asking people questions, bugging old lady Berber and sticking your nose in Granger's bank records.''

''I've been exercising my rights of free speech and assembly. Did Joleen complain to you about my visit?''

He shook his head. ''No.''

''Then how did you know about it?''

''My deputy saw your car parked outside her house.''

Jed didn't for a moment believe Joleen's place was

on a regular patrol, which meant he was being followed. The knowledge didn't bring comfort.

"This is a murder investigation, Louis," Fielder continued. "I'm warning you for the last time. Stay out of it."

"Or what?" Gwyn snapped, unable to remain silent any longer.

Jed tried to wave her to silence, but she wasn't about to be quiet.

"Or I'll put him under arrest."

"On what charge?" she demanded none too calmly. If this wasn't a murder investigation involving the man she loved, it might have been amusing to watch the two strong male personalities slug it out verbally. Under the circumstances, however, she didn't find any humor in the situation.

"The law is on my side, Miss Miller. It would do you well to remember that."

"You didn't answer my question. On what charge would you arrest Mr. Louis if he continues to talk to people who might have information pertinent to Mrs. Granger's death?"

"Witness tampering," he said smugly.

The ready response stopped her for a minute, but not a very long one. "I'm no expert regarding legal matters, Sheriff, but my understanding is that that particular statute pertains to trying to influence witnesses during a trial. I also believe your having a deputy follow us, as well as your gratuitous threats, constitute harassment and intimidation. Perhaps you're the one who ought to be more careful." She looked him straight in the eyes. "Unless you want to face charges of civil rights violations."

The rolling of Fielder's fingers into tight fists suggested he wasn't having a good day.

"If there's nothing more, Sheriff," Jed spoke up calmly, "I think you had better leave."

"I'll be back."

"Bring a warrant next time."

For the first time Fielder's expression softened, not in a smile, but with a kind of cunning sneer. "Count on it, Louis. Count on it."

FOR GWYN the rest of the day dragged by in slow motion. Her actions were routine and should have been mechanical, yet she had to concentrate to accomplish every single one of them. Her call to Dallas was highly encouraging; she was finally making the inroads into the advertising business she'd worked so long and hard for. Yet her mind kept dwelling on Jed.

He'd put on a good front with the sheriff that morning, but she hadn't missed the worry in his eyes. Jed was convinced he was going to be arrested for murder, that somehow the sheriff was holding back information that could convict him of killing the woman who'd brought him up.

Over and over Gwyn reviewed the information Jed had given her—about the argument he'd had with Frannie the day she disappeared, his ditching school that day—the only time he had—about Frannie's car still being at the house.

One of the most damning facts was that Frannie

had been buried on the grounds of Beaumarais, the estate Jed knew he would inherit in three years. His adamant refusal to let Tessa Lang dig there reinforced the premise that he was aware what the archaeologist would find. It all fit neatly into place if one believed Jed was guilty, which the sheriff clearly did.

None of that, however, explained why Frannie had been murdered to begin with. Fielder seemed to hold her in disdain, while Jed held her in high regard and affection. The truth was probably somewhere in between, though Gwyn was confident Jed was closer to it, since he'd lived with the woman for nearly twelve years—unless he'd idealized her over the passage of time.

Gwyn thought about Jed's aspiration to become a concert violinist and his trip to New York. Frannie had apparently been right—he didn't have the requisite skill, yet Gwyn had to wonder how the woman, unschooled in the finer points of classical music, as Jed claimed she was, could judge his talent so accurately. Of course, Gwyn hadn't heard Jed play. Maybe his amateurishness was obvious for anyone to hear. Or maybe Frannie had refused to support his ambition because she was afraid of losing him. Which would mean she was more manipulative than Jed realized.

Unfortunately, this kind of speculation played right into Fielder's hands. Even if Jed had had the requisite talent when he went to the Juilliard, Frannie's disappearance could easily have distracted him and prompted his counselor to discourage him.

They'd never know now if he might have succeeded had Frannie not disappeared.

JED WAS COMPLETELY off balance all day. He did what he had to do, but he couldn't seem to feel any of it. His mind kept wandering to the sheriff's visit, to the look on Gwyn's face when Fielder had promised to come back with an arrest warrant. She was scared. He only hoped she didn't know how nervous he was, too. Suppose the sheriff hadn't been bluffing. Suppose he really did have sufficient evidence to charge him with Frannie's murder. It was all circumstantial, but people had been convicted of murder— even executed—on no more than circumstantial evidence.

Jed had the uncomfortable feeling Tessa Lang, the archaeologist, might have found something at the burial site that would further reinforce Fielder's case against him, something incriminating the sheriff had sworn her to secrecy about and that he wouldn't reveal until the very last minute. What it might be baffled him, but in his gut Jed knew there was something, if only he could remember what it was.

He took Gwyn to Santiago's that evening for dinner. It was the best Mexican restaurant in town and, as far as Jed was concerned, within a hundred-mile radius. He'd gone to school with Rico Santiago. The family business had started as a strictly mom-and-pop operation, the food served literally out their kitchen back door. Rico's mother and grandmother had expanded the operation over the years until now it was run in a sprawling complex of added-on rooms and intimate patios. Mariachis strolled the crowded dining areas on weekends, entertaining and lending an air of festiveness to the boisterous atmosphere.

Rico had returned to Uncertain a couple of years ago. His grandmother had been convinced from the day of his birth that he was destined for the priesthood. Then Rico reached puberty, discovered girls, and his life took a different course. His considerable straying from the path of celibacy was still a butt of friendly razzing. After graduating from medical school he'd returned to Uncertain, opened his own family practice and married his high school sweetheart. If Abuela Santiago was disappointed in his rejecting her choice for his vocation, she seemed to have gotten over it—and, as soon as she found out she was going to be a great-grandmother, to have forgiven Layla for tempting him away from holy orders.

As always the Tex-Mex fare was spicy, generous and mouthwatering.

"Something wrong with the cinco-cinco nachos?" Rico's mother, Carlita, asked when Jed and Gwyn ate only half the platter of crispy tortilla chips piled high with seasoned beef, refried beans, chopped onions, tomatoes, melted cheese, jalapeños and guacamole.

"The only thing wrong," Gwyn told her with genuine pleasure, "is that I can't eat more of them. Jed tells me your chicken mole is to die for, so I have to leave some room."

Rico's mother smiled happily. "I'll wrap the nachos up for you to take with you." She turned to Jed. "You seen Rico?"

"Not lately," Jed admitted. "How are he and Layla doing?"

"She has the morning sickness."

"Again? Have you told her they've found out what causes it?"

Mama Santiago chuckled richly. "I don't think my daughter-in-law is looking for a cure."

"They're nice people," Gwyn commented nearly two hours later when they were pulling out of the parking lot.

"I always envied Rico his big, close-knit family. They're very kind people."

The tangy aromas of cumin and sharp cheddar wafted through the car. "And generous," she added. "We have enough food in these doggy boxes to feed a small convention."

Jed shook his head. "I've often wondered how they earn a profit. They certainly don't make one on me. I always seem to come away with twice as many leftovers as I've paid for."

He slowly pulled up the driveway of Beaumarais and parked the Jaguar in the garage behind the house. Each took a foam container from the rear seat, and they walked hand in hand toward the back of the stately mansion. He paused and stared across the broad lawn leading down to the lake's edge. The full moon was just rising, an oversize golden disk that sparkled above the mist seeping across the water between moss-draped cypress trees. Crickets chirped. An owl hooted and somewhere off in the distance a whippoorwill called. A beautiful night. A beautiful woman at his side.

They deposited the leftover food in the refrigerator.

He turned to face her. "I love you, Gwyn."

Her heart leaped. She gazed up into his eyes. There was wariness there as well as desire. She understood both.

"I love you, too, Jed." She waited for him to say more, but instead he brought his mouth down to hers and kissed her sweetly on the lips. Oh, there was passion, but it was banked, held in reserve. "Let's go upstairs," she whispered.

SEVERAL HOURS later, she stirred. He was still beside her, his arm extended across her naked belly. She looked over and found his eyes wide-open.

"Did I wake you? I'm sorry." He withdrew his arm. "Go back to sleep."

"What's wrong?" she asked, dismayed by the troubled expression on his face.

"Nothing," he said softly, and repeated, "Go back to sleep."

She pulled herself into a sitting position and rearranged the pillows behind her head more comfortably.

"Tell me what's bothering you, Jed," she urged him.

He hesitated, then drew himself up beside her.

When he remained silent, she prompted, "Speak to me, Jed. Whatever the problem is, we'll work it out together."

His expression was forlorn. "Talking with Carlita Santiago last evening reminded me how much I've missed—marriage, children."

She leaned over and laid her head against his shoulder, her hand sliding across his chest. She could feel his heartbeat under the coarse hair that overlay the warm firmness of muscle. "Family," she said. "I know."

He snaked his arm around her and planted a gentle kiss on the top of her head. "I want to spend the rest of my life making love to you."

The murmur of his smooth, deep voice so close to her ear sent erotic little vibrations tripping through her. She felt herself floating the way she had in his boat on the lake, gliding effortlessly through a misty forest of half-hidden trees.

With his free hand, he touched the long coil of auburn hair that cascaded over her shoulder to her breast. He combed his fingertips through the silken strands gently, as if they were something delicate, sacred and magical. "I want to share my life with you, Gwyn. I want to make babies with you."

She cuddled against him, pressing herself into the reassuring shelter of his body. This kind of contentment was new to her. It wasn't a neutral thing, like having no worries or the absence of pain. It was a positive force that brought her serenity. She'd dreamed of having a home, a family, a husband and children, but she'd never thought such fantasies could come true. Not for her. "Me, too."

"I wish I could ask you to marry me, Gwyn," he

muttered in quiet defeat, "but as long as this murder charge is hanging over my head—"

He might as well have dashed the love boat smack into a sandbar—or maybe an iceberg. The fog immediately cleared. She lifted her head and stared at the handsome profile of the man who'd become the center of her world. There was no denying the sadness in his eyes. It made her ache. She knew why he was doing this. To protect her. To spare her the pain of losing him if things didn't go right. His damn nobility made her furious. She'd spent her life alone, and now he was abandoning her, too. Never mind that he thought it was for honorable reasons. Her parents were always doing things "to help" her, "for her own good." When she wanted to be close instead of "safe," she was called selfish.

"Jed, we've had this conversation before." She pulled away from him and propped herself on the pillows crowding the headboard. Instinctively, she tugged the sheet up to cover her naked breasts. "And frankly I don't see any point in having it again."

He shifted, and she felt his startled gaze sweep her face. Refusing to meet it, she looked away, toward the windows, where morning light was spilling into the room like gold dust. His perplexity at her response further fueled her temper.

"Besides, who said I wanted to marry you?" She swung her legs over the side of the bed, away from him, so he couldn't see the tears her anger was causing.

He ran his hand down her spine, sending shivers along the vertebrae. "Gwyn..." he implored.

She jerked away. The sensation of his fingers on her skin distracted her from her rage and she didn't want it to cool. Confrontation had never been in her makeup. Her parents had been very efficient in nurturing it out of her, but maybe it was time for nature to take over.

"The sex has been great, Jed, so let's leave it at that," she announced, and started to get up.

This time, he grabbed her arm. She stared down at the hand that had only minutes earlier stirred such glorious passion in her, but that now held a different kind of force. She turned toward him. He was glowering at her as if she had three heads.

"Is that all this is about? Sex?" he asked in a low voice. There was an edge in his words now, and disappointment, as well.

It's about love and trust, devotion and steadfastness, she wanted to yell at him. But what good was anything if it had to be spelled out. She dragged her fingers through her hair. She'd given herself to him, not just physically, though that had also been more complete, more unreserved, than she'd ever imagined possible, but she'd left herself totally vulnerable when she'd presented him with her heart. She'd told him she loved him, and it wasn't enough.

Drawing in a deep breath, she yanked her arm out of his grip. "Damn you, Jed Louis."

She rose from the bed and padded naked to the bathroom. At the door she paused and glanced back at him. "I'll be gone for the next few days. I have to go to Coyote Springs to check on some miniature donkeys, or maybe they're jackasses, for a kiddy show. I'll see you when I get back, and maybe we can have another romp in your bed.''

JED WAS IN his office in Jefferson, studying a contingency contract for a piece of property he was buying on the outskirts of Longview. He'd put in long hours the past three days, leaving the house before June arrived, so he could feed Gwyn's miniature horses in addition to his own, repeating the process in the evenings.

He barely registered the outside office door opening until he heard his secretary greet the visitor by name. He jumped from his seat and went to the doorway.

She was wearing a shirt of butter yellow—a color that perfectly complemented the long braid of auburn hair slung over her left shoulder. Her jeans hugged her slender hips the way he wanted to.

Had she come to rail at him? To announce she was leaving Uncertain? To tell him that since he didn't want her in his life she was going away forever? He'd replayed his last conversation with her over and over, trying to figure out where he'd gone wrong. Why could she not understand it would be unfair, selfish and irresponsible of him to ask her to tie herself to him when his future was so tenuous? Of course, she had free will, and he respected her right to make her own decisions. But he couldn't contribute to an error of judgment that could ruin the rest of her life. He loved her too much.

''Hello, Jed.'' It wasn't a hostile greeting, but there was skepticism in it.

"Hi, Gwyn," he replied lightly, partly for the sake of his secretary, partly because he was unsure of himself, of her. "I'm glad you stopped by."

"I was in town picking up mineral blocks for my horses," she said, justifying herself.

He waved an arm, inviting her into his office. She entered. He closed the door behind her and forced himself to keep his hands at his sides while he waited for her to speak.

"About the other morning," she said tentatively. "I'm—"

"No," he cautioned her, then realized he didn't know why she was here. "Before you say anything, please let me apologize, explain."

"I—"

But she didn't get a chance to utter another word before he had her in his arms and was kissing her madly.

"Gwyneth," he said in a husky voice as he buried his face in the crook of her neck. The smell of her skin, the silky softness of her hair, were aphrodisiacs, stirring, arousing, tormenting. She squirmed in his embrace.

"I—" she started again.

The slam of the outside door had them both jumping apart. Almost immediately, there was a rattle of the doorknob and the office door flew open. Logan Fielder filled the available space.

Jed's secretary, trying to see around the tall sheriff, whose arms were akimbo, called out, "I'm sorry, Mr. Louis, but he—"

"That's all right, Nicole." He stared at the intruder. "You want something?"

"It's not me, Louis. It's the D.A. He'd like you to come to his office at your earliest convenience—that means now—to answer a few questions."

Gwyn began trembling. "Are you putting him under arrest, Sheriff?"

"Depends on what he tells the D.A.," Fielder responded. "Grab your hat," he said to Jed. "You might be a while."

Jed was tempted to resist, to tell the sheriff to go to hell, but he knew this showdown had been coming. It was time to face it head-on.

"Call Thorndyke," Jed told Gwyn. "Tell him what's happening and ask him to meet me at the district attorney's office. Tell him I won't say a word until he shows up."

Jed reached over to the hat rack, snagged his Stetson, set it carefully on his head, leaned over and kissed Gwyn familiarly on the lips and followed the sheriff out the door.

CHAPTER FOURTEEN

GWYN'S HANDS SHOOK as she dialed the number of Dexter Thorndyke's office in Dallas. He wasn't there.

"I have to reach him immediately," she told the secretary at the other end. Images of Jed sitting at a scarred wooden table with a bright light shining in his eyes flashed across her mind, though she was fairly certain the notion was ridiculous. They wouldn't be using rubber hoses on him, either.

"Have you tried his cell phone number?"

In the excitement of the moment, Gwyn had completely forgotten about it. "No. What is it? I don't have my planner with me." Actually, her appointment book was out in the Rover, but it was parked a block away. She didn't want to take the time to retrieve it.

Thorndyke's secretary rattled off his number. Flustered, Gwyn had to ask her to repeat it while she scribbled on a piece of paper on Jed's desk.

He answered on the second ring. "Hey, take it easy," he advised a moment later. "Calm down and tell me exactly what's happened."

She felt her face grow warm at the realization that she'd been babbling. Giving herself a moment to collect her wits, she recounted the turn of events.

"So he hasn't been arrested," the attorney noted. "Just invited to the D.A.'s office." He paused a moment. "Could be worse."

"You will help him, won't you?" She hated the note of panic in her voice, but there was no hiding the fact that she was scared. Jed had been sure the authorities were out to get him, and he'd been right. He'd wanted to shield her from this, but how could he? Whether they were married or not, together or not, didn't matter. When he suffered misfortune, she suffered with him. Wasn't that what love meant? Experiencing emotions together?

"Actually, I'm in Uncertain right now," the voice at the other end said. "In Riley Gray's office. It'll probably take me half an hour or so to get to Marshall."

"So you'll come?" she asked anxiously, though he'd already told her he would.

"Gwyn, relax."

"That's easy for you to say," she replied with a feeble attempt at wry humor.

He laughed. "You'll be okay. Look, go over to the D.A.'s office and wait for me. They probably won't let you see Jed, but that's all right. I'll be there as soon as I can. If you do see him, tell him to keep his mouth shut."

"He told me to tell you he wouldn't say anything until you arrived."

"Good man. Now, go about being your usual cool self, Gwyn. Nothing ticks off cops and lawyers more than people who aren't afraid of them."

It was her turn to laugh. "Got it. Thanks, Thorny."

She hung up the phone feeling somewhat relieved. Jed always kept his cool with the sheriff. No reason to think he wouldn't with the D.A., as well. But with Fielder their confrontations almost had the element of a game. Raised to this new level, the stakes were higher.

She tore off the piece of paper with Thorny's number on it, just in case she needed it again, stuffed it into her purse and left the office. Jed hadn't been officially arrested or charged, she reminded herself. Maybe this was just another bluff, an attempt to intimidate. To what end? To get him to confess to a crime he didn't commit?

The county prosecutor's offices were in a brick municipal building across the street from the courthouse. The suite was small, shabby and cramped, not at all what Gwyn had expected, though her only knowledge of such places was from movies and television. When she informed the woman at the reception desk that she'd like to see the D.A., she was told he was in a meeting. She asked to see Jed Louis and received the same bland response.

"I'll wait," Gwyn announced as she took one of two hard wooden chairs in front of a wall of leatherbound books. There was a stack of out-of-date magazines on a small table nearby. She casually paged through one, totally unaware of its contents.

Thorny showed up within twenty minutes, carrying a thin attaché case and wearing a lightweight suit of pale beige and a power tie of red-and-blue stripes.

Gwyn suspected he might have violated the speed limit on his way, but by his easy, almost nonchalant gait one would never know he was in a hurry. His air of confidence was infectious.

He came immediately to her, his hands outstretched. ''This shouldn't take too long.''

''Can you tell me what's going to happen?'' she asked, the feeling of panic she'd managed to suppress again reasserting itself when she pictured Jed behind the closed doors.

''Probably nothing. They're on a fishing trip and the weather is about to close in on them,'' he said with a grin.

She managed to return a smile, but it didn't fool either of them.

''Keep the faith,'' he whispered in her ear as he gave her a gentle peck on the cheek. ''I'll have your man sprung in no time.''

Was it bravado, or did he really mean it? She chose to believe him. ''I'll be waiting.''

The high-powered attorney went up to the reception desk. ''I'm Dexter Thorndyke,'' he said smoothly, ''representing Mr. Louis.''

''Yes, sir,'' the woman said. ''Mr. Philpott said you'd be coming.'' She rose from her chair and led him to a door behind her.

JED SAT in a room that was too small for the long, polished conference table that dominated it. Milky daylight streamed in from the row of unwashed wood sash windows that lined one long wall. Overhead, lights burned, but their weak yellow glow did nothing to alleviate the gloom that seemed to pervade the room. Except for a framed lithograph of the first president of the United States, the walls were bare.

Daniel Philpott, fiftyish but fit looking, in white shirtsleeves, his blue tie askew, sat at the head of the veneered table. By his side was a younger woman, whom he'd introduced as Tracy Simms, an assistant district attorney. Logan Fielder, taciturn and scowling, sat across from her.

They'd offered Jed coffee, which he'd declined. They'd tried asking him questions about Frannie and him, which he'd politely but pointedly refused to answer until his lawyer arrived. There was a quick tap on the door, it opened, and the D.A.'s secretary held it for Dexter Thorndyke. He came first to Jed and shook his hand.

"Gwyn called me. You all right?" he asked quietly.

"Fine," Jed said, though he didn't feel fine. He'd done his best not to show discomfort, but he doubted he'd succeeded. These people were experts at applying pressure and reading reactions.

Thorndyke did an about-face and went up to the man at the head of the table. "Mr. Philpott. I'm Dexter Thorndyke. We've never met, but I know you by reputation. It's an honor to meet you."

Probably without realizing it, Philpott beamed, if only for a second. "Call me Dan," he said, extending his hand.

Jed wondered if Thorny had actually heard anything about the country attorney, or if the statement was a routine disarming tactic. The rest of the introductions were made, though Thorny already knew Fielder.

"Now, perhaps you will tell me why Mr. Louis has been asked to come here," he said as he removed a yellow legal pad from his attaché case, placed it on the table and took the seat beside Jed.

"There are some facts pertaining to the disappearance and murder of Frannie Granger," Philpott announced, "about which we would like to ask your client. Since he has been unwilling to cooperate with the police—"

"That's not true," Jed objected.

Thorny raised a hand to silence him, his eyes never leaving the other attorney's. "Why do you say he's been unwilling to cooperate?"

"He's refused to answer the sheriff's questions," Philpott declared.

"I'm afraid you've been misinformed, Mr. Philpott...Dan. Mr. Louis has answered all the questions put to him by Sheriff Fielder."

Philpott said nothing, but his glance at the sheriff begged for an explanation.

Fielder clearly wasn't pleased at being put on the spot, but he answered evenly. "The day after the skeletal remains uncovered by archaeologist Tessa Lang were positively identified as those of Mrs. Frances Granger, I approached Mr. Louis and asked him to recount the events surrounding her disappearance on May 4, 1982. He refused."

"That's not true," Jed said again.

"What Mr. Louis did," Thorny enlightened the D.A., "was tell the sheriff his recollection of the circumstances surrounding his foster mother's last days were already a matter of record and that he had no reason to change them. After nineteen years, Dan, I'm sure you'll agree memory of such a traumatic event can be hazy, incomplete and subject to time's distortion.''

"Time can also provide deeper insight," Philpott pointed out in a weak attempt to rescue the sheriff.

Thorny easily agreed. "But," he added, "the sheriff didn't offer Mr. Louis a copy of his previous statement to review in order to ascertain if there were any inaccuracies in it or if he had more information to impart.'' He addressed the sheriff. "Did you even research the record of statements taken at that time?''

Taking obvious umbrage at the counselor's insulting tone, Fielder flexed his jaw before he answered. "Of course I did.''

"Were Mr. Louis's statements incomplete or unclear in some way?''

"They were clear as far as they went," Fielder grudgingly acknowledged. He was about to add something, but Thorny didn't give him a chance.

"However, you didn't recount a specific event or fact in Mr. Louis's statement that you needed clarification on. Is that correct? You simply wanted him to repeat to you what he'd already told you at the time of his foster mother's disappearance.''

Fielder sucked air through his nose. He was smart enough to know where the defense attorney was going with this. "I wanted to find out if Louis had thought of anything since then that might be relevant to my investigation.''

"But you didn't tell Mr. Louis that, did you?" Thorndyke reminded him in a tone that was so easy-going it was deceptive. He picked up the uncapped fountain pen he'd laid beside the pad and held it by its ends between his hands. "I don't think that's what you were really after, Sheriff. Since you didn't ask any specific questions or elicit clarification or elaboration of any of his previous statements, I think you were hoping he would say something that varied in some small detail with what he'd said previously, so you could call him a liar."

Fielder's large hands gripped the edge of the table. "That's not—"

"You were on a fishing expedition."

"You've no call—" Philpott started to interrupt.

Thorndyke turned directly to him and fixed him with a hard glare. "You still are."

Philpott stiffened in his chair. "Now, just a minute, Thorndyke—"

Thorny ignored him. He didn't raise his voice, but there was enough force in it to prevail. "For the record, we are willing to concede that Jed Louis, then seventeen years old, had an argument with his foster mother, Frances Granger, at their residence on the morning of May 4, 1982. That sometime after this verbal altercation, Mrs. Granger disappeared and was never seen again until her remains were recently uncovered by Ms. Lang."

"What was the nature of this…altercation?" the woman across from the sheriff asked. Jed had watched her taking in the exchange among the men. Tracy Simms gave the impression of a student absorbing everything and filing it away. The curtness in the way she asked her question, however, suggested she wasn't nearly as acquiescent as she appeared.

"Mr. Louis asked her to sign a form so he could travel to New York to attend the Juilliard School of Music. Mrs. Granger refused, and Mr. Louis, in understandable disappointment, accused her of ruining his life. Contrary, however, to the hearsay information that has been given to the press, he did not threaten her in any way."

"Where did he go that day?" she persisted.

Thorny continued in his formal manner. "For the record, we also stipulate that on that particular day Mr. Louis did not attend school. He went fishing on Caddo Lake."

"By himself?"

"Yes." Thorny bequeathed her a wide grin. "And that's all the fishing you're going to be able to do, as well. Unless you have questions you have not asked before, this meeting is over." He pushed back his chair. Taking his lead, Jed did the same.

Thorndyke didn't immediately stand up, however. As he returned his unused pen to an inside pocket of his suit jacket, he looked across the table to the district attorney. "Dan, unless you have information you're not sharing with me, all you've got against my client is circumstantial. Clearly you don't have an indictable case. Otherwise you would have a warrant for Mr. Louis's arrest."

He clutched the arms of the stiff wooden chair. "It might be a good idea for you to review with Sheriff

Fielder the elements that constitute police harassment and intimidation.'' He retrieved his attaché case and slipped the yellow pad back inside. "And don't forget to cover the penalties associated with those crimes.''

Fielder's eyes widened, and he nearly came out of his seat.

Philpott reached over and pressed down on the hand splayed on the table closest to him. "Mind telling me what are you're getting at?'' he asked Thorny.

"Your sheriff has been stalking my client.''

The D.A. looked over at Fielder. "Is that true?''

"No,'' Fielder snapped.

"Isn't it? My client informs me you called on him several days ago and accused him of intimidating Ms. Joleen Berber.''

"All I did was ask him why he went to see her.''

Thorny's dark eyebrows went up in a simulation of surprise. What the expression more convincingly said was "Gotcha.''

"I have a witness who says you told him to stay away from her.'' Thorny clicked the attaché case closed. "By the way, did Ms. Berber contact you about Mr. Louis's visit and register a complaint?''

Plainly, Fielder knew he'd just been tricked. In a low and angry undertone, he said, "One of my deputies happened to be passing by and saw his car parked in front of her house. Louis has the only Jag in town,'' he added, as if that explained everything.

"My understanding is that Ms. Berber lives in a remote part of town, one well off the beaten track. The coincidence of a deputy just happening to patrol that road at the same time my client made his one and only visit to her residence strains credibility, Sheriff. I'm quite certain a judge would find it highly suspect, as well.''

Jed studied the body language of the people at the table. They weren't happy.

Thorny finally rose and moved toward the door. Jed followed and muttered something in his ear. The attorney nodded and turned back to the D.A.

''When can Mrs. Granger's remains be released, Dan? The true victim in this case deserves the dignity of a decent burial.''

Philpott looked blank for a moment. ''I'll check and get back to you.''

Thorny nodded. ''I'd appreciate it.'' He started for the door but again stopped short. ''One other thing, Dan. Since the sheriff here has obviously not been completely forthcoming with you, I feel it's my duty to inform you he's apparently made no good-faith effort to explore other possible leads in this tragic case. He's done nothing, for example, to find Hank Belmonte, who had means, motive and opportunity. Locate him and you may well find the real killer.'' He motioned to Jed for them to leave. ''Now, if you'll excuse us…''

Jed preceded Thorny though the door. The last thing they heard was Philpott asking Fielder, ''Who the hell is Hank Belmonte?''

WHEN JED EMERGED through the doorway, Gwyn jumped to her feet, then worried that her legs wouldn't hold her. Heart tripping, she ran to him and threw her arms around his waist. The warmth of his body as he hugged her to his chest reassured her and gave her strength.

"Let's go somewhere and talk," Thorny said as he kept moving past them to the hallway door, his tone amused and encouraging.

Outside the building, he glanced up at the pearl-gray sky. "Have to drive to Dallas this afternoon and haven't eaten a thing all day, so let's go to the family restaurant I saw a couple of blocks from here."

Gwyn left her Rover parked in the street and climbed into Jed's truck a few spaces away. They followed the lawyer's shiny black Mercedes. It was the middle of the afternoon, so the restaurant wasn't crowded. Nevertheless, they chose a booth in the rear, where they could be reasonably sure of privacy.

Jed ignored the menu the hostess placed in front of him. "Thanks for your help back there."

"That's why you pay me the big bucks." Thorny gave him a toothy grin. "Actually, it went very well."

Gwyn wrinkled up her nose. "You sound almost pleased it happened." Jed had given her a quick run-down of the meeting on the drive over.

"Oh, I am." He scanned the menu quickly.

The waitress came by with pad and pencil in hand. "What can I get y'all?"

Jed ordered coffee, Gwyn iced tea and Thorny a Reuben and a Coke.

"Would you care to elaborate?" Jed prompted after the waitress left.

Thorny repositioned the paper napkin and flatware in front of him. "Okay, let's consider what just happened. The sheriff obviously told the district attorney you were being uncooperative. Philpott knew they didn't have enough for an arrest, but the sheriff must have convinced him that inviting you in for an informal discussion would yield some benefits.''

''But Fielder knew you'd been retained,'' Gwyn objected. ''Jed told him often enough that he wouldn't talk except in your presence.''

The lawyer shrugged. ''Maybe Fielder didn't tell Philpott that. There's a tendency among some cops to hold back on prosecutors, to tell them only what they think will help their case.''

''It'd be damn stupid of him not to let the D.A. know about you, wouldn't it?''

Thorny cocked an eyebrow. ''People do stupid things.''

The waitress delivered their drinks, momentarily interrupting the discussion.

''Maybe Fielder or Philpott thought I was unavailable,'' Thorny speculated, ''and this would be a good time to scare Jed. Calling someone in for a voluntary interview is a not-so-subtle form of intimidation that's often successful. Even if Jed had stood mute, they could have regaled him with the consequences of his failure to cooperate. They'd also remind him he wasn't under arrest and therefore the Miranda warning didn't apply. Theoretically anything he said couldn't be used against him.''

''But it would have been,'' Gwyn concluded.

''It would have given them leads they could exploit.''

''I refused to discuss even the weather with them,'' Jed reminded both of them.

''Which was exactly the right thing to do.''

Jed chuckled for the first time and grinned at the man across the table from him. "I don't think Fielder did tell him you were my lawyer. Philpott seemed surprised when I announced that you were."

The waitress brought their orders. Thorny slathered mustard inside the grilled corned beef, Swiss cheese and sauerkraut sandwich and took a big bite of it, using his napkin to wipe his mouth as he chewed.

"So why was this business good for us?" Gwyn asked.

Thorny swallowed. "First, it showed the D.A. and his people that the usual tactics aren't going to work." He finished off the first half of his sandwich.

"Second, it drove a wedge between Fielder and the D.A. Philpott will think twice now when the sheriff comes to him with information about this case. He'll want to make damn sure it's accurate and indisputable before he's willing to go out on a limb."

He bit into the second half, chewed and swallowed. "Third, it allowed me to plant a seed of doubt in his mind. He's more likely now to push Fielder to find Belmonte." He wiped the corner of his mouth.

"Fourth, it gave me the opportunity to put them on notice that police harassment won't fly and will not be tolerated." He turned to Jed. "I want you to keep me informed of everything that goes on or that you think might be going on—cars following you, unexplained phone calls, letters or threats—"

"God, you don't think he's in danger!" Gwyn exclaimed.

Thorny finished his sandwich and crunched the dill pickle that had been served with it. Gwyn watched him wash it down with the soft drink. The sour-sweet combination made her stomach lurch.

"I'm not trying to frighten you, but let's face facts," the lawyer said as he wiped off his hands on his nearly shredded ball of paper napkin. "Somebody murdered Frannie Granger. That person may be miles away from here now—or dead."

"Like Hank Belmonte."

He nodded. "Or he could be someone who still lives around here and who is now in danger of being revealed. Desperate people do desperate things."

Gwyn tightened the grip she had on Jed's hand under the table.

"I've got to be honest with you," the man across from them said seriously. "This homicide may never be solved. If this Hank Belmonte, for example, killed Granger, hightailed it out of here and is now dead, we'll probably never get enough evidence to prove he did it."

"What are we going to do?" Gwyn cried.

"I'll have a private investigator do some checking on Belmonte, see if we can't find him ourselves."

Gwyn bit her lip to stem the emotions going through her. Jed's hand holding hers under the table helped. "It's this never knowing…having people always wondering if Jed is a murderer."

"You want my advice?" Thorny asked as he pushed back his plate. "Get on with your lives."

CHAPTER FIFTEEN

THEY'D BOTH brought vehicles to the county seat. Marshall wasn't exactly a high-crime area, but Jed didn't want to leave his truck on the street overnight. A brand-new, shiny pickup might be too much of a temptation for joyriders. The Rover was Gwyn's only means of transportation, and she had the mineral blocks she'd bought in the back of it. Under the circumstances, they had no choice but to drive home to Uncertain separately.

Jed was disturbed. Despite his lawyer's upbeat advice, the events of the past few hours had imparted a sense of gloom and foreboding that seemed endless.

He ached to have Gwyn by his side. He'd never needed another human being, never wanted a woman as much as he needed and wanted her. He'd been fooling himself when he thought he could do the noble thing and send her away. He couldn't fool himself anymore.

He wondered about the unhappiness he'd seen in her eyes when they'd left the D.A.'s office. Was it the same disappointment he felt that nothing had been resolved in the legal arena, or was it disenchantment in him as a man?

Get on with your lives had been Thorndyke's counsel. It sounded positive and encouraging—until he remembered Gwyn's observation, that life could never be normal or content as long as people kept wondering if he were a murderer.

Gwyn led the way back to Caddo Lake. Her old Rover plumed blue smoke as she chugged along the nearly deserted country road. She needed an overhaul badly, or better still a new van or truck. Obviously, she couldn't afford either. He'd offer to fix it for her, but he knew she'd turn him down. The independence of the woman amazed him.

What was equally astounding was that her strength didn't weaken his but bolstered it. They'd started off by clashing wills. Now their energies complemented each other—and not just in bed. In spite of their opposing backgrounds, they understood each other.

He'd grown up in modest circumstances and come into a fortune. She'd been raised in the lap of luxury and walked away from it, choosing instead a frugal life. He'd seen the lack of money as a burden. She'd seen the possession of it as a much heavier millstone. He smiled at the ironic term.

Jed remembered a saying attributed to Sophie Tucker, a comedienne from the age of vaudeville: *I've been rich and I've been poor. Rich is better.* Apparently, Gwyn would disagree.

Of course, it wasn't the wealth she had rejected but what she'd seen it do to people who possessed it. Gwyn worked hard as an animal agent, and she no doubt had ambitions of making money at it. Whatever capital she might accumulate, however, would be an indication of her personal success, not greed for someone else's.

She drove past Beaumarais and continued on to her place. Jed followed up the narrow cracked driveway and made a mental note to have it repaved. Romeo scampered out from around the side of the building and barked ferociously until he recognized the people who got out to greet him. Then his tail wagged with equal enthusiasm.

Jed moved up to Gwyn's side and bent down to give the dog a friendly rub behind the ears.

"I have animals to feed," she said, straightening up. "And so do you. I guess I'll see you later."

The warmth they'd shared at the D.A.'s office had been supplanted by a coolness that sent an icy chill down his spine. His worst fear was being confirmed. The squirming he'd felt when he took her in his arms at his office in Jefferson had been to get away from him, not to ask that they reconsider their differences. Her distress at the D.A.'s office had been real enough, but the short trip from Marshall had given her a chance to reevaluate the situation. Clearly, he'd come up wanting.

"Hey, you're not trying to give me the brush-off, are you?" He tried to sound playful, but her somber expression made it difficult. Taking another tack, he drew her against him and looked down at her, at the deep blue of her eyes under long lashes. "We have things to talk about, decisions to make."

"Decisions?" she asked warily. She didn't pull away or resist but passively allowed him to hold her. The giveaway that her indifference wasn't total was the delicate tremor he could feel beneath the surface of her skin. It rallied his sagging confidence.

"We'll start off with the easy ones. Where shall we eat?" He smiled invitingly. "My place or yours?"

She chuckled then. "Trust me, you don't want to experience my lack of culinary skills. Your very survival could be at stake."

Should he tell her she already held the key to his survival, to any chance he might have for happiness?

"I guess that means my place for dinner." He grinned smugly. "How about we compromise and have cocktails here beforehand?"

"Here? Cocktails? My offerings are rather meager, I'm afraid."

He stroked her cheek and touched his lips lightly to hers. "Let me be the judge of that."

The guardedness was back in her eyes. Did she think he was talking about sex? Of course he was, but more, much more. Somehow he had to convince her of that.

Gwyn studied him, trying to fathom the full depth of his thoughts. Was he saying he wouldn't marry her but saw no reason why they couldn't share a bed from time to time? Would she accept him on those terms until he was cleared of murder? And what if he never was?

"I might have a bottle of white wine in the back of the fridge," she murmured. "No fancy vintage, though."

"We can always pretend."

What else are we pretending? she wanted to ask.

That every time we touch each other it isn't with the secret fear that it might be for the last time?

"Will two hours be enough for you?" he asked, looking at her as if he could see the turmoil coiled deep inside her.

"I guess so—"

"Good." He released her, turned toward his pickup and called out over his shoulder, "I'll see you then."

GWYN WAS STEPPING out of the shower when Jed tapped on the back door. She called for him to come in. "I'll just be a couple of minutes."

She would have been ready in time, except one of her horses had managed to cut a foreleg. Not badly enough to require phoning a vet, but treating it had thrown her off schedule.

After using the blow-dryer on her hair, she gathered it, still slightly damp, at her nape with a powder-blue ribbon. She donned loose-fitting tan slacks and a baggy cotton blouse, applied a mere touch of mascara and lip gloss and went out to the kitchen.

He was bent over the open door of her refrigerator, his narrow, jean-clad backside projecting.

"Can I help you?" she asked lightly.

"Thought I'd get out the wine," he muttered, reached inside and removed a bottle of low-priced California Chardonnay.

"I told you it wasn't vintage," she observed when he checked the label.

He shrugged indifferently. "At least it has a cork instead of a screw cap."

She chuckled softly and got a couple of plain wineglasses from an overhead cabinet. "You're obviously a connoisseur." She dug a corkscrew out of a drawer just below it.

His eyes swept her body. "You look very pretty," he said appreciatively. "Gold suits you."

She glanced down at her shirt. "It's ordinary yellow, Jed," she objected.

"Is it?" He cocked an eyebrow. "I guess I was thinking about the glow of your skin."

It was a clumsy compliment, but it made her blush nevertheless.

Smiling at her discomfort, he opened the wine, poured, raised his glass and held it between them. "Here's to making beautiful music together."

A cliché wasn't the toast she'd expected from him. It made her wonder if he was as nervous as she was. Why? Because he was saying he only wanted to share pleasure with her, but not pain. His body, but not his soul. Could they be separated when you were in love? Wasn't it all or nothing? She certainly didn't know how to compartmentalize her emotions so easily.

"I'll drink to that." She lifted her glass and smiled at him over the rim.

"So are you ready?" he asked after their virgin sip.

"Ready?"

"To make music?"

Bewildered, she gazed at him, at the erotic sparkle in his blue eyes. Is this what their relationship had sunken to? Appointments for sex? The worst part was she suspected if that was the condition of their staying together, she just might agree. Making love with Jed Louis wasn't exactly a hardship, she consoled herself.

Then she saw the violin case sitting on the kitchen table. It took another minute for her to register its significance. He'd literally meant making music. Her face grew hot this time at the realization that she'd completely misconstrued his meaning, his intentions.

"I thought we'd start with something a little less ambitious than the 'Double Concerto,'" he said in a soft, intimate voice. "Maybe 'Liebenstraum.'"

Gwyn loved nineteenth-century romantic music and Franz Liszt's sentimental composition was one of her favorites.

"Jed, I haven't held a bow in several years." The admission didn't please her. She hated disappointing him, disappointing herself.

"Neither have I," he confessed. "So we can warm up together."

Warm up? She could feel herself heating up from the inside out. "I don't want to embarrass you."

He smiled intimately. "By your expertise?"

"By my ineptitude," she replied humbly, then saw the gleam in his eyes. She didn't believe they were still talking about stringed instruments.

He took her wineglass and put it with his own on the counter. Hands free, he cradled her hips and held her in front of him, not quite touching, except for the tension that practically crackled between them like an electrical force field.

"I'm willing to take the chance," he murmured, his eyes focused on her lips. "Are you?"

She smiled up at him, the corners of her mouth curled impishly. "I don't think you know what you're letting yourself in for."

"I'm looking forward to finding out."

She laughed, then brought her hands up to his shoulders. They were warm and broad and solid. She caught a whiff of his aftershave, woodsy, fresh, arousing. Raising herself on tiptoe, she planted a playful kiss on his lips. Unsatisfied, he wound his arms around her and pulled her closer.

He kissed her, hard, hungrily, impatiently.

She took a deep breath when they finally broke, her eyes wide. It certainly was convenient, she thought, that her cello happened to be in a bedroom.

They tuned for several minutes, then Jed warmed them up with a rousing version of "Turkey in the Straw." They segued into tunes ranging from early-eighteenth-century baroque to late-twentieth-century jazz. Short pieces mostly, many of them upbeat, a few nostalgic. Time slipped by.

At last, he began the sweet-sad strains of *Liebenstraum*. Gwyn filled in the harmony and could have wept at the melancholy beauty of the piece. She glanced up at Jed, who stood tall and straight, his chin tucked against his instrument, eyes closed as he absorbed the sweeping lyricism of the music.

He'd claimed to be a mediocre fiddler, and maybe Frannie had been objectively correct in her assessment of his talent and technique, but there was a passion in his interpretation that was moving and sincere. Yes, Gwyn liked making music with him very much.

The last strains of Liszt faded into silence. He lowered his fiddle. "Love's dream," he said, translating the title of the rhapsody.

"What's yours, Jed?" she asked.

"Being with you."

Strangely, the admission seemed to throw her into a funk. He took up his bow once more and fiddled an upbeat version of the Beatles's "Yellow Submarine." It made her laugh, and she sawed at a fathoms-deep accompaniment.

"You ready to eat?" he asked brightly when they'd finished.

"I forgot all about food. Now that you mention it, I'm starved. What's on the menu?"

"Pizza."

She did a double take. "Pizza?" Neither of them was averse to fast food on occasion, but every time she'd eaten at his house, the cuisine had approached gourmet status.

He looked practically insulted. "Something wrong? Don't you like pizza?"

"Of course I like pizza. Do you want to call from here?"

"Call? Who?"

"The pizza parlor."

"Why would I call them?"

"To deliver."

"You misunderstand. We're not fixing to have someone else's pizza. We're fixing to have mine."

"Excuse me," she drawled. "I didn't know I was fiddling around with an Italian chef."

"Boy, are you confused. I'm not Italian. I'm Texan, and you can be sure the likes of my pizza have never been seen anywhere on the Italian peninsula."

"Ah, crayfish and pineapple, I suppose."

He drew back. "Anybody ever tell you you're weird?"

"Not lately."

"Well, take it from me." He kissed her quickly on the lips. "You're weird."

He encased his musical instrument and they left the room. She felt wonderful, though there was just a niggling sense of letdown that they hadn't taken advantage of the twin bed.

They departed the house through the back door, Jed carrying his violin case, and walked in the dusky light through the stand of oak and sycamore trees. In his kitchen, Jed removed a piece of cloth from a ceramic bowl, punched down a yeasty ball of dough and flattened it on a floured pastry board. From the refrigerator, he retrieved several covered containers and an enamel pan containing tomato sauce.

Gwyn helped him arrange them on the stainless-steel worktable. "June sure is well organized."

"June?" He shook his head, clearly affronted. "I did it all myself with my trusty little paring knife. Except for the dough. I used my hands to knead that. But it's all right. I washed them just the other day."

She snickered. "That's a relief. Jed, you didn't

really make the dough from scratch, did you? It's frozen, right?''

He gave her a haughty, withering glance. ''It's not nearly as complicated as you think.''

''I find that hard to believe.''

This time he went still. ''That I made it?''

''No, silly. That it's not complicated. I still haven't completely mastered the can opener.''

''Poor baby,'' he chided. ''You truly did have a deprived childhood, didn't you?''

At first she thought he was mocking her, but a glance at his teasing smile and she knew he was laughing *with* her, not *at* her.

''It was terrible,'' she agreed, playing along. ''While other people were allowed to enjoy tuna salad on toast for lunch, I had to eat fish eggs on crackers. And instead of chicken noodle soup, I was given clear turtle broth.''

He took her in his arms. ''I'll make it up to you, Gwyn. I'll give you all the things you were deprived of. I'll teach you to make macaroni and cheese and sloppy joes.''

''You're so good to me,'' she crooned against his chest.

He held her away with his big hands. ''But I draw the line at tuna fish casserole and creamed eggs over toast.'' He looked quite ferocious. ''I'm sorry, sweetheart, but there are some things even I can't abide.''

She laughed now, imagining him being served those traditional, economical meals by Frannie on a routine basis. Gwyn had tried making a tuna casserole once. If hers in any way resembled the real thing, she wouldn't miss having one again in the least.

She watched him pat out the dough, stretch it, then pick it up and spin it in the air.

"Where'd you learn to do that?" She didn't mind showing how impressed she was.

"I worked part-time in a pizza joint one year during college."

"In that case, I'd expect it to be on your most hated list."

"It wasn't one of my favorite food groups for a while," he acknowledged, "but abstinence made the palate grow fonder."

He spread tomato sauce. She dotted it with sliced mushrooms. He caught her attention when he spread shredded barbecued beef brisket on it. She suggested adding jalapeño peppers.

He raised an eyebrow. "A woman after my own heart."

Finally, they added generous amounts of mozzarella cheese, before he popped it into the preheated oven.

They slaked their thirst with tall glasses of chilled spring water. He opened a bottle of Chianti while she tossed a salad. She set up a tray with napkins, silverware and plates. The room filled with the mouthwatering aroma of baking bread and tangy spices. The timer dinged. He removed the bubbling pie, cut it into wedges with a wheel, and they carried their dinner to the library.

Although the day had been long and draining, their pleasure in the music they'd made still lingered in their heads. They ate in contented silence, devouring most of the pizza and all of the salad.

"Today made me think—about us," he commented as he rose from his end of the couch to replenish their glasses with red wine.

"And what did you conclude?" she asked, eager for the answer and afraid to hear it.

"That Thorny is right. We ought to get on with our lives."

He made it sound so easy, so ordinary, but she knew it wasn't. More unsettling was her awareness that they were at a crossroads. Was he saying they should go their separate ways? That he wanted to spare her the anguish of waiting for him to be formally charged and arrested? That until the real killer was exposed, they couldn't continue on together, even as lovers? Were "Liebenstraum" and pizza his way of saying goodbye?

"And how should we do that?" she asked after a sip of Chianti.

He put aside his glass, rose on his long legs, came over to her and sat beside her. The depth of his blue eyes betrayed the frustration that comes from uncertainty, but there was passion, as well, and an ache they shared. He lifted her hands to his lips and kissed them.

"I have so little to offer you, Gwyn," he said, imploring her understanding.

The sensation of his hands holding hers, possessive yet strangely undemanding, ignited both desire and fear and had her heart pounding. *This is his farewell,* she thought. *He's sending me away.*

The sharp point of anger prodded her. "Let me be the judge of that. What other people think isn't important, Jed."

She could see in his glance that he wanted to argue with her. He'd earned wealth and prestige precisely because he wanted to change how people thought of him. And didn't she camouflage her heritage in part because of what people would think?

"These aren't the best of times." He kissed her fingers. "Except that I found you."

A glimmer of hope played like a minor chord in her head. "They're not the worst, either, Jed."

He almost retorted that the worst might be yet to come, but she knew that. He lifted a hand to caress her cheek, a soft, gentle touch that washed warmth through her. "There's that silver lining again."

"Sometimes you have to look."

"I wasn't looking when I found you."

She tipped her head against the palm of his hand. "Neither was I," she whispered. "I never thought I'd find you."

With a wry grin, he asked, "Why would a woman of your breeding want to be associated with the bastard son of a dead gambler?"

She curled her hand around his wrist and felt the heavy throb of his pulse. "And why would a man of your moral integrity want to be associated with a member of a dissolute and corrupt family?" she countered.

"Because she's a beautiful person. Because I love her."

"In spite of her family's fame, fortune and power?"

"Maybe. After all, it contributed to her education."

She rewarded him with a tiny laugh. "And you accuse me of seeing a silver lining."

Their eyes met and held. She brushed back a shock of dark hair from his forehead. How could she tell him what she felt? She couldn't explain it to herself. She knew only that she loved this man, and that the prospect of living without him was more unbearable than anything she'd ever experienced. She'd given up hope of finding a man who would love her for herself. Now, it seemed, it was too late.

"What are we going to do?" she asked, doubts and fears giving her voice a muted, unhappy sound.

He gathered her hands between his again and rested his arms on her thighs. His soul-searching gaze captured her, suspended her in space, then drew her into his. Her heart fluttered. Her breathing became shallow. He was her world, her life, and she didn't want to let him go—ever.

"Will you marry me, Gwyneth Miller? Will you be my wife?"

Breathless, she stared. Surely she hadn't heard his words correctly. It was just her mind playing tricks on her, making her hear what her heart wanted to hear.

"I—" Her heart pounded viciously, painfully, in her chest. "What did you say?"

He smiled uncertainly. "I love you, Gwyn. I

promise to do everything in my power to make you happy. Will you marry me?''

Great tears formed in her eyes and cascaded down her cheeks. Through them she saw the confusion and despair on his face.

Laughing, she wrapped her arms around his shoulders, pressing his face to her breasts.

"Oh, Jed," she cried. "Yes. I'll marry you."

His head shot up. "You will? I was afraid..." He stood, tugged her by the elbows, then pulled her into his arms. "I thought—"

"Shut up and kiss me, Jed."

He arched back far enough to let her see the wide grin on his face, then his mouth came down on hers with a passion and hunger that left them both panting.

He swept her toward the hallway, flicking out lights as he went.

"What about the mess?"

He laughed. "I think June will understand when we tell her she has a wedding to prepare for." He swung her around into his arms at the foot of the stairs. "Kiss me, my love."

"Mmm," she moaned as he covered her mouth with his before she had a chance to reply. His hands stroked her side, her hips, her buttocks. She held his face as a flood of sensations raced through her.

In one clean sweeping motion he picked her up and carried her up the stairs, their mouths joined. She flipped off the light switch at the top of the landing as he transported her to his bedroom. Inside, he kicked the door closed, only then letting her feet touch the floor.

They stood before each other, grinning like candy-cotton-crazed kids at a carnival. He touched her breasts, felt their warmth and fullness and vowed to possess them more intimately, to taste them in his mouth. She ran her hands across his chest, feeling the hard hot muscle, knowing she was the cause of the heavy thud of his heartbeat.

He made a move to turn out the single bedside lamp he'd left burning earlier, but she stopped him.

"I want to see you as well as feel you," she murmured, and delighted in the erotic gleam in his eyes as he started to undress her.

They took off each other's clothes in fits and starts, one moment impatient to remove a barrier, the next savoring the feel of exposed skin. He planted wet kisses along her neck, across her shoulders. She teased the fine sheen of hair on his chest and giggled as he sucked in his breath when she tickled her fingers across his ribs and taut belly.

Naked, aroused, biting his lip against the pressure building inside him, he lifted her into his arms and carried her to his bed—their bed. Suspending himself above her, he kissed her mouth, then brushed his lips down the center of her body, between her breasts, through her belly button.

Dragging in ragged breaths, she placed her trembling hands on the top of his head as he wended his way down her torso. She melted under his lavish tasting.

Little moans of pleasure escaped when his tongue

lashed her. She arched against him, sensations assaulting her, throwing her into the delirium of lust when he found her center.

"I want you inside me." Her voice was a gasping plea.

He retraced his route up her quivering body, pausing this time to suckle her enflamed nipples.

"Please," she begged, unable to keep from squirming under the intensity of his stimulation.

His smile was wicked when he rose above her. Wicked and loving and filled with erotic desire.

Unable to keep from smiling back, she reached over to the bedside table drawer, extracted a foil packet, removed the rolled latex and sheathed him. She watched his eyes glaze as she guided him, surrounded him. Then began the ancient rhythm, the building crescendo. She cried out at the dramatic climax and surrendered to the explosion of sensations rocketing through her.

His release came a moment later, making him shiver and groan. At last there was silence, peace, contentment and joy. They lay in each other's arms, spent, fulfilled, complete.

"This is only the beginning," Gwyn murmured in his ear, his hand stretched across her middle.

He nuzzled her closer, savoring the taste and touch and smell of her body close to his. He swallowed the words he dared not speak.

Until they arrest me for murder.

CHAPTER SIXTEEN

IT SEEMED a little strange to Jed that the first person they would tell of their impending marriage was the housekeeper, but why not? After so many years, June was like family. He'd discussed some of his business dealings with her from time to time, as well as social events. He was fond of her and trusted her discretion, but he'd never seen her more ecstatic.

"We've decided on a small wedding in two weeks," Gwyn confided. "Nothing too elaborate, just a few friends."

June nodded with seeming approval, then started in on what he was sure would become a litany of questions. "Where is the ceremony going to be?"

"Here at Beaumarais, on the veranda," Gwyn responded. "A late-afternoon affair. The weather should still be cool."

"And the reception?" June asked, then ran on without waiting for an answer. "I hope you're planning on having it here, too. The formal dining room can seat twenty-four comfortably, or we can get more in if we go with a buffet. That way you won't have to worry about bugs or being rained out."

"A wonderful idea, June. As soon as I've worked out the numbers, we can decide on the menu."

June beamed and clapped her hands. "Lordy, I can't remember the last time we gave a dinner party. I'll have Josiah help me polish the silver, and we'll need to get in a crew to clean the chandelier." She looked apologetically at Jed. "If that's okay, sir."

He laughed. "Whatever you and Gwyn decide is fine with me."

"About the food," Gwyn said tentatively.

"You tell me what you want, miss, and you'll have it."

"Well, I was thinking…" Gwyn continued as she walked out to the kitchen with the housekeeper.

Jed chortled happily and went in the opposite direction to the library. Giving in to a secret compulsion for proprieties, he'd slipped downstairs while Gwyn was in the shower that morning and removed the remnants of last night's meal to the kitchen. Now he picked up the phone on his desk.

"How about dinner this evening?" he asked when Riley Gray answered.

"You planning to fill me in on what happened in Marshall yesterday? Thorny was in my office when Gwyn called him, but he didn't come back, and I have to admit I'm curious about how things went."

"Sorry," Jed replied. "I should have called you myself."

Riley chuckled. "Not to worry. I figured I'd find out eventually." There was a pause, in which Jed could practically see his friend's sly grin. "Besides, you probably had other things on your mind. I enjoyed the concert."

Jed's smile carried in his voice. "I'll explain everything when you get here. You can make it, can't you?''

''I'll get a sitter for Alanna.''

''Bring her along.''

''Are you sure, Jed? Four-year-olds can be a handful, especially at dinnertime.''

''Bring her,'' Jed repeated. ''Between the three of us, I bet we can keep her entertained and out of trouble.''

''Famous last words. Okay, what time? We usually eat around six. If it's going to be much later, I'll have Mrs. Yates give her a snack this afternoon around five.''

''No need. Six will be fine.''

''You're sure?''

Jed chuckled happily. ''Positive. See you and Alanna at six. Don't be late.''

GWYN'S DAY was a joyously mad scramble to get things organized. She went to a stationer in Jefferson, not far from Jed's office, and ordered wedding invitations. Thanks to computers and the payment of a slight inconvenience fee, they were ready that afternoon for him to pick up on his way home.

They had already discussed the list of guests. Their wedding wouldn't be a sumptuous affair—in numbers, at least. Gwyn would send invitations to her parents, a couple of cousins she still kept in contact with and, of course, her best friend Clarice. Jed, naturally, had a more extensive list. The Jenningses, including their daughter, Amanda, though he would have avoided inviting her if he could diplomatically have done so. Several business associates and dignitaries in town with whom he felt comfortable.

"What about Joleen?" Gwyn asked, unsure what his response would be.

"Invite her," he said.

"Do you think she'll come?"

"Probably not, though I wish she would. She's the only person left who was part of my life with Frannie."

Gwyn felt a tug of sadness. The only family he'd known was gone. Hers likely wouldn't show up.

"Joleen might not have proper clothes to wear," Gwyn commented.

"She probably wouldn't be very comfortable here, anyway."

"I'll send her an invitation nonetheless," she assured him, and decided to deliver it personally.

JED CONCLUDED that Riley already knew what he was about to announce because when he greeted him at the door at precisely six o'clock, his friend was sporting a sly grin.

"My, don't you look pretty," Gwyn commented to his daughter as they entered the hallway. Alanna was wearing a bright pink T-shirt and lavender shorts.

"This is my most favorite shirt." The little girl twirled around to show everyone. "When are we fixing to eat? I'm hungry."

Gwyn's laugh bubbled out. "Do you think you can wait five minutes?"

"Is that a long time?"

"Not very long at all," Gwyn assured her, and reached for her hand. The child gave it willingly and allowed herself to be led back to the morning room.

"Heard any good rumors lately?" Jed asked his friend as they trailed behind.

"This and that." Riley smirked.

Jed screwed up his mouth. "I hate small towns."

"They are a treasure, aren't they?" Riley offered with a laugh.

He gave his friend a bear hug and Gwyn a more gentlemanly embrace when Jed announced that they were getting married.

"Will you be my best man?" Jed asked.

Riley placed his hand on Jed's shoulder. "It'll be an honor, my friend. It's about time the last class-A bachelor in Uncertain bit the dust."

Gwyn knelt in front of his daughter. "Mr. Jed and I are going to get married in a couple of weeks. Would you like to be my flower girl."

"Oh, yes. Can I?" the little girl asked, wide-eyed, then paused more seriously. "What's a flower girl?"

Keeping her amusement to a smile, Gwyn explained, "You get all dressed up in a pretty new dress—"

"Is it going to be on a Sunday?"

Gwyn cocked her head to one side. "It'll be on a Saturday."

"Oh," the little girl responded unhappily. "My daddy only lets me wear a dress on Sundays."

Taking the child's hands in hers, Gwyn said, "I think he might make an exception in this case."

"Can I, Daddy?" She looked up adoringly at her father. "Can I?"

"You bet you can, pumpkin. It's an honor to be asked to be a flower girl at a wedding. Be sure to say thank-you."

Alanna turned to Gwyn. "Thank you, Miss Gwyn."

Without thinking, Gwyn hugged the child. "You're welcome. I'm so glad you can do it for me."

"Do I have to pick flowers? Mrs. Yates doesn't like it when I take one from the yard."

"You can help pick them, but your real job is going to be dropping the petals on the floor."

The girl's eyes widened. "You won't get mad?"

Gwyn hugged her again. "No, I won't get mad. But we'll practice with you so you'll know exactly what to do."

Alanna screwed up her mouth in an attitude of superiority. "I don't think I gots to practice. My daddy says I'm real good at spilling things."

Gwyn chuckled. "Well, practice'll make you even better."

"Oh, okay. Is it five minutes yet? Can we eat now?"

THE FOLLOWING MORNING, Gwyn mailed out the wedding invitations and spent most of the morning in the kitchen with June, planning the menu for the dinner to follow the wedding ceremony.

"Where are you going on your honeymoon?" the housekeeper asked. She was snapping green beans she'd put on to cook with salt pork and onions. The southern-style vegetable would be ready by the evening meal.

Gwyn continued paging through a bride magazine. She hadn't decided yet whether she wanted a traditional long gown and veil or something more contemporary. As a child and young adult she'd dreamed of a fairy-tale wedding. The gown her mother had selected for her near marriage had been just that— an elaborate confection of silk and lace, with a monstrously long train and flowing veil.

"Or is it a secret?"

Gwyn looked up. "I'm sorry, what did you ask?"

June grinned and broke off the stem of another bean. "Your honeymoon."

"Oh—" Gwyn felt her face flush "—we thought we might drive to the Ozarks for a couple of days. I understand they have some wonderful spas there. I've never been."

"It's pretty country," June agreed.

Jed had suggested Mexico. They'd even considered Victoria, British Columbia, but then they'd decided they didn't want to venture too far from Uncertain. For one thing, there were the animals to consider. Jed had a local man he routinely called upon to tend to his horses when he was away on business. The neighbor agreed easily to care for her miniatures, as well. But there were also Romeo and Cleopatra. Riley volunteered himself and Alanna to take care of them even before Gwyn had a chance to ask him, but the kittens were beginning to roam, and she hesitated to leave him with the burden of minding them for very long.

So she and Jed agreed this first honeymoon would be for only three days. Neither of them explicitly said they also didn't want to be too far away in case something new developed in Frannie's murder investigation. After the unsuccessful attempt by the D.A. to interrogate Jed, word got back to Riley that the sheriff was more convinced than ever that Louis was "guilty as sin, otherwise he wouldn't need some high-powered lawyer to speak for him." Fielder was positive Belmonte was a diversion herring, and he was determined to find the evidence that would prove Jed had murdered Frannie Granger.

TWO DAYS LATER, Gwyn received a polite letter from her mother. Senator and Mrs. Miller had a prior commitment and, unfortunately, wouldn't be able to attend the wedding. Claudia Miller wished her daughter the best of luck and happiness in her impending marriage and announced that a present would be forthcoming.

Gwyn tried to brush the matter aside, but the one person she couldn't hide her feelings from was Jed. He came into the room as she was placing the expensive stationery back in its envelope and trying hard not to give in to the knot of anger and pain in her throat.

It shouldn't matter, she told herself. She and her parents had never been close. Having them attend would only have made her uncomfortable, as well as everyone else, and would have broadcast that she was one of *the* Millers. It was just as well they'd declined. Uncertain didn't need the disruption of a U.S. Senator showing up.

Though she had her back to him, Jed must have seen something in her posture or the clumsiness of her movements that prompted concern.

"What's the matter?" he asked softly.

She shook her head. "Oh, nothing. Mother wrote. She and Father won't be able to make it. They send their good wishes."

"May I see it?" He indicated the letter, but made no move to pick it up.

Gwyn knew if she said no he'd drop the matter. That, at least, was some consolation. In spite of the intimacy of their relationship, he respected her privacy. Whether he liked it or not, however, he was part of her family now, too. He might as well see firsthand the type of people he could one day have to deal with. Getting up from the small writing desk she'd appropriated by the window in the front parlor, she handed him the envelope and quietly left the room.

Jed watched her go through the doorway, head held high, then leaned against the table and opened the vellum letter. He scanned it once, then settled into the stiff Victorian chair and read it more closely. The senator and his wife, it turned out, had been invited that same weekend to Camp David, the presidential retreat in Maryland, and simply couldn't get away. Gwyn's father was apparently being considered for a cabinet post in the new administration, so declining such a prestigious invitation was out of the question. Nevertheless, Claudia Miller wrote, she hoped Gwyn's nuptials would be a happy occasion and the newlyweds would be able to find an opportunity in the not-too-distant future to visit Washington.

Jed slouched against the back of the upholstered chair. For so many years he'd felt rejected—which he had been by his indifferent father and high-handed uncle—but he'd also been blessed with his mother's and Frannie's unconditional love, by the family that included Emmy Monday and Will McClain. Frannie was dead and his foster siblings were not to be found, but his memory of them was positive and rich. Holding the offensive letter in his hand, he realized that he, the illegitimate son of a naive young woman and an irresponsible gambler, had been more blessed than had the heir of a powerful dynasty.

Heavy-hearted, he found his fiancée in the library, making out yet another list, or going through an old one, he wasn't sure which. He walked up behind her, placed his hands on her shoulders and kneaded the tense muscles he could feel cabled there. "I'm sorry."

She tilted her head to brush her cheek against his fingers. "I guess I am, too," she murmured. "They're never going to know the joy of being grandparents, Jed. They'll probably live to ripe old ages and die very, very rich. Their names will appear on many buildings and monuments, but they won't be in anybody's hearts."

It was a sad epitaph, he thought, and one that was no doubt true.

CLARICE QUINCY arrived two days before the wedding. The flamboyant redhead had put on a few pounds over the years, but it was an improvement over the skinny kid she'd been when she and Gwyn were in college together. The pert, slightly irreverent candor hadn't changed, though. Which may have had something to do with her having had three husbands and being on the prowl for a fourth. Gwyn often thought the first marriage might have succeeded if her friend had been able to have children, but she hadn't, and the man she'd fallen in love with—and possibly still loved—insisted he needed a blood heir. Blood was thicker than love in his hierarchy of values.

It took about fifteen seconds for Gwyn to find out how Clarice and Jed would get along. They hit it off like long-lost pals. By the second sip of her usual dry martini, Clarice was making playfully snide comments about big men in small towns. He swallowed beer and returned a quip about society dames slumming it in the sticks.

THE CEREMONY was set for Saturday afternoon. To Gwyn's and June's immense relief, the weather turned out to be not only clear but still and cool. The Reverend Briggs, who'd been a good friend of Frannie's and had known Jed all his life, officiated. Gwyn had met him the day before when he'd visited to go over the ceremony and rehearse the participants. Remembering her earlier suggestion that he might have misappropriated church funds now made her laugh. The diminutive clergyman with his rosy cheeks and liver-spotted hands was so sincere and kind that he couldn't possibly have done that, much less killed anyone and buried the victim in an unmarked grave.

At the rehearsal the previous evening, Alanna had been giddy and hyper. Today she was quiet and shy, taking her role as flower girl very seriously.

Her father looked devilishly handsome in his tuxedo. He'd been offered the opportunity to bring a date but had chosen to come alone. Clarice was also unescorted, so the numbers worked out fine. For a very fleeting moment, Gwyn wondered if the divorcée and the widower might hit it off, but it didn't take even that long for her to realize they had absolutely nothing in common. Riley was a laid-back small-town lawyer whose greatest ambition centered on his daughter's welfare and happiness. Clarice was a born-and-bred big-city girl whose idea of living in the country was spending more than three days at a posh ski resort.

Ray Jennings and his wife, Catherine, were among the last to arrive. Their daughter, Amanda, had sent a present but regrets, claiming a previous engagement out of town. Neither Jed nor Gwyn was convinced it was true, but they didn't care. If anything, they were relieved that she wouldn't be attending.

Joleen, as Jed predicted, had likewise declined. Gwyn had visited the reclusive old woman to extend the invitation but, sensing the former nurse's discomfort, hadn't pressed. Joleen had sent a card and a modest but thoughtful present.

Because Gwyn's parents had chosen not to come to Texas for their daughter's wedding, she and Jed had asked Dexter Thorndyke if he would give away the bride. The renowned attorney showed rare humility in accepting the role and kissed Gwyn more fondly on her cheek than her father ever had.

June, eternally cool and calm, was uncharacteristically jumpy as she directed the small staff she'd assembled to deal with the final preparations. Her husband, Josiah, had festooned the veranda with ribbons and flowers that added still more to the vibrant colors of spring. Azaleas, camellias and roses contributed their tints and scents to the soft air.

Jed's friends buzzed with snickering amusement as he circulated among them. No one had ever seen him nervous before, at least not this rattled. If it wasn't for the smile he didn't seem to be able to wipe off his face, people might have thought he dreaded the ceremony ahead.

At last the moment came. The chamber quartet they'd hired sounded the traditional chords of Mendelssohn's "Here Comes the Bride," and the assembled rose from their folding chairs. In a crinolined pink dress, Alanna walked an imaginary tightrope from the library, first too fast, then too slowly, strewing white rose petals in tiny clumps.

Clarice followed in a lavender above-the-knee dress, her radiant hair fanned out in a copper halo.

Finally, Gwyn appeared on Dexter Thorndyke's arm. She wore an elegantly simple ankle-length gown of cream satin and seed pearls, without a veil or train. Her luxuriantly thick auburn hair was piled high and dotted with larger pearls.

Jed looked about ready to pop his buttons as he took her hand and stood before the preacher.

The traditional questions were asked; the traditional responses were given. Yes, they took each other as lawfully wedded spouses to love and cherish till death do them part.

The dinner that followed was a combination of formal and country fare. Crayfish étouffé and prime rib of beef. French champagne and Texas wine. German cheesecake and mulberry compote. Jed and Gwyn smiled and clutched hands under the table when the chamber ensemble played an adaptation of Brahms's "Double Concerto for Violin and Cello" during the leisurely meal.

Later, everyone retired to the high-ceilinged living room, which hadn't been used in years. Most of the furniture had been removed to the garage and the Aubusson carpet taken up. Within a circle of smiling faces, Jed and Gwyn glided to the "Anniversary Waltz" over the glowingly polished hard cypress floor. Later when everyone was dancing to CDs of big band tunes and more contemporary arrangements, he led her out onto the veranda. In the distance, the moon sparkled silver on the placid lake.

"Like the beginning of time," Gwyn murmured, remembering Jed's description of it when she'd first glimpsed it from his morning-room window.

He raised his hand and caressed the back of her neck. "The beginning of our time," he murmured in her ear.

She let him continue his expert massage for several minutes, luxuriating in the feel of his skillful, probing fingers. Finally, she crossed an arm over her breasts, placed a hand on his and turned to look up at him.

"I want to have children, Jed. Lots of them."

Joy radiated on his face and brought a playful smile. He pursed his lips and narrowed his eyes. "Exactly how many is lots?"

She draped her arms on his shoulders. "I want us to have a couple of our own, of course," she said with a lightness that matched his, but then she grew serious. "But I want us to take in more. There are children who don't have parents, Jed, or whose parents don't want them, don't love them. I know we can't save them all, but I want to help those we can. Your foster mom devoted her life to kids that other people didn't want. In her memory, Jed, can't we do the same?"

He smiled broadly, clearly pleased with her dream. But she detected a lingering sadness in his clear blue eyes, and for a moment, he seemed to close up, retreat from her.

"I know what you're thinking," she said softly. "Frannie's murder still hasn't been solved."

"It wouldn't be fair to you or any children we might have if I'm convicted of killing her."

"You didn't kill her," Gwyn declared quietly but with absolute conviction. "And we're not going to let other people dictate who we are or what we do." She raised her hand and stroked his cheek. "Remember? We're going to get on with our lives."

He curled his hands along both sides of her neck and peered into her eyes.

"I love you, Gwyn," he whispered. "I love you more and more each day. I know Frannie would have loved you, too. She'd be very pleased and proud of what you want to do."

He kissed her sweetly and held her in his arms. Their hearts beat softly against each other. Then he murmured seductively in her ear, "So you want to make babies, huh?"

Turn the page for an excerpt from
WHO IS EMERALD MONDAY?
by Roz Denny Fox, the second book in the
RETURN TO EAST TEXAS *trilogy.*

Emmy Monday has just arrived in Uncertain and discovered that the house she'd lived in as a child—Fran Granger's house—is for rent. She has also discovered that Riley Gray Wolf, the boy she'd loved as a teenager, is still living in town, a lawyer now and more attractive than ever.

As SHE DROVE to the phone booth, Emmy's thoughts were consumed by Riley. How good he looked. How successful. How difficult it would be to see him around town. Living in a small town increased the odds of future meetings. Darn, why hadn't she asked him for Josey's address? At one time, Riley's sister had been Emmy's best friend. The two of them had spent hours on crafts. The girls had been friends long before Emmy took notice of boys. Of Riley in particular.

Angling into a parking spot on the street adjacent to the booth, Emmy deliberately thrust Riley Gray Wolf, or Gray as he called himself now, behind a carefully walled off section in her brain.

She punched in the number she'd copied from the For Rent sign in front of Fran's house. The phone rang three times before a woman's lilting voice sang out, "Hel...lo."

"I'm calling about a house you have for rent. A small place off Moss Road. Is it available? It looks vacant."

"It is, although there are still boxes in a back bedroom that need moving. The house belongs to my husband. He's away on business. I expect him home by dinnertime. Say, seven-thirty, if you'd care to call back then.''

Emmy twisted the phone cord. ''Oh. I'm afraid I can't really wait. Perhaps I'll just go ahead and rent one of the Kit and Caboodle Cottages.''

The owner's wife sounded curious. ''You'd rent a house based on a drive-by?''

''I…uh,'' Emmy stammered. ''Know the place. I used to live there. Although it looks nicer now than it did then.''

''Are you sure you have the correct house in mind? Jed, my husband, has owned the place for some time. He grew up there.''

''*Jed?* Jed Louis is your husband? He owns the old Granger house?''

''Yes. You know him? I don't believe I caught your name.'' The voice sharpened—unless Emmy had imagined that.

''He probably had no reason to mention me. My name is Emmy Monday. A long time ago we both lived there as foster kids.''

''Emmy!'' A happy cry followed. ''Jed's told me about you. He'll be so pleased when he hears you've come home. I know he'll want you to stay at Beaumarais with us. I'm Gwyneth, his wife—please call me Gwyn.''

''Oh, I couldn't impose on you.'' Emmy recalled what Cassie had said about Jed's recent marriage. ''I heard you're newly married. Besides, Jed and I haven't spoken in years. We're virtual strangers.''

''I guess I understand how you feel. But you two have so much catching up to do. Tell you what, I'll meet you at the rental. Jed would never forgive me if I turned away the only family he has.'' She lowered her voice. ''I'm assuming you've heard what a mess he's in?''

''Bits and pieces. Enough to know that what they're accusing him of is totally absurd. I'm not only Jed's only family, by the way. There's Will. Will McClain. Is he around?''

''No. But I'll let Jed fill you in on everything that's happened since you, Will and Frannie Granger disappeared. If you won't stay with us, Emmy, promise you'll at least come to dinner tonight. Eight-thirty. I'm ten minutes from the rental. If we meet and you find the house suitable, that'll give you time to unpack and rest a bit before coming over.''

''Wait. I'd love to see Jed, but I'll have to reserve judgment on renting the house.'' Emmy felt bowled over—things were moving too fast—and yet her words reflected a smile.

Meet 50 loving dads in

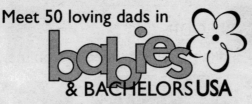

babies
& BACHELORS USA

Take 4 FREE BOOKS,
Plus get a FREE GIFT!

abies & Bachelors USA is a heartwarming new collection of reissued
ovels featuring 50 sexy heroes from every state who experience the
ps and downs of fatherhood and find time for love all the same. All
f the books, hand-picked by our editors, are outstanding romances
y some of the world's bestselling authors, including Stella Bagwell,
ristine Rolofson, Judith Arnold and Marie Ferrarella!

Don't delay, order today! Call customer service at
1-800-873-8635.
Or
Clip this page and mail it to The Reader Service:

In U.S.A.	In CANADA
P.O. Box 9049	P.O. Box 616
Buffalo, NY	Fort Erie, Ontario
14269-9049	L2A 5X3

ES! Please send me four FREE BOOKS and FREE GIFT along with the next four
ovels on a 14-day free home preview. If I like the books and decide to keep them, I'll
ay just $15.96* U.S. or $18.00* CAN., and there's no charge for shipping and
andling. Otherwise, I'll keep the 4 FREE BOOKS and FREE GIFT and return the rest.
I decide to continue, I'll receive six books each month—two of which are always
ee—until I've received the entire collection. In other words, if I collect all 50 volumes,
will have paid for 32 and received 18 absolutely free! 267 HCK 4534
467 HCK 4535

lame	(Please Print)		
ddress			Apt. #
ity	State/Prov.		Zip/Postal Code

* Terms and prices subject to change without notice.
Sales Tax applicable in N.Y. Canadian residents will be charged applicable provincial taxes
and GST. All orders are subject to approval.
RBAB01R © 2000 Harlequin Enterprises Limited

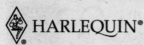

HARLEQUIN *Super*ROMANCE®

RETURN TO EAST TEXAS

**After twenty years, they all come back—
Jed and Emmy and Will—to find the solution to
a long-buried mystery:** *Why did their foster
mother, Frannie Granger, die? Who killed her?*
**After twenty years, they're looking
for answers...and for love.**

Join them in the town of Uncertain, Texas!

Enjoy this captivating trilogy

The Millionaire Horseman by **K.N. Casper,**
on sale in April 2001

Who Is Emerald Monday? by **Roz Denny Fox,**
on sale in May 2001

A Man of His Word by **Eve Gaddy,**
on sale in June 2001

Available wherever Harlequin books are sold.

HARLEQUIN®
Makes any time special ®

Harlequin invites you
to walk down the aisle . . .

To honor our year long celebration of weddings, we are offering an exciting opportunity for you to own the Harlequin Bride Doll. Handcrafted in fine bisque porcelain, the wedding doll is dressed for her wedding day in a cream satin gown accented by lace trim. She carries an exquisite traditional bridal bouquet and wears a cathedral length dotted Swiss veil. Embroidered flowers cascade down her lace overskirt to the scalloped hemline; underneath all is a multi-layered crinoline.

Join us in our celebration of weddings by sending away for your own Harlequin Bride Doll. This doll regularly retails for $74.95 U.S./approx. $108.68 CDN. One doll per household. Requests must be received no later than June 30, 2001. Offer good while quantities of gifts last. Please allow 6-8 weeks for delivery. Offer good in the U.S. and Canada only. Become part of this exciting offer!

Simply complete the order form and mail to:
"A Walk Down the Aisle"

IN U.S.A	IN CANADA
P.O. Box 9057	P.O. Box 622
3010 Walden Ave.	Fort Erie, Ontario
Buffalo, NY 14240-9057	L2A 5X3

Enclosed are eight (8) proofs of purchase found on the last page of every specially marked Harlequin series book and $3.75 check or money order (for postage and handling). Please send my Harlequin Bride Doll to:

_____

Name (PLEASE PRINT)

_____

Address   Apt. #

_____

City   State/Prov.   Zip/Postal Code

_____

Account # (if applicable)   098 KIK DAEW

HARLEQUIN®
Makes any time special ®

Visit us at www.eHarlequin.com

A Walk Down the Aisle
Free Bride Doll Offer
One Proof-of-Purchase

PHWDAPOP